SELENA IR DRAKE

THE ARCHFIEND ARTIFACT

CASE ONE OF THE AEON FILES

A DRAKE BOOKS & MEDIA BOOK

Cover design by Selena IR Drake
Author photo by Robert Berry.

Drake Books & Media
901 62nd Avenue NE, Suite B, Minot, ND 58703
Visit us online at www.DrakeBooksMedia.com

Published in the United States of America

First published: October 2013

ASIN: B07W4D3KHV
ISBN: 978-1-088-66410-0

PUBLISHER'S NOTE
The characters and events in this book are fictitious. Any similarity to real persons, living or dead, is coincidental and not intended by the author.

The views and opinions expressed by the author are not necessarily those of Drake Books & Media.

For those who believe.

Parathrope *[par-uh-throhp]*
noun (from Greek, *para-* beyond + *ánthrōpos* man):
1. an individual with abilities beyond those which are considered natural;
2. a superhuman

Cowan *[kou-an]*
noun
1. an individual of the species *Homo sapien*
who lacks any power or knowledge of supernatural origins;
2. a mortal human being

Aeon *[ey-on]*
noun (from Late Latin, Greek)
1. one of a class of paranormal beings charged with protecting the people, animals, and things of the Mortal Realm
2. a guardian spirit

INTRODUCTION

There is an ancient Lie still spoken in every language in every nation on earth:

"There are no such things as monsters."

If you believe the Lie, here is a word of caution: Stop reading right now. Believing the Lie is your only camouflage. Your ignorance protects you from them—but the very moment you realize the creatures from your nightmares aren't just stories but real, live monsters…well, that's when they have you. That's when the true terror begins.

Few Cowans realize there are beings in this world who predate the Roman Empire, the Pharaohs, the Mesopotamians…even humanity itself. They've gone by many names. Apparition. Fiend. Demon. Monster. *Spook*. There are some who are revered for their wisdom and benevolence, and we came to call them angels or gods. Others have a darker nature, and we were witness to their evil and malice and named them devils and demons.

But no matter what you choose to call them, the fact remains: these creatures exist. And they used to exist everywhere—dwelling in the darkest caves, roosting atop the highest mountains. Walking the vast plains and scorching deserts. Soaring the empty skies and lurking in the densest forests. Swimming the swiftest rivers and slumbering deep in the endless icy seas.

Of course, this was before mankind swept across the globe and claimed it for their own, before the rise of the Church, and its endless Holy Wars that threatened to destroy these ancient beings for good.

The Cowans almost succeeded.

In the beginning of the eighteenth century, a secret, world-wide partnership between man and monster was forged, and the power of the Lie was renewed. The next several decades saw a decline in public awareness of the realm of the paranormal. By the dawn of the twentieth century, almost every living human believed that monsters were merely the fruit of frightening stories told to scare children into good behavior. Eventually, these so-called stories evolved into the monsters of literature and the silver screen, fading from the collective unconscious almost entirely.

But the *real* monsters refused to fade away.

They persist. And they walk among you. A parathrope—for this is their true name—could be anybody. A neighbor. The barista behind the counter of your favorite coffee house. Your teacher. Your child's imaginary friend. A lover—or a hated enemy.

I know this because I'm one of them.

Since you've read this far, I now present you with a Choice. Keep believing the Lie, or accept everything I have just told you and pretend not to notice the subtle tells that betray even the craftiest parathrope. A trick of the light, or a twitch of shadow. A sudden chill that shoots up your spine. A change in the air. The feeling of unseen eyes watching your every move. I promise: when it happens, you'll know. And you'll wish you didn't.

But there is a third option, open only to a select and secret few. If you believe that you, yourself are a parathrope, one of us, I implore you to seek me out. Don't hesitate—for the Cowans may already know of your existence. You can find me—and sanctuary—within a secret archive.

An archive called:

THE AEON FILES

I'll be waiting.

1

STARR THRIFTS & GIFTS, OBSIDIAN GROVE
MONDAY, OCTOBER 20
6:43 AM

Rain fell in cascading sheets, pummeling the fire escape outside my second-story window, splashing on the streets and sidewalks in a relentless torrent. Gray fog rode the air like roiling smoke, veiling the world outside until everything appeared as little more than shadows. Lightning flashed, close and blinding, and thunder rumbled on its heels.

Perfect weather.

I sat alone in the dark, watching the storm as it battered every inch of my hometown. An hour, probably more, had passed since the first roars of thunder had awoken me. It hadn't been fear that had roused me. No. It had been the storm's song; the serenity of rainfall and thunder amid the raw, unbridled energy that danced from cloud to cloud. I always found the sounds peaceful, especially on days like today.

Unfortunately, that peace never lasts long. Footsteps were already approaching my bedroom door. Sighing in annoyance, I reached up without looking to brace the mirror that hung just over my desk.

"*Golanv! Ayega!*" the usual loud and repetitive banging on my door promptly followed. Then another yell in Cherokee. "You'll miss the bus!"

That's *agilisi*. My grandma. I'm required to endure imprisonment in the tiny spare room of her one-and-a-half bedroom apartment. I hate the place with the fiery passion of a thousand suns. The walls are paper thin so I can hear everything going on in and around the complex. The noise of cars racing by with their stereos on max bass or drunkards stumbling home from the bar just up the street often kept me up at night. I couldn't even have my friends—if I actually had any that is—over to hang out because we'd make too much noise merely talking about how we hated homework. Not that you could fit more than one person in this minuscule space.

The prison cell that is called my room used to be an office, which agilisi had been forced to convert when she got dumped with me. It is filled to the brink with a twin bed and small desk that doubled as my vanity. The drab, olive green wallpaper had started to curl up years ago, so I hid the eyesore with dozens of drawings or coloring pages. I kept the hideous, worn yellow-orange carpet covered with my second-hand clothes and a few battered knickknacks I had managed to save from the dumpster. The only attractive feature of the room is a single, dingy window. It leads out to the fire escape, where I hide when I need some time alone.

Like this miserable room, agilisi had been the only constant in my life since I turned five. On the good days, she and I got along about as well as two feuding warlords. I think it's because she blames me for what happened to my parents. Sometimes, I think she wishes I had joined them. Sometimes, I wish I had, too.

I cut off that line of thinking as quickly as it had come, hollered over the insistent drumming. "*Howa*, *elisi*! I'm awake!"

Agilisi gave my door one final whack, hard enough to set the wall quivering. I waited until I heard the door to the bathroom squeal as it opened and closed before I finally let go of the mirror.

Truthfully, I didn't want to go to school today. Not just because Principal Roan despised me or because I am the new girl with a bad rap. I didn't want to go because today is the twentieth of October, and that is never a good day. Not going, however, would be even worse. Agilisi would force me to work all day in her thrift store downstairs, but not before she turned her switch on me. I'd sooner live in school or on the street than have to endure another of her torture sessions.

Running away wasn't an option. I've tried twice already, and she had been able to find me after only a few hours. It's not like I could get far with no money and being too young to be employed. Those jerks from Social Services and my shrink were no help either. I honestly believe agilisi paid them off to keep me in her custody.

The sooner I get out of here, the better.

I tore my gaze from the storm to delve into my would-be closet—a stack of cheap, wire shelves mounted to the wall over my twin mattress—in search of attire. I dug out a plain, black tee and my only pair of pants: black Levi's. I had resorted to stealing them after my last pair got tore up in a fight—that I did not start—and agilisi refused to buy me another pair.

Before you ask, yeah, I felt like a total dirt bag afterward. But how can someone seriously expect a teenager to make one pair of jeans last her entire high school life? Besides, I swore I'd never do it again.

And I *always* keep my promises.

I laced up my shoes, slung my tattered, old backpack over my shoulder, and made for the back door, pausing just long enough to grab an umbrella from the hook. Agilisi stood waiting for me at the bottom of the stairs, next to the stockroom door of her store. I had the great misfortune of looking almost exactly like her. Both of us had round faces with high cheekbones and slightly bent noses. Heavy, almond-shaped eyes the color of milk chocolate. Smooth reddish-copper skin. Thick hair that fell like a moonless night down the middle of our backs.

Honestly, the only difference between us is her hair had streaks of gray.

Agilisi held out some crumpled bills for my lunch along with a couple bus tokens. I stuffed the money in my pocket, rolled my eyes as she told me to behave for once. With a mumbled goodbye, I shoved the heavy security door open and stepped outside.

The rain plastered my hair to my skull before I even had a chance to open the umbrella. It's a cold autumn rain, too. Not that that bothered me any; I am incapable of feeling cold unless it's something like liquid nitrogen. I've never been able to figure out why, and I'm too afraid to ask agilisi about it. She'd probably sell me to some laboratory or something.

Without bothering to look, I started for the opposite side of the street. Chances of getting run over in a town of two hundred and eleven people during rush hour are almost zero. See, Obsidian Grove is a Podunk town known for nothing except it's now defunct drive-in movie theater. For a teenager like me, this place is as dull as a weekend in a convent. The main strip is Main Avenue, which is a whopping three blocks long. The town's only cafe (aptly named Oh! Gee) is a tiny thing at the west end. Agilisi's store stood at the east. And a quaint convenience store sat right in the middle, across the street from the post office slash bank slash town hall.

There's no bus stop in Obsidian Grove (not an official one anyway), so all the people who need to go to the big city during the day tend to congregate at the convenience store. The usual crowd had already arrived, coffee and doughnuts or other fat pills in hand, and bus number seventeen had just pulled to the curb when I arrived.

The driver, a twenty-something college kid, greeted everyone by name as they boarded. "Good morning, Cye."

My name is Cybil Golanv Starr, but everyone just calls me Cye. I'm fourteen-years-old and half Cherokee. If you believe the hype, I'm the kid your parents warned you about. You know: the playground bully, the emo-fueled loner. The troubled kid. The bad influence. Yadda, yadda, yadda.

Let me set the record straight once and for all. I don't know what the heck emo is. Yes, I am a bit of a loner. No, I don't set out every day looking for a fight. In fact, it's the bullies who often pick a fight with me. I'm just usually the last one standing when the dust settles. And to the victor goes the spoils.

"*Osda sunale*." I dropped my bus token in the slot, made for my usual window seat. Moments later, we were on the highway heading to Mabon City.

2 PRIVATE PARKING LOT, MABON CITY
MONDAY, OCTOBER 20
7:07 AM

Mabon City is a study in contradictions. New, lean skyscrapers of glass and metal stood beside stocky, century-old brick buildings. There are waterways and highways, concrete industrial parks and thick, luscious forest, dingy slums and luxurious mansions. All existing within stones throws of one another.

The parking lot across the street where my bus drops passengers off is a prime example of the peculiarities of the city coming together. The buildings flanking either side of the lot were squat, old apartment complexes. The elder of the two, a red-bricked heirloom, sported the scars of a hundred years' use. The other, a thirty-something with orange-creamsicle vinyl siding, had only just begun to show its age. Behind me, a sparkly new high rise pierced the sky. Across the parking lot from me, a quaint public garden—still alive with a riot of colors despite the recent cold snap—stood defiantly in the face of the urban jungle around it.

When my bus arrived, everything surrounding the lot flickered with the lights of the emergency vehicles. My fellow riders were quietly inquiring each other what they thought happened. Me? Well... Let's just say I had some specialized knowledge no one else did; not even the cops.

Okay, I confess; there's something I neglected to mention earlier.
I'm not exactly... normal. I realize teenagers say that a lot, but trust me when I say I'm in a whole different, freaky category. It's hard to describe what I am, but I think psychic comes close. I have this weird ability to feel things. I don't mean with my fingers, either. It's more of a sixth sense; like warning bells that trip when something weird and inexplicable is going on. I'm sure

you've experienced something similar at some point—that moment when the hairs on the back of your neck rise and your gut tells you that you're not alone. For me, it's a bit different.

Every living thing has a unique corona of ever-changing energy around them. It's commonly known as an aura, prana, chi, ki… you get the picture. Whatever you call this energy, I am able to sense it the same way a metal detector in a steel box would pick up on metal. Sometimes, I can even focus on the signature and know whether a person is your everyday stranger just going about their business or a cold-blooded killer looking for their next victim.

Freaky, right? Guess what: That's only half of what I can do.

The other half is where the term psychic applies. Ever since I can remember, flashes of events that are going to happen or those that have already passed have appeared in my dreams. I have no way to control these visions, but I do know they are accurate one hundred percent of the time. I've lost count of how many times the things I see in my dreams become the top news stories. I've seen it all—from natural disasters and man-made catastrophes to devastating plagues and never-ending droughts. Trust me; it's horrible.

That's the reason why I'm always saying the name Cybil fits me. And why the kids in grade school called me Jinx all the time (they believed I had been cursed).

Since Mabon City is such a vast space with a couple hundred-thousand inhabitants, it has a wide variety of energy signatures. So it came as only a mild surprise when an abnormal sort-of pressure began to settle over me the instant the bus entered the city limits. The closer I got to downtown, the more the pressure continued to build. Combined with a tingling chill that left me barely able to breathe, I knew something terrible had happened. And very recently.

A sinister energy that screamed of anguish and revenge struck like a knife on raw nerves the moment I stepped off the bus. Yelping in surprise at the unexpected intensity prompted a few fellow bus riders to ask if everything's okay. It wasn't, but I declared everything hunky-dory and sent an apprehensive look towards the source of all that horrible energy.

It emanated from the parking lot.

Crap.

As a general rule, I avoid the places where negative energies materialize. That negativity has a tendency of latching on to people like leeches whenever they get close. Don't worry; there are ways to get rid of it, but it can be time-consuming if you're not practiced at it. I'm not, so I definitely did not want to bring that nastiness home with me (I have enough problems in my life). Unfortunately, the route I take to school passes right through the parking lot, and I didn't have the time to navigate around it if I wanted to make it to school before the first bell.

I quickly slipped into the trickle of commuters in the crosswalk and made for the edge parking lot furthest from all the police activity. Every step closer caused my heart rate to spike more and more. The very air seemed to come alive with marrow-chilling tension. Tendrils of malicious energy reached out in ragged threads, desperate to take hold of anyone foolish enough to wander too close.

I hated being one of those fools.

But I despised that something compelled me to stop.

Frowning, I sent my senses out in search of the reason. The garbled mess of the police radio and the cacophony of voices from those gathered around were the only things I picked up. Whatever had reached out for my attention had become so faint that it could no longer pierce the noise. I had only moments before it drowned in that turbulent sea of evil energy.

Ignoring the instinct that told me to just keep walking, I moved in for a closer look. Onlookers and press teams vied for position along the yellow police tape. I knew I'd never get anywhere near enough to see beyond the wall of their backs. Instead, I hopped up on the concrete ledge of a nearby light pole.

Cops were everywhere, snapping photographs, measuring stuff, taking notes. A few stood by their squad cars, talking over the radio. Two detectives in cheap suits were being interviewed by the press. Uniformed officers stood guard on the sidelines, intent on keeping out anyone who might interfere with the scene.

The usual controlled chaos.

The wreck that had been a Cadillac Escalade caught my attention first. The roof had been struck by something substantial enough to cave the windshield and blow out the driver's window. I scanned overhead, measuring the rooftops. Even an Olympic athlete couldn't leap the forty-some feet to land on the roof of a car in the middle of the lot. Shards of glass littered the ground beside the SUV, telling me that the vehicle hadn't been moved.

And, judging by the body bag the two guys in blue jumpsuits were jostling onto one of those wheeled beds, this wasn't a meteorite or weather balloon. I knew the corpse couldn't be a stunt skydiver with a faulty chute. If that had been the case, there would be evidence of the chute somewhere. Ropes. Cloth. Something.

You can probably tell that I aspired to become a police officer one day. (Not that that would ever happen with my "mental instability.") This crime scene served as a test for my fledgling investigative skills, but I didn't have the time to be this wound up in it. I took a deep breath to calm my racing thoughts and wished I hadn't. Something else lurked among the blending smells of colognes and perfumes, car exhaust, and rain. This scent reminded me of last week's geology lesson when we studied the properties of little, yellow lumps. Though faint, I recognized this as the pungent odor of sulfur.

I wiped my nose. *How in the world does sulfur wind up in a parking lot?*

The back of my neck tingled, and a heated wave crashed over me. I held my breath, ready for the plunge knew I couldn't stop. Everything went numb, and the world fell away like a dream…

> *A guard moved through the halls, confident in his stride despite the dimness of the estate. He had these halls memorized, and knew he could navigate them even without the security lights. He paused at a doorway, chuckled at his younger colleague. She stood ogling the half-dollar sized jewel on the pedestal. He shook his head and moved on. He hadn't even gone three paces when suddenly the few lights that remained on began to flicker.*
>
> *A heartbeat later, they went out entirely, and darkness swallowed everything. A sudden, icy chill made him shiver, and he could swear he saw his breath escape in a cloud of mist.*
>
> *He heard someone stumble, and called out to see if they were okay.*
>
> *Glass shattered.*
>
> *An alarm blared.*
>
> *The guard quickly pulled his sidearm from its holster and rushed back to the hallway he had just passed. The air turned freezing and rank with the stench of rotten eggs. His colleague lay on the floor; dead or unconscious, he couldn't tell in the constricting dark. But someone… No. Something stood over her. A mass of black darker than a moonless*

night. It could have gone unseen had it not been moving, taking the dazzling gemstone from the display gingerly into its claws.

The guard trained his SIG on the dark mass and shouted as boldly as he could, "Freeze!"

The shadow whipped around with a hiss that no human could possibly make. Two glowing orbs the color of blood were instantly trained on him. The thing bared startling white fangs in a grin that reminded him of an evil Cheshire cat. He aimed for the thing's trunk and squeezed the trigger. He felt his heart plummet into the pit of his stomach when he heard the bullet ricochet off the far wall. The shadow chuckled, dark and mocking. It lunged at him, and he screamed as he emptied the clip.

The next thing he knew, his entire body had gone numb, and he shivered uncontrollably, just as if he had been caught outside during a blizzard in Antarctica. He barely caught a glimpse of the shadow before it blinked out of existence; it had kept that same horrible grin in place.

When at last sensation began to return, he instantly knew what had happened. Wind ripped past him, tearing away the breath from his lungs and water from his eyes. It reminded him of his days in the Air Force's jump school. Only this time he plummeted in free fall towards the ground without a lifeline.

A car alarm erupted as metal crumpled and glass blew.

Snapping back to reality as if someone had dumped a barrel of ice water on me nearly cost me my footing on the narrow concrete ledge. My breath came in shaky gulps like I couldn't get enough air. Goosebumps covered every inch of my skin while sweat traced a trail down from my temples. And the hair on the back of my neck tingled from the slightest touch of the morning breeze. I tried desperately to shake it off, but the strange feeling only remained to plague me.

Movement on my left finally stole my attention, and I watched the two guys in jumpsuits load the body in the back of an ambulance. I knew precisely who lay underneath the black plastic of the body bag. I could see his face in my mind in crystal clear HD, though I had never laid eyes on him before. He had bright, hazel eyes beneath bushy eyebrows. He had a crooked from that time he got punched in a bar fight in Korea. A faint scar ran along his chin, a reminder from when he fell out of a tree as a kid.

That's why you stopped me, isn't it? Because I could see what happened to you?

The faint presence finally lost its battle against the seething energy.

Sorry to waste your effort. I don't have the power to help you.

The ambulance doors closed, and I looked away.

My gaze shifted to a guy with shaggy, brown hair watching me as he spoke into his phone. I figured him for one of the police officers on the scene since he wore a suit similar to the other detectives. He must have been eyeing me because of my visibility above the crowd. I put on what I hoped looked like a sweet smile and waved a little. He continued to stare at me, but his expression changed from sour to curious.

I don't need any more trouble from the police, and it was past time I got out of here anyway. Agilisi would have me enslaved in her shop for a month if I arrived late to Homeroom and slapped with another detention.

I rushed away from the scene before anything else could stop me, continuing my usual walk to school but at a faster pace. I couldn't escape the weird feeling of being followed. A few times, I thought I even heard footsteps or breathing, but every time I looked over my shoulder, the sidewalks would be empty. Already aware that the intense negativity had more than likely latched on to me, it made sense. Now I just had to remember to get rid of it before my day could get any worse.

3 MABON CITY CAMPUS, MABON CITY
MONDAY, OCTOBER 20
8:03 AM

With someone shadowing me and the school bell just minutes away from ringing, I jogged the last few blocks. I made it to the school grounds just as the first bell sounded. On the outside, Mabon City Campus is an H-shaped building not worthy of description. It's just a pile of gray bricks surrounded by a white-washed, wooden fence. The only thing uglier than it right now was the jalopy of a station wagon that pulled to a stop at the curb.

The car might have had a lovely, royal blue paint job once—back in the Eighties when it was new. Now rust and mismatched primer overtook much of the original paint, and the hood and passenger door had been replaced from two different donor cars; one green, the other red. I had no idea who drove such an eyesore, but, with just moments before the tardy bell rang, I couldn't stick around to find out.

The front doors of the school had become crowded with other late arrivals, so I made for entrance on the southeast side of the school. *It's definitely shaping up to be one of those days. I just hope it doesn't end like the last one.* My back spasmed, and I stumbled a step as the memories shot through my mind like a runaway bullet train. I quickly shoved them away. *Not today, Cye.* I found my stride again. *Don't think of that today.*

I passed through the side entrance, bolted straight down the empty hall to the theater doors, and gagged the moment I crossed the threshold. The stench of new construction and fresh paint hadn't dissipated in the slightest over the weekend. *Stupid remodel.* I found the offending plastic buckets of paint and the pile of well-used brushes atop cheap card tables a few feet to the left of the door. A couple of the lids sat askew, indicating that the work would likely resume after homeroom cleared out.

The tardy bell rang and I made for my usual seat in the back row, far enough from the teacher to avoid her prying eyes. She never could tell whether or not I had been paying attention to the Media Club's version of the morning news (News my wrinkled rump! It's just school gossip the club found juicy enough to share.). I needed to exploit that little bit of privacy this morning if I were to have any hope of dispelling the negative energy that had latched onto me. I just hope it's not too late.

When you work with as much negative energy as I have, you learn that running water is the best way to cleanse it. Well, that, and reiki—though I'm not sure if that technique would work in this situation—or a variety of crystals and herbs. And since I couldn't pop down to the gym for a shower, I'd have to resort to grounding. Grounding works sort of like a water wheel. I send any bad energy I have into the earth while, at the same time, siphoning off some of the earth's bountiful good energy. My biggest problem with grounding is that I suck at it. It requires a level of concentration I just can't achieve most of the time. I require a focus to, well, focus on my intent, which is why I always keep one with me.

I dug into the side pocket of my bag as I flopped into my seat, and removed the old railroad spike I kept there. Why a railroad spike? Simply put, iron sucks away negative energies like a black hole devours light. Hence the ole horseshoe-over-the-door thing. I have no money to buy a horseshoe, but I could afford a free railroad spike. Since workers leave the old ones lying around when they fix the tracks, finding one is extremely easy. I picked this one up during my last escape-from-home attempt. It's rusty and pockmarked, but that's fine for what I use it for.

At the head of the spike I had tied three ribbons, each three feet long (before you ask, no, I didn't steal them; I got them from my art teacher) and a different color. Each color represented a specific purpose. I used white for balance and cleansing; purple to drive away evil; and black for grounding and banishing negativity.

This is my focus.

It also makes for a pretty decent improvised weapon, but we won't get into that.

I waited until after roll call, when no one would be paying any attention to the back row. Then I got to work. I started with spinning the spike between my hands as if I were making a Play Dough snake. This got the iron tuned to me and my intent. That done, I took the ribbons and began to braid them. With each knot, I imagined the negative energy affecting me being bound into the strands, where it would remain until it could be grounded into the earth proper.

I managed to get half-way through the lengths of ribbon before the doors behind me squeaked open, thus breaking my concentration. I heard the vice principal, Mrs. Nygarde, tell someone to take a seat before she strode past me. I cast a quick glance at the late arrivals as they sank into a pair of seats just opposite the aisle from me.

I recognized the younger of the two girls as a classmate of mine, but her name escaped me. I believe we shared science and math classes. She had an inch or two on me in height, and shoulder-length caramel-colored hair. Her second-hand jacket bunched awkwardly at her left elbow, and an almost glowing white cast covered her forearm. I couldn't remember if she had had the cast when I last saw her.

The elder girl I knew as Anjelah Cross. She had the preppy attitude one would come to expect from the new Prima Donna of the Theater Club. Anjie stood taller than the other girl by about six inches, and that's without her famed knee-high, stiletto boots. She had on a short skirt and a maroon sweater over a white blouse. She kept her chocolate and caramel-colored hair in an asymmetrical pixie cut. The look flattered her, but I'd never tell her that.

Unfortunately, their late arrival had interrupted the grounding procedure at a crucial time, and I couldn't simply pick up where I left off. I exhaled my frustration, glanced at the clock above the doors. If I could regain the concentration I had a moment ago, I could redo the entire grounding before first period. I might have to rush it a little, but that's a risk I'd have to take. So I broke the braid, releasing the half-bound energy I had gathered. At least this time I wouldn't have to tune the railroad spike to me. I blocked out all thought except my intent and started the braid again.

Not three knots in, I heard a hissed whisper that shocked me out of the correct state of mind for a second time. "How many times are we going to have this conversation? I told you, I'll take care of it."

"I don't like how you *take care* of things," came the equally whispered reply.

"You don't think the bitch deserves it?"

"Yeah, she needs to be punished. Just… Just not in the way you're talking."

Intrigued, I extended my senses towards Anjie and the other girl. What I picked up gave me the willies. I'm talking spiders-climbing-up-your-spine freaky. Unfortunately, they were sitting too close to each other for me to positively identify which of them gave off such a creepy vibe. Chances were remote they were both radiating it. Even identical twins aren't completely capable of synchronizing their auras like that. If I wanted to figure out the culprit behind this vibe, I'd have to get either Anjie or What's-her-name alone, and that's not likely to happen during school hours.

The bell rang just as I thought that, and a muttered curse slipped past my lips. I had forgotten about the grounding ritual. I could always skip class and finish it, but agilisi would be notified and that's the last thing I wanted. I sighed, returned the spike to its side pocket. It would have to wait until lunch period.

And I prayed to the gods that nothing went horribly wrong for me until then.

4 MABON CITY CAMPUS, MABON CITY
MONDAY, OCTOBER 20
12:19 PM

The morning drew on and on, as if time could only move at half the pace of a snail. Yet it kept surprising me. Just when I thought I had forgotten my homework for composition, I found it neatly folded between my notes. None of the usual jock bullies tried to challenge me. I didn't get yelled at by teachers, sent to the principal's office, or slapped with detention. I had to pinch myself a few times to make sure I hadn't gotten trapped in some twisted dream. And even then, I had a hard time extinguishing the anxiety that something really bad was about to happen. So when lunch time finally rolled around, I found myself sitting at one of the tables on the outdoor patio, staring at the railroad spike and wondering if grounding this negative energy away was the right choice. Ever since it latched onto me, things have been looking up.

But I knew some things were too good to last.

And this might all be just a huge coincidence.

Movement out of the corner of my eye captured my attention. I shot a glance sidelong, towards the lawn between the school's patio and football field. A handful of people were setting up a large tent. Others were piecing together stalls and a stage. That's when I remembered the Autumn Festival kicks off this Friday, which coincided with the Great New Moon Festival.

The old Cherokee tales say that the world had been created in the autumn, so the Great New Moon Festival marks the start of our new year. There's days and days of feasting, dancing, and praying. Then, ten days later, the Friends Made Ceremony is held, which is when old friendships are renewed and new friendships are forged. The first white settlers combined these traditions into what is known today as Thanksgiving.

I hope agilisi has plans of going this year. She might let me tag along.

An approaching presence jostled me from my thoughts, and I shot a look to my right. The girl with the cast—the one whose name escapes me—paused only briefly, and brazenly came up to me. She smiled, but it didn't reach her tawny eyes.

"Hi," she managed to squeak out. "I'm Aiden."

"I don't care." My gaze returned to the spike. *That's right. Aiden Cross. Anjie's little sister.*

"You're Cybil, right?" She sank into the chair opposite me. "Did you know the other kids call you J—"

"Jinx. Yes." I sipped my soda.

"Mind if I ask why?"

My attention returned to my unwanted visitor. She looked miserable, and she hadn't so much as touched her lunch.

"Because I'm not normal."

She made a face. "So, um?"

I sighed. "What?"

"There's something kinda important I'd like to talk to you abo—"

Six shadows suddenly fell upon us like vultures on a carcass.

Not today. I exhaled my annoyance as I scanned the faces of the boys that surrounded us. Just as I expected, they were school's precious football players. At least, that's what the school believed. They're a bunch of racist egomaniacs. I had previously exchanged blows with a couple of them—off school property of course—and come out the victor. My guess, they were looking for some kind of revenge when they approached.

Their captain, a stub-nosed boy with freckles and horrible pimples, spoke first. "What do you think you're doing here, injun? Don'cha know this is our table?"

I clenched my fists and tried to ignore the little voice in my head screaming at me to punch his lights out.

"Funny, I don't remember seeing any names written on it," Aiden said in an acid tone of voice she probably developed as a defense against her older sister.

"Like we really gotta put our names on it," said the captain. "Everybody just knows that this is our table."

"Yeah," added a tall boy that looked like he could turn into a kite if a soft breeze blew in. "Do you know what we do to little twerps like you that sit at our table?"

I rolled my eyes, muttered, "*Wena.*"

"What did you say to me, bitch?" For emphasis, the captain slapped my drink aside. The bottle gushed soda before rolling off the table to clatter against the ground.

I stood so quickly the boys flinched. A smirk traced its way across my lips as I faced the captain. "I said, 'Go away!' There are several empty tables, so how about you be good little boys and go sit at one of those instead of irritating me."

The next thing that I knew, someone held me pinned against his chest. The captain balled up his fists and closed in. Before he even got within striking distance, something within me roared to life. The air around me turned heavy. Colors grew more vibrant. My limbs tingled with static. My muscles tensed. I soaked up this feeling like a desert consuming a welcomed rain.

I slammed my foot on the knee of the guy holding me, smirked at the sharp crack. He released me in an instant, dropping to the ground with howls of agony. Two of the other footballers swooped in. I dropped one with a kick to the nads and kite-boy with an open-hand strike to his eyes. Then their pathetic, little captain stepped up. He apparently had something to prove because he dove right at me with a yell, intent on bashing in my face.

I swung my foot up to catch him in his ugly, little kisser. His head would have been ringing when he kissed the concrete, but someone else threw himself between us. The stranger caught the captain's punch in the same instant he snatched my ankle. His grip clamped on me like a vice, and I worried he'd snap my foot off like a dry twig from a tree. I glared up at the intruder, ready to kick his face in too, and his emerald green eyes stared coolly at me from beneath a mop of muddy brown hair.

I realized I recognized him. And the high I had been riding suddenly evaporated.

"Hey, you're the detective I saw at the crime scene this morning." *He must have been the one I sensed following me.* "What are you doing here?"

The fierceness in his eyes ebbed, and he studied me with a guarded stare. The vice-like grip he had on my ankle slackened ever so slightly. He moved his lips to speak but a shout interrupted before he could utter a syllable.

"Starr!"

I rolled my eyes upon recognizing the principal's growling shout. I finally bothered to look around. Several students had stopped what they were doing to see little me kicking the butts of the school's precious athletes. A couple of them even had their cellphones out, probably to record the fight. And at least one of them had run to get Mr. Roan.

Son of a—!

"Fighting again?" Mr. Roan stopped to observe the scene before him. Then he turned his fiercest scowl upon me, which, for a nerdy, bald, toothpick of a man like him, wasn't very intimidating. "That does it! You are out of here, young lady!"

The detective finally released my foot, and I brought it carefully down to earth. He faced the principal, flashed his badge. "My name is Quinn

Calloway. I am a detective with MCPD, here to speak with Miss Starr."

"Good!" snapped the principal. He knelt beside the big guy, whose knee I had kicked in, and told him that the nurse will be here in a moment. "That means you can escort that little hooligan from the school grounds before she tries to beat up any more of our students."

"Actually, sir, she only defended herself. These boys," the detective picked out the guys on the football team, "they started the fight."

"We did not!" proclaimed the captain.

I glared at him. "Shut-up, you squeaky-voiced pansy."

The principal shot the dirty look he usually held in reserve for me at the detective. "These boys are the school's star athletes. They do not go around bullying other students. They know they will be removed from the team if they do. Miss Starr there, has a long record of violent—"

That does it! "Oh, yes! I am so guilty!" I screamed at him. "All I ever do is step in to stop bullies like you and your pathetic jocks and preppy egomaniacs from beating up other kids! And what do I get in return? Expelled!"

"That's enough, young lady!"

I snatched the textbooks from my backpack, hurled them at him. "Bite me, you conceited jackass!"

I didn't bother waiting for a response; I just grabbed my railroad spike and stormed off.

5 MABON CITY CAMPUS, MABON CITY
MONDAY, OCTOBER 20
1:03 PM

Here's an interesting little factoid for you: There are no swear words in Tsalagi. If we Cherokee wanted to cuss, we used English. And I unloaded every single one of them in a flowery bouquet of profanity, each syllable emphasized by the pounding of my feet against the sidewalk. I probably made quite a spectacle of myself to the people driving by, but I didn't care at that point. I had a much, much larger problem. I'm not saying that four expulsions in two years isn't something to be concerned about, it just pales in comparison to what awaited me at home. Just the very thought of it brought tears to my eyes and an old, familiar pain to my back.

"Stupid jocks. Stupid principal. Stupid school!" I kicked the school ground fencing as hard as I could, and the boards gave with a loud crack. Another lovely curse slipped past my lips and I struck the busted plank with a rapid one-two punch.

When the next solid strike broke the skin on my knuckles and set them bleeding, I forced myself to walk away. Some more logical part of my brain told me to go to the police; that they'd protect me. But fear and experience told me otherwise. Just like with Social Services, agilisi very well could have a few cops in her pocket, which meant they'd ignore my claims of abuse and turn me right back over to her custody. Or they'd release me to Social Services, in which case, I'd still end up back with agilisi.

Terrified of returning home and with nowhere else to go, I wandered aimlessly. I knew I was only delaying the inevitable, and my punishment would be even more severe as a result, but at least I could pretend things were fine for a little while. It also bought me some time to figure out what the heck happened during the fight.

I can't recall how many times some sort of alternate personality took over whenever I got into a fight. When it did, it made me faster. Stronger. And I don't mean it made me *feel* that way. I actually became superhuman. If I wanted to, I could have done a lot more damage to those boys than give them a few bruises and spotty vision.

That side of me also enjoyed causing pain, and it felt superior to those stupid humans.

I paused mid-step, made a face. '*Stupid humans?*' I lightly laughed. *What a weird thing to say.*

Sure, I've repeatedly said that people are stupid because, lets be honest, we do a lot of stupid stuff for stupid reasons. Don't believe me? I'll introduce you to a guy who stole a stop sign to impress a girl, bragged about it to the whole school, and now wonders why he has a juvie record. Or that pair of geniuses who wrapped their faces in duct tape, robbed a store, and wound up getting arrested when they went to the hospital for help getting the tape off. Or the drunk guy who stripped naked and rolled through a cactus patch to see if the needles really did hurt.

I could go on for a while. But my point is: I never once said *humans* were stupid. How strange to suddenly say that now. Stranger still was where this line of thinking had given me cause to stop: right at the edge of the parking lot and the vortex of negative energy. I had been unknowingly weaving my way back to it as if called by something. Though the energy had dissipated some thanks to the morning sun, the lot still had a feeling of someplace haunted.

The hairs on the nape of my neck prickled and stood on end. I shivered, and swept the blighted parking lot with a questing gaze. Only a handful of cars now dotted the space. A UPS truck sat parked a few feet from the old soldier of a building, hazards blinking and door ajar. Puddles from this morning's storm pooled in low points of the pavement. Some old soda bottles and autumn-painted leaves lay in crevices where the masonry had crumbled away. Yellow police tape encircled the now empty section of the lot where the crumpled Escalade had been parked.

Everything was as it should be. Yet… Something just felt… *wrong*. The air had come alive with a strange energy, not quite evil but not wholly good either. The scent of fresh rain carried on the breeze yet there were only scattered clouds in the sky. I tried to tell myself that it might just be the remnants of this morning's storm or, perhaps, the negative energy that had clung onto me, but that did little to ease the feeling.

"Man! Can this day get any more F-ed up?" I moved into the parking lot with exaggerated care. A stench like rotten eggs on a hot day filled the air where it had not been a moment ago. Something must have had died in one of the trash cans, and the rain from this morning had activated the stench. Perhaps the wind had simply changed directions, pushing the stench towards me.

Yeah. Right. And I might have just won the Powerball and a free lifetime stay at the Ritz.

The wind hadn't changed; only my position along the street. To be sure, I sent my senses out in a wide search pattern, grasping for any hints of inexplicable energy. Only the normal pulse of the planet and its people came back to me.

How odd.

Something drew me further into the parking lot. Curiosity, maybe? Or, perhaps, an outside influence? The latter thought terrified me. So much so that the sudden slamming of the door on the UPS truck made me jump. I must have yelped too since the driver shot me a strange look before driving away. I let out a long, shaking breath, and covered my face with my hands. I stayed that way for a bit, berating myself for being such a coward.

When, at last, my heart rate slowed, I started across the parking lot with renewed determination. I had just passed an old Eighty-Eight when the entire car lurched. I jumped back with a wordless yell. The car creaked, and metal caved with a thunderous complaint. My heart leapt to my throat, and I dared a peek out of the corner of my eye. A monster, vaguely humanoid and blacker than any moonless night, stood hunched over on three limbs too long for it's body. It held a fourth aloft, reaching outwards as if trying to touch me. Two ruby-like orbs floated in the ebony abyss above a stark white smile of needles. I couldn't breathe. I couldn't run. My fear had frozen me. And the thing just stared right at me.

It growled like some wild predator and slowly crossed to the hood of the old Eighty-Eight. I finally found the courage to move and stepped back as slowly as I dared. Metal complained as the mass of black moved off the car, never once breaking eye contact with me. It crept closer and closer, and the stench of rotten eggs grew stronger and stronger. It stopped about five feet away from me, where the shadows cast by the buildings gave way to late afternoon sunlight. I tried to move another step back, and it hissed venomously, showing me every needle-like fang in its twisted smirk of a mouth.

I swallowed the lump in my throat. "Yo-you're that thief, aren't you? The one who stole the jewel?"

It continued to grin like an evil Cheshire cat but cocked its head to one side like a dog does when it hears something funny. The fire in its ruby eyes seemed to grow curious, or perhaps puzzled.

Is it wondering how I knew of the gem? Or is there another one of these things out there, and I'm confusing this one for the other? That thought terrified me, and I felt tears of panic burn at my eyes. "P-please just leave me alone."

Its creepy grin faltered slightly, almost as if it considered leaving. For that moment I allowed myself to hope that this… this *terror* would retreat back to wherever it had come from. Then it snorted. The shapeless lips peeled back even further, flashing its stark white mouthful of needles. And then it leaped towards me.

A brown streak zipped past my legs, heading right for the shadowy monster. The two collided in midair with a clap of thunder. They fell to the ground in a mix of flailing limbs and bestial snarls. Car alarms blared then promptly malfunctioned, victims of the strange energies the creatures radiated.

I didn't stick around to see which one would win. I raced across the street, narrowly missing becoming a street pizza when a jalopy of a car sped past. The driver yelled a few choice words at me, but I didn't listen. Bus Seventeen had pulled to the curb, and I was determined to reach it. I did. And just in the nick of time. I dropped my token in the slot and the bus started moving before I even took a seat.

I finally dared a look back at the parking lot. There weren't any signs of a battle, but an enormous, brown husky sat on the sidewalk, watching the bus as it pulled away.

6 STARR THRIFTS & GIFTS, OBSIDIAN GROVE
MONDAY, OCTOBER 20
3:33 PM

Agilisi had just hung up the phone when I walked through the door and into her domain. She looked absolutely livid, and wasted no time grabbing my arm and pulling me to the back room. Once there, she ordered me to take off my shirt as she got her switch cane. I folded my shirt neatly, laid it aside. Agilisi's fury broke upon me within seconds.

The arrival of customers spared me from more of her rage. By then, I had already fallen to my knees in a desperate, defensive ball. She hissed at me that this wasn't over, and left. I slumped forward to lay on the hard concrete, biting the back of my hand to keep the sobs back. I couldn't let the customers hear me. It would only make things worse with agilisi.

It was a long while before I forced myself to move. Excruciating pain shot through my body like lightning. My back protested with even the slightest move, and I could feel liquid oozing from the wounds. My legs were wobbly. I couldn’t stop shaking.

Grabbing my shirt from where it had been laid, I quietly slipped into the tiny employee bathroom and locked the door. The orange-ish light flickered to life automatically when I stopped at the sink. My reflection showed me puffy, reddened eyes and cheeks stained with tears. I opened the tap and threw cold water on my face. My hand stung. The skin had broken in several places along the bite marks, and blood pooled in the divots. I ran it under the cold water to numb the pain, but it wouldn't stop shaking. Eventually, I worked up the courage to turn around for a look at my back.

I wished I hadn't.

It looked more like a slab of raw meat than human skin. Enormous, red welts and dark purple bruises covered my back from shoulders to waist. A patch of skin the size of my fist had been torn off, leaving an angry and bloody canyon between my shoulders. At least three of the strikes had broken through the old scars and left bloody slashes running the full width of my back. They hadn't stopped bleeding yet and part of one looked deep enough to require stitches.

I unraveled several sections of paper towel from the dispenser and expertly folded them into a thick belt. Gritting my teeth against the burning bite of moving, I wrapped the belt around my waist to catch the blood before it could soak my jeans. Even if I could reach all of the strikes, I had no way to treat them. There's no way in hell I'd ask agilisi for any help. And I couldn't go to a hospital.

It's not fair! Why am I being punished for what those stupid boys started? I left the tap open and let myself cry. Even if I had to do it quietly, it was the only comfort I could give myself. There's no medication in the world that could ease this pain. *Why? Why do I keep coming back to this?* I studied myself in the mirror, marveled at how pathetic I looked. *Come on, Cye! You're stronger than this!*

I had to find some way out of this nightmare that didn't end in my funeral. There had to be a way to disappear without a trace. If I could just figure out how. The neighbors weren't likely to help me, and I wasn't about to place my burden on anyone else.

What had my shrink said? Rely on no one but yourself.

"Golanv."

I flinched, bit the back of my hand to keep from screaming at the agony that knifed through me. My pulse raced as panic consumed me, and I felt blood once again ooze from my wounds. Agilisi had come to fulfill her threat to continue the beating. I'm just a rat in a corner in here; she had all the keys. So I croaked out, "*G-gadousdi tsaduliha?*"

She spoke in an emotionless voice, using Tsalagi to order me to carry in some boxes for a customer.

"*Howa*, elisi." I silently and slowly counted to fifty, all the while straining my ears to hear even the softest of footfalls and worried when there weren't any. I fashioned another belt from the paper towels, and struggled into my shirt. Every time it barely whispered over my abused flesh, I had to bite back screams. I took a minute or two to compose myself, preparing myself for the worst.

Rely on no one but yourself.

Unlocking the door, I poked my head out to take a look.

She had gone.

I released the breath I had been holding, and moved as swiftly as I could to the key rack. The bells on the front door jingled, and I hoped it was agilisi leaving. Daring a peek through the storeroom door, I spotted broken-arm-girl, Aiden if I recall correctly, exchanging hushed words with agilisi. She looked upset as agilisi talked to her, most likely feeding her lie after lie. Aiden waved goodbye with a disappointed frown before she quit the store. She followed the sidewalk westward and disappeared beyond the shop windows.

What in the world is she doing here? I thought back to our last conversation. Something had been bothering her, and she had been about to tell me, but those little bastards started the fight. With the day's hectic activity, I had completely forgotten about it. If she had convinced her parents to drive all the way out here, it must be something extremely important. I wonder if I can move fast enough to catch up to her.

Agilisi hissed like an angry cat. Only then did I realize that she had spotted me watching through the door. The look in her eyes conveyed the message: Do as I said, or you'll end up worse than just a bloody piece of meat. Then she went to the dark-haired man browsing through the old lamps.

His amethyst gaze found me in the doorway, and I forced what I hoped passed for a friendly smile before slipping away.

With a heavy sigh, I headed towards the back stairs and shoved the heavy side door open. Searing hot agony knifed through me, and I berated myself for being so stupid. Stupid for body slamming the door open. Stupid for returning to this hell to be tortured and abused. Just stupid. If it hadn't been for that monster in the parking lot, I'd still be in the city. I'd be safe. And my back wouldn't be a torn up, bloody mess.

So why did I come here?

It doesn't make any difference now.

But I refuse to let it happen again. I had to escape this. I had to disappear. Now. Otherwise I doubt I'd live long enough to graduate high school—If I *could* graduate.

I'd be fifteen in eleven days, barely old enough to get a real job. A real life. The biggest challenge would be getting a place to live. I'd need a fake ID or else I might as well live under a bridge or in a… My gaze snapped to agilisi's burgundy Taurus, parked in its usual spot behind the store, and a light bulb suddenly clicked on.

Agilisi had no idea that I had discovered the hiding spot of her spare master key ring—the keys that unlocked every door and safe and lock box in the building—in the trunk of the car, just under the spare tire. It's probably the most insane idea I've ever conceived; crazier and stupider than my last two attempts. I never would have considered it if not for the driver's ed class I'd started this school year. If my plan worked, I'd be long gone before agilisi ever knew I left.

Perfect!

I couldn't risk getting the keys now, not with a client waiting for a pick-up, so I'd have to sneak in a way to get them without agilisi knowing. I set that line of thinking on the back burner for the moment and turned my focus to the job at hand.

A fancy, antique car had parked a few yards from the hydrant at the corner, and I mean *really* fancy. It looked like it belonged in a museum under high security. It had custom-made, wire spoke rims with white-walled tires. On the side facing me, a matching full-sized spare had been fixed to a mount that left it hovering just above the chrome running boards. The length of the hood probably matched my height, and it had been fitted with a highly polished chrome ornament I didn't recognize. It had three windows on each side, of which the back two on both sides as well as the rear windshield were so heavily tinted that no one could see inside. Even through that level of tint, I could tell that it had an enormous back seat, like that of a limousine's.

A tall woman in a white pant suit stood at the rear passenger door. One glimpse and I instantly hated her. I hated her cascading golden hair, her modest makeup, her creamy skin, even the aquamarine gaze she turned on me as I approached. I mean, I wanted to rip her into itty bitty pieces and dump them in a septic tank and light it all on fire. And the feeling had come on so strong and so suddenly that it left me reeling. I'd never felt this way about anything or anyone before; not even agilisi.

Whatever it was about her that caused this feeling, I had to ignore it. Agilisi gave me a job to do, and letting my personal feelings get in the way would only make things worse. So I approached the woman brazenly and introduced myself.

"Do you have a box that needs to be brought in?"

She didn't say a word; just opened up the back door (Backwards! That's really cool!) and gestured inside. Vast is as accurately as I can describe the size of the antique's unusually dark back seat. In fact, you could probably park a Fiat 500 in the space and still have room for groceries. I rappelled down onto the leather-upholstered bench seat and took the monorail to the other side, making sure to keep my abused flesh away from any surfaces. I showed up eventually, and found a filing box sitting on the floor. I peeked inside.

Books. Great. Just what my back needed.

I took the elevator back up to the surface, bouncing the hefty box along with me. The sudden onslaught of sunlight blinded me for a moment and the box tipped. While I took a moment to wrangle the books back into order, I heard a phone ring. Then the woman began to talk in a hushed but hard tone.

"Yes, sir?" A pause. "That report is mostly accurate. I fear that a few important details have been… omitted." I heaved the box from the car, grit my teeth to keep from screaming in agony as the weight stretched the muscles and skin of my back. The woman curtly nodded when I slipped past her. As I made my way to the store's main entrance, I heard her mutter, "Worse than we thought."

I'm not very graceful on a good day, and this certainly wasn't one of those. So I struggled to balance the box on my thigh long enough to pull the door open and nearly succeeded in falling through the window instead.

The man I had seen among the lamps rushed over to hold the door. "My goodness. Are you all right?"

I wanted to say no, but I put on a smile and said, "Yeah, I'm fine. Just a little clumsy." I paused for a moment to adjust the box again, and got a good look at him in the process. He had extremely pale skin, like he had never seen a beach or tanning salon his entire life. I couldn't guess his age, but he looked somewhere between thirty and fifty. He had piercing, upturned eyes, high cheekbones and an angular chin. A low ponytail kept his long, dark hair out of his face and he was dressed in an expensive, tailor-made suit. This close to him, I detected a hint of a spicy, but not at all offensive, cologne. "Thank you for the help."

"My pleasure," he said with a friendly smile. The sparkling white of his teeth made his skin look like a rich suntan. And he spoke with the memory of an accent. It might have been Russian, or something more exotic from that area. “I’m Duncan Thatcher.”

“Nice to meet you, Mr Thatcher,” I said and set the box on the counter by Agilisi, who immediately started looking through the collection of books. It would take her maybe ten minutes to comb through the books and appraise them then another few minutes to pay Mr Thatcher. That gave me enough time to myself to put my escape plan into action.

Before agilisi could shoo me, I excused myself and slipped into the back room. Moving as quickly as I could, I grabbed one of the recycle bins and popped open the hidden spare key section of the door frame. Just as I had hoped, the two old Ford keys still hung on the short nail within. I snatched them, resealed the compartment. I exited through the side door a moment later, under the pretence of taking the blue bin to the recycling dumpster. Heading away from Main Avenue, there's a short gravel driveway that cuts a path to the back of the store where agilisi keeps the Taurus parked. It’s usually an easy walk, but the awkwardness of the recycle bin played havoc on my back. I wasn’t about to let the pain stop me. Not this time. I just grit my teeth and kept walking.

At last, I could see the two dumpsters. Right between them sat the Taurus.

The old Ford hailed from the early nineties. It’s a four door burgundy heap riddled with hail dents and rust. The windshield had been chipped and cracked, and the muffler had fallen off. Its passenger-side mirror had been amputated in a small collision during a particularly bad storm last winter.

It may not be the belle of the ball, but the old girl had the spirit of a Mustang.

I felt as if eyes were upon me as I crossed the driveway. Not wanting to betray even the smallest portion of my plans to anyone, I strode past the car and up to the recycling dumpster. I set the bin on the ground to unload it and used the opportunity to look around. When I didn't find anyone, I extended my senses to feel for someone. I thought I picked up on something for a fraction of a second, but the presence and the feeling vanished as suddenly as it had appeared. I waited a moment, senses still extended, but the feeling didn't return.

Seizing the opportunity, I rushed to the rear of the car. The deck lid opened with a quick turn of the key, and a mess of second-hand junk greeted me. I shoved it out of the way to expose the spare tire compartment, lifted the cover. Luckily, the donut wasn't locked down making it simple to access the cradle underneath. The ring of keys lay there, gleaming like diamonds in a forbidden treasure. I took them and let everything fall back into place. A half-eaten box of granola bars tumbled out of the mess. I snatched them, stuffed all four in my pockets along with the keys. Then I softly closed the trunk and continued dealing with the recycling as if nothing had happened.

The moment I returned to the store room, I switched out the empty recycling bin for a full one. It took me less than two minutes to set it outside, slip upstairs into my room to hide the stolen keys and granola bars, and return downstairs to take the bin out. As I did, I smiled.

My plan is progressing nicely so far. No matter what happens today, I'll be out of here by tomorrow.

7 STARR THRIFTS & GIFTS, OBSIDIAN GROVE TUESDAY, OCTOBER 21 5:43 AM

The world was gray with the oncoming dawn when I carefully, silently slipped out the window. The delightfully cool air carried a whiff of the last wildflowers of summer. The gekkering of foxes erupted from somewhere in the distance. The pinkish-orange glow of the street lights did little to scatter the remnants of dark. For a single, fleeting moment, I worried about the return of that ruby-eyed monster and of the ever-watching gaze that I had been under. But out here, none of that mattered. Whenever I came out here, particularly at night, whatever bothered me seemed to just melt away. This little fire escape had been my sanctuary for the last decade. This morning, however, it represented much more than that. This morning, it marked the first step along the road of my new life.

I looked forward to the freedom. I could get a job that actually paid, find a school that would accept me, or maybe enroll in one of those online ones. I could buy my own clothes and food, get the stuff I've always dreamed of having, and live where I wanted to. Most importantly, I'd never have to be afraid of coming home ever again. I'd never be beaten or starved or locked up because some despicable woman resented my existence.

I'd finally feel human.

I had just one last thing to do before I left, and my heart raced at the very thought of it.

Quickly reaching through the open window, I grabbed my stuffed backpack. There were a few things I wished I could bring with me but, because agilisi had locked me in my room, I didn't have access to them. I stuck with what I had, which consisted of a couple shirts, extra socks, my hair brush, and a couple of well-used notebooks. With a final look back at my prison cell and the misery it represented, I shouldered my bag and stepped towards the ladder.

I felt my back pang in protest as I struggled to release the ladder silently. I ignored the pain, unwilling to succumb to any delay.

Within moments, I found myself on the ground and making for the side door of agilisi's shop. I paused, pressed my ear to the door to listen. Silence greeted me. At last, I unveiled my secret weapon: agilisi's spare master key ring. With it, I easily got into the shop's storeroom, where I quickly made for the makeshift office. Half-concealed behind a wall of shelves, in a small corner of the room, sat a secretary desk and an old iron safe. Agilisi never uses a computer, so the top of her desk is always riddled with log books and office things. The desk has a secret that agilisi believes I don't know about, but I had seen her do it half a dozen times.

I walked right up to it and shoved everything off the top. A satisfied grin spread across my face, and I fought the urge to upend everything in the store room. I had to remind myself this morning wasn't about revenge. I needed to escape.

A tiny keyhole in the top of the desk gleamed in the dim light. Quickly finding the old bronze key among those on the master ring, I jammed it into the lock. I heard a soft click, and pulled up on the key. The cubicle hidden inside the desk measured roughly half the size of a shoe box. Two things were kept in it: a sizable roll of dollar bills held together with a rubber band and a single Polaroid.

Smiling, I pulled the photo from the box. Years had passed since I had last seen it. It showed a happy family at the beach, posing behind an enormous sand castle. The father had long raven hair and skin like bronzed caramel. The mother had a fairer complexion and eyes of emerald green. Between them, a dark-haired girl in a pink swimsuit made a face at the camera.

I only vaguely remembered that day. We had been on vacation in Florida. The three of us spent the entire morning building that castle, and my dad had paid a guy five bucks to take our picture with it. We flew back to Mabon City later that afternoon. It was the last time we were together.

The twentieth of October, 1999.

I wiped the tears from my eyes, tucked the picture safely between the pages of one of my notebooks. *Now. Now I am ready to leave this nightmarish place behind me.*

As I returned the notebook to my bag, I considered taking the money as well. I knew I shouldn't, but if I really wanted to escape agilisi, I'd need to get away as fast as I could. That would be impossible without money. It would be a necessary evil to ensure not just my escape, but my very survival.

I seized the money, jammed it into the side pocket of my bag. *I'll consider it my wages for all the years I slaved away in her shop.* Then I went to the rear door of the back room and removed the car keys from the secret compartment in the frame. With that, I walked out of the side door for the last time.

Sticking to the shadows, I headed away from Main Avenue, to the back of the store and the parked Taurus. Like the cash, I needed it. Twenty miles separated Obsidian Grove and Mabon City; much too far to walk. And the bus wouldn't be here for another two hours. I had to get out of here *now*. The money had changed my plans slightly. I had originally intended on taking the car and driving until it broke down. Now I had a much better alternative.

I'd take the car and leave it parked somewhere downtown before going to the train station. When agilisi reported the car stolen and her "precious" granddaughter missing, the cops would find it but not me. I'd already be on a train heading somewhere far, far away from this nightmare. I could decide where I‘d go later. Right now, I just needed to get out of here.

I unlocked the driver’s door and slipped inside. My hands were shaking as I stuck the key in the ignition. I had to tell myself again and again that I could do this. I could drive. I *needed* to drive. Then I stuck the shifter on D and slowly let off the brake. The first few feet were exhilarating, and I almost forgot that I had to turn to get out of the parking space. My knuckles were white from gripping the steering wheel as I crept the car up to the cross street. My hands were clammy and still shaking, but I somehow managed to pull onto Main Avenue without hitting anything. A huge smile lit my face as I went past the convenience store. Before I knew it, I was cruising down the highway toward Mabon City, and my smile widened as Obsidian Grove grew ever smaller in the rear view mirror.

8 DOWNTOWN, MABON CITY TUESDAY, OCTOBER 21 6:21 AM

I stuck to familiar roads as I navigated the city, diverting only once so as to avoid that blighted parking lot. The sun had just begun to paint the horizon in fiery colors when I ditched the ole Taurus at the airport. I made sure the security guards and cameras got a good look at me when I went inside. A few minutes later, I emerged a different person.

Not literally.

I had slipped into the ladies room to switch shirts and release my hair from the messy bun I had put it in. I also burned a couple of minutes counting out the money I had taken. The roll of bills totaled just under two grand (happy birthday to me). I ended up pocketing a couple fifties and twenties and storing the rest in my bag. By then, the plane I had been waiting for had come in, and I had vanished into the crowd to slip out the exit.

As I did, I couldn't help but notice the blue and silver Rolls Royce Phantom that slowly cruised by.

"There's something you don't see every day," I muttered, watching out of the corner of my eye as it pulled into a parking spot not far from the ole Taurus. Why would anyone park a half million dollar car in an unsecured lot? Only the gods knew. Still, I extended my senses towards the car to feel for anything abnormal. I got nothing back. Nothing. No life force. Either the driver and any occupants were dead—in which case, he or she did a spectacular job driving—or they left without me noticing.

I pulled my senses back and kept walking.

Less than a hundred paces later, I felt a gaze settle upon me. I still found nothing when I stretched out my senses, so I called upon my Second Sight. Some people refer to it as opening the Third Eye. You become aware of things that normal senses could never detect, and it is impossible to filter out what is real and what isn't. Beings of spirit and shadow that lurk just beyond the physical world become as real and as solid as you and me. The intentions and feelings, both good and bad, of everyone and everything become swirls of dancing light. You can see the ebb and flow of life energies as they were, as they are, and as they will be. And what you See never really leaves your memory. People have been driven insane from it.

It's a challenging thing to do; walk and *See* everything around you. Trust me when I say it's nowhere near as simple as rubbing your belly and patting your head at the same time. It's more like juggling flaming knives while riding a unicycle in an off-road BMX competition while wearing a blindfold.

Needless to say, I didn't leave my Sight open for very long; just long enough for a quick glance around. Unfortunately, it wasn't long enough to discover who had their eye on me. I turned my focus back to making my way to the train station, my pace a little faster due to my desire to escape. Once or twice, I thought I heard someone behind me, but I never saw anyone. I kept walking.

The vision struck without warning.

Cold, light-drinking marble stretched onwards, disappearing into the darkness ahead. Its footsteps echoed, quick and sure despite the constricting black.

Out of the void, two pinpoints of light materialized. Braziers. Each alight with azure flames. Betwixt them, twin doors of solid, ebony metal. Centuries had passed since last the doors had been opened. If it had its way, it would be centuries more before they opened again.

A key forged of the same strange metal unlocked the doors, and hinges screamed in protest as each crept inwards. It shoved them fully open, already knowing nobody would hear the noise. Only a select few knew of this location.

It strode in.

Azure fire burst into existence with a roar like a wild cat. The flames traveled along grooves in the floor, illuminating a cavern of a room in dancing light. The enormity of the space had been hand-hewn from ebony stone over several lifetimes, and boasted three stories and several separate antechambers. Stockpiles of weregold and dazzling gemstones filled the space on the main floor. Ancient texts and scrolls and treasures long forgotten by the Worlds had been stored in the upper levels.

Except for one.

That particular artifact sat in the center of the main room, perched atop a dais of solid gold. At its heart, black glass that reflected nothing until the spell could be used. Around it, the pitted and twisted bone of an ancient beast that had been stained dark with age and use. The mirror had been broken long before it found its way here.

At long last the two remaining pieces had been found. The artifact could once again be used. And the Worlds would suffer as they so deserved.

The presence strode right up to the dais and snatched the mirror from its pillow.

It turned to leave, froze in place.

Something stood haloed in the cold light of the doors.

Something with blazing, ruby eyes.

I snapped back to myself at about a zillion miles an hour. The vision had come and gone so abruptly that it left me dizzy, disoriented. Walking became impossible. I wound up flat on my ass on the sidewalk, clutching my head in my hands and praying for the world to stop spinning so wildly.

I have no idea how much time passed, but three cars had crawled by at half the pace of a snail. The horrific thought of them being a single police cruiser passing by three times is what finally got me moving. I had to use the wall for support during the first several shaky steps. By the time I crossed the first alley, everything had returned to normal.

My body may have forgotten the vision, but my mind sure didn't. In fact, it was so wound up in trying to figure out the meaning behind it that I almost missed the appearance of a strange presence. It danced on the edge of my senses like a butterfly around a flower. I stopped, sent my senses out towards the presence. The energy it emitted wasn't quite human, nor did it feel completely animal.

Could it be whoever is behind the ever-watching gaze? I wondered.

That's when a creature stalked out of the shadows ahead of me. I say 'creature' because 'siberian husky on steroids' just doesn't do it justice. It had a shaggy coat in river mud brown and eyes that glowed as blue as the midday sky. It must have been a foot, foot and a half taller than me at its shoulders and at least ten feet long. Its chest was broader than any canine's, as if packed with a hundred pounds of pure muscle. Ears that resembled spearheads protruded from the top of its head, upright and focused forward as the canine searched for something. I saw the gleaming white of its saber-like teeth, heard the clicking of its ebony claws against the sidewalk as it drew nearer.

I noticed all those details in the span of a second. My reptilian brain admired the canine's savage beauty, but my logical brain told me I had seen it someplace before. Then its glowing, pale blue gaze zeroed in on me, and it crouched, ready to pounce. Panic gripped me. Hard. And it took every ounce of self control I could muster not to double back on myself.

Its tail wagged.

I blinked.

It whined, pawed the ground twice.

I allowed myself to relax a little. "Are... Are you lost?"

It cocked its head, sat.

"I guess that's a no," I muttered. Louder, I said, "You'd better go home before animal control comes after you."

It chuffed. Then it got up. I stepped to the side as ginorma-dog circled around behind me. It nudged me, nearly knocking me over.

"Oh, no. I'm not taking you home." I faced the canine with my hands on my hips. "I'm going to the train station. I don't have time for you." With that, it pivoted on my heel and strode away.

I heard ginorma-dog follow, glanced over my shoulder at it.

"Sure, you can follow me to the station, just don't expect to get inside. Or on a train."

It gave me a soft woof and fell silent.

I tried to ignore it as the mile passed. It's nearly impossible to do with a beast that size. Where had it come from? Why had it chosen to follow me? These are the things that kept going through my head as I walked. The feeling of being watched remained over me, but the canine wasn't the source.

At long last, the squat, red-bricked building loomed before me. Only when I reached the glass doors did I finally slow down. I bade the enormous canine farewell and entered. The ever-watching gaze melted away. A few groups of people mulled about the lobby, which had a decor that went out of style some time in the 1870s. Only one man sat quiet and apart from everyone else, thumbing through an old magazine. I ignored them all, made for the Arrivals and Departures board. My footfalls on the hardwood floor were like thunder rising over the din of quiet conversation. My breath like gales of wind before a storm.

I stared at the board not really seeing it and trying to calm my hammering heartbeat. Now that I had arrived, the reality of what I had just done hit me. I had robbed a business and stolen a car. All for a dream I wanted more than anything to come true. I tried to convince myself this was all worth the risk, the potential jail time if I got caught, and that I had nothing to fear. My freedom from that wretched woman was finally within my grasp. I just had to decide which direction to go.

Then a voice from behind said, "I'd suggest Chicago."

9 13TH STREET STATION, MABON CITY TUESDAY, OCTOBER 21 7:05 AM

I jumped, spun around ready for a fight. The man with the magazine just stared at me with a piercing, amethyst gaze. I realized then that I recognized him from agilisi's store. He had come by yesterday afternoon with that antique car of his and that blonde woman.

"Duncan Thatcher," he said, business-like, and extended a hand for me to shake. "Please, call me Duncan."

"I remember." I relaxed my fighting stance slightly, took his hand. A cold, tingling sensation shot up my arm. In that instant, I threw up my mental barriers, jerked my hand back, and took several shaky steps back and away from him. "What the hell was that?"

"Interesting," he thoughtfully muttered, staring at his fingers. His gaze returned to me, and I could practically *feel* him reassessing me. After a minute or two, he said, "That, my dear, vas a test. And you passed vith flying colors."

"What kind of a test?"

He flashed a too-white smile. "One vich proves that you and I have something in common. Something that ve need to address."

Something in common? I stretched my senses out to him, searching for that commonality. What I detected frightened me almost as much as the thought of agilisi hunting me down. He had no aura. No life force. That, by itself, didn't make sense. Every living thing has an aura of some kind. Insects, plants, animals. Everything. And that reaction just now, when we shook hands, meant an interaction of some sort of energy. So either this guy had managed to find a way to mask his life force, or… Or he wasn't a *living* thing.

I studied his features again. Skin as cold and pale as white marble. Long hair as black as an abyss. Upturned eyes of an unnatural color. That a piercing gaze, like a lion trying to pick out the weakest in a herd of zebras.

I swallowed, my throat suddenly dry. In as level a tone as I could manage, I asked, "What are you?"

He nodded, impressed. "You are quick, Miss Starr. Have you had training?" He considered me again. "No. I guess not."

"Look, Mr. Thatcher, Duncan, I'm busy. I don't have time to be playing fifty questions with you. Either tell me what you want with me or get lost."

"Actually, I vould just like to talk vith you for a few minutes." He flashed me some delicate-looking golden broach pinned to a leather backing. A badge perhaps? "Vould you mind coming vith—?"

We felt the bone-chilling energy in the same instant, but he proved to be the quicker to react. He blurred then suddenly, he stood between me and a woman quickly approaching. She had on the most spectacular costume, and I couldn't help but drink in the details. She had the kind of beauty that would make super models jealous. I couldn't tell her age, but she had to be at least in her twenties. Her skin had been painted a blue so pale it almost appeared white, yet it shimmered in the light like new fallen snow. Her ears were elongated and came to a point like an elf's, and a tiny, silver snowflake sat upon her brow. Ice blue eyes with feline pupils and a dusting of purple eyeshadow expertly scanned her surroundings. Hair that looked like liquid platinum cascaded in sweeping curls down to her hips where the color shifted to ocean blue. She wore a long vest of shimmering blue and purple tones, its coattails reaching down to her ankles, and leather pants that matched the blue in her hair.

"Khione," said Duncan, his voice straining to sound friendly. She came to a stop just out of arm's reach, regarded him with haughty superiority. "I believe you are outside your jurisdiction."

She scoffed, and a small plume of steam sped past her grape-colored lips. "You AEONs and your jurisdictions." She crossed her arms, cocked out a hip. "You should know by now, Revenant, that I go wherever NEST sends me."

His fists clenched. "You're here under orders?"

Khione nodded.

"Vhat are they?"

"I am here to meet someone. The identity of which is none of your concern." Her icy, feline gaze slowly shifted to me. Her eyes narrowed slightly. "Interesting company you keep."

Duncan shielded me with his body. "Vhat is so interesting about her?"

Khione's attention returned to his face. "You know what she is. Perhaps I could be persuaded to return her to the Netherworld for you. After all, a Bloodless is not one of your kind."

I almost laughed out loud. She had to be on drugs. Or she took her LARPing way to seriously. I mean, come on! The Netherworld? Seriously? And she had to be mistaking me for someone else in her troupe of role players.

"Bloodless?" He shot me a quick glance. "Are you certain of that?"

She gave him a look that said 'did you really just ask me such a stupid question?'.

"Are you certain?" he demanded.

She waved her hand in dismissal. "Her face holds the memory of a demon I knew. As for whether or not she is truly a Bloodless half breed, I cannot say."

"I see," he muttered thoughtfully, cast another glance back at me.

"I am still willing to deliver her to the Netherworld for you. All you need do is ask."

I growled, stepped past Duncan. "Listen, lady, I don't know who you are, but I sure as hell ain't going anywhere with you." I shot Duncan a look. "Or you." I turned back to the woman. Her frigid gaze gave me the willies, but behind the aloof mask she wore, I could see a burning curiosity.

Her mask fell back into place, and her features took on the air of aloof superiority once more. "It's for the best, I suppose. After all, I can't be dragging every lost demon you AEONs dredge up back to the Netherworld. And I doubt that petite thing could handle herself there."

I fought the sudden, overwhelming urge to sock her in the jaw. Man! What has gotten into me lately? It's as if I had been possessed.

That's when the lights suddenly cut out. All of them. At the exact same moment. And the emergency lights, which should have come on automatically, didn't. The first rays of the cresting sun seeped through the windows, casting shadows that resembled withered fingers upon the floor.

"Is this you?" they demanded of me at the same time.

"What?"

"Are you doing," Duncan gestured to the air, "this?"

"Like I know where the freaking light switches are!"

"I vas afraid of that," he darkly muttered, glowered at Khione.

Her eyes scanned the darkness. "It is not one of mine," she said, her tone flat.

Someone screamed.

Duncan loosed what sounded like a curse in some other language. With a command to me to not move from this spot, he rushed away.

I scoffed. "If he thinks I'm waiting here, he's a bigger idiot than I thought."

I had expected a remark from Khione, but none came. I turned to face her only to realize she had vanished. I hadn't even felt her leaving.

“Nothing like a pair of crazies leaving a kid alone in the dark.” My frustration bubbled over in a growl.

Something else echoed it.

Unnerved by the sound, I sent my senses out in search of the source. I found the groups of people, huddled together and murmuring. Their life energies were a turbulent storm of fear and unease. Panic took hold of me when a pocket of intense cold suddenly appeared beside a family. I recognized the signature and started for the family, intent on keeping that monster away from them. The signature vanished without a trace. I skidded to a halt on the waxed hardwood, scrambled to pick up the icy energy again.

Suddenly, the darkness before me grew even darker. Two blazing rubies appeared in the air. From one heartbeat to the next, I realized they weren’t rubies; they were eyes. And they had locked on me. My heart leaped to my throat. I fell back a step. The mass of black took a step forward. I cautiously stepped to my left. It stepped to its right.

A child screamed. The monster’s focus on me broke. The instant it looked away, I ran. I heard it snarl behind me, felt something grab my bag. My wounds cracked open with shocks of hot agony as I struggled to free it from the grip. Fabric tore. I surged forward, clutching my bag to my chest. The monster roared its frustration. I made for the exit, not daring to look back to see if it had taken up the chase.

I had nearly reached the doors when a shadow crossed in front of it. It was a man, and he stood with one armed raised. A barrel gleamed in his hand. A gun.

“Get down!”

I dropped to my right side with a pang of pain and a grunt. My momentum kept me going, and I slid across the floor a good six feet or so.

The ruby-eyed monster sailed clean over me. The gun roared as the man fired. The monster loosed a horrible screech and crashed to the ground.

Another deafening shot from the gun sent it skittering away.

Silence fell.

The lights flickered on, bright and blinding.

My eyes adjusted slowly. The man in the doorway padded inside, tucking the gun into the waistline of his gray sweatpants. He wore no other clothing, and I couldn't help but admire his healthy physique. Even his shaggy brown hair looked good on him.

He got within arm's reach and extended a hand towards me. That's when I realized I recognized him.

"Detective Calloway?"

He grinned. "You can call me Quinn."

I gave him my hand and let him help me up. Why would he be here? Especially dressed like that.

A woman, probably a supervisor for the station, started asking around if anyone had been hurt. People murmured. A child cried about a red-eyed monster. The parents told her it had just been her imagination.

Must be nice to be that ignorant, I thought bitterly and retrieved my bag from the floor. My backpack bore the evidence of that red-eyed monster's presence. One of the straps had been torn to shreds from where that thing had grabbed it. At least the other strap survived with only a minor cut.

"Ah, Fenrir," I heard Duncan say as he approached. My attention shifted to him, then to the nearly naked hunk that stood nearby, watching me. "I had a feeling you vere skulking about outside."

"I did tell you that I would find her."

"Indeed you did."

I pointed between Quinn and Duncan. "You two know each other?"

A small smile flashed over Duncan's face. "Fenrir vorks for me. You'll see ven ve are settled in the car."

"The car?" I blinked. "After what just happened, you still expect me to go with you? How do I know it wasn't you who cut the lights? Or summoned that monster? Hmm?!"

"I can assure you, I had nothing to do with the Shadow or the lights." He looked grim as he said, "And vith vhat Khione said, it is more important than ever that you come vith us."

"You don't seem to understand," I snapped. "I'm. Not. Going. Anywhere. With you." I shouldered my bag, strode away. "I am getting on a train and getting the hell out of here."

"Vhat if I gave you ten thousand dollars in cash?"

I stopped. That much money would keep me set for a long time while I got my new life sorted out. Rent. Groceries. New clothes. I could afford it all and still have some left over for emergencies. I could even pay tuition for online school with it. But…

I sighed. "It sounds too good to be true."

Something tapped me on the shoulder. I glanced sidelong. A one hundred dollar bill glimmered at me from atop a stack almost half an inch thick. My heart fluttered at the sight.

"Ten thousand," said Duncan, taking the bills back. I turned to watch him stuff the money in his inside coat pocket. "It's yours if you stay vith me until Saturday."

I could suffer a few more days. That's provided agilisi never found me. At last, I said, "Under one condition."

Duncan anxiously awaited my next words.

"You keep me hidden so that my grandma doesn't find me. Ever."

He considered it for a fraction of a second. "Done."

10 SOMEWHERE IN MABON CITY TUESDAY, OCTOBER 21 8:02 AM

"I want answers," I said as I joined Duncan in the back seat of the car. I had been expecting the antique he brought to the shop yesterday, but this was a bit more modern. If you call a mid-1950s Chevrolet Bel Air modern. Nice gray and candy apple green paint job on it, too. The windows were so heavily tinted that I could barely see out of them. And a semi-transparent divider of dark material separated the front seat from the back.

"We all want answers," said Quinn as he sank into the driver's seat. Then he shrugged into a black tee shirt.

"I want to know," and I ticked them off my fingers as I spoke, "why you're so desperate to get me to come with you; what the heck you're doing," I eyed Quinn, "wandering around the city almost naked; who that Khione woman is; and I definitely want to know what that red-eyed thing is and why it's been following me."

Quinn shot a glance back at Duncan, who nodded. Quinn licked his lips as his gaze shifted to me. "You know that big, brown wolf that was following you earlier?"

I said that I did and briefly wondered where it had run off to. The lumbering canine hadn't been outside when we exited the station.

"That was me."

I had been about to blurt something nasty about liars, but, with the way things have been going for me recently, I just knew that attitude would only cause me more problems. Instead, I chose to simply say, "Prove it."

The shade of his eyes faded from dark to almost nothing as he said, "You asked if I was lost then told me I could follow you to the station, but not inside or onto a train."

I just stared at him. As I did, the paleness of his eyes melted away and they returned to the original shade. My mind raced with a bajillion questions and all ended with the same answer. Werewolf. Quinn was a werewolf.

Then I frowned. "I thought werewolves were more…" I pursed my lips as I tried to think of the word. It escaped me. "Well, human-shaped."

He chuckled. "I have three forms; full human, half-man-half-wolf, and full wolf." With that, he turned around and started the car.

"So is the silver thing true?"

"Some of my kind are deathly allergic to it, but not all." He put the car in gear and got us moving. "It's a long story, and we have more important things to discuss."

My attention turned to Duncan. "Yes, we do."

"You must understand," he said calmly. "I don't have all the answers."

Quinn suddenly slammed on the brakes. The Bel Air didn't have seat belts (they weren't required back then), so Duncan and I braced ourselves against the front seats. Quinn muttered a curse. "Sorry. Some student driver in their ugly beater cut me off."

"All right." Duncan sat back in his seat. "Where should we begin?"

I winced as my abused back brushed against the leather. "Let's start with what that red-eyed thing is."

"It is a Shadow," he said plainly, as if expecting me to understand. When it became obvious that I had no idea what he meant by that, he continued with the details. "They are a type of elemental demon. They have the power to bend shadow and darkness to their will, and they are far more powerful at night."

I nodded and thought back to my vision about the stolen jewel. "And these Shadow things walk in and out the dark like we walk through doorways?"

His eyebrow quirked. "Yes."

"Why do you ask?"

I wanted to say I had no particular reason. That it only made sense since those things could manipulate the dark. I got the feeling they would see right through that. So I went with the truth. "Because I saw it do just that yesterday morning."

"When was this?"

I looked at Quinn's reflection in the rear view mirror. "Remember when you saw me on the base of the light pole in the parking lot?"

He said that he did.

"That was when I had a vision of Robert Patterson—that's the guy the cops scraped off the roof of the Caddy—being dropped by one when, just the instant before, he was shooting at it in some museum-looking place."

"Vell," said Duncan, clearing his face of surprise. "At least now ve know vhy they keep coming after you."

"Care to share?"

Duncan looked at Quinn. I followed his gaze.

"Remember me staring at you that morning?"

"Hard not to," I replied. "You had that look on your face that said you were going to haul me to jail."

"Close." He nodded. Then he looked at me through the rear view mirror. "I was staring at you because your eyes were glowing red."

"Yeah, right."

His gaze returned to the road ahead. "It's true. It's why I followed you to your school."

"And you say your vision of the Shadow occurred at the same time."

I looked between them. "What are you getting at?"

"You are not just psychic, my dear," said Duncan. "You are also a demon."

"Half demon," Quinn corrected.

"Heh. What?"

"Technically, half Shadow."

"Your psychic abilities make you a very rare breed of Shadow. Add to that vhat Khione said about you possibly being a Bloodless, and I can see vhy everyone has been after you."

"Khione?" Quinn shot a glance over his shoulder. "Khione was here?"

"Unfortunately. She came on NEST business, saw Miss Starr, and offered to take her to the Nehervorld for me."

"For what?"

I finally came out of my stupor to ask, "What is a Bloodless?"

Duncan pursed his lips in thought for a moment. "From vhat I understand, a Bloodless is a child of a High Born, vhich is a demon of royal status, who vas conceived outside a recognized marriage."

"Sin could explain it better," said Quinn. He looked at me over his shoulder. "But he's someone you want to avoid at all cost."

"Let me see if I got this straight," I said, turning in my seat so that I faced Duncan more. I moved the same time Quinn turned a corner. Physics took hold, forcing my back to lean against a part of the car door. My back explode in absolute agony, and I tried desperately to keep the pain from showing. I hoped. "You're telling me that these Shadow things are after me because I'm some psychic demon princess?"

He made a face. "I don't know about 'princess,' but if you truly are the daughter of a High Born, ve vill need to place you in protective custody."

"No kidding," injected Quinn. "If the demons of NEST and any bounty hunters catch wind of who and what you are, they will just keep coming after you."

"I already have that Shadow thing after me."

"Wonderful," Quinn muttered, pulling the car to a stop at a red light.

He looked back at me. "We definitely need to get you in protective custody."

I scoffed. "Somehow, I don't think any law enforcement agency is quite prepared to handle keeping a kid safe from those uber powerful demons you spoke of."

"AEON is," replied Quinn. And he got the car moving again.

"What's AEON?"

I detected a hint of pride in Duncan's voice as he said, "The Assistance and Enforcement of Othervorldy Natives Agency. Ve are a secret government group set in place to protect the Mortal Realm from supernatural disturbances and to aid our fellow parathropes."

I had to beat down a guffaw of laughter as I stared at him. What ridiculous nonsense!

"A parathrope," my gaze wandered to Quinn as he spoke, "is a being or creature of paranormal origins and or with supernatural powers and abilities."

"Uh huh." I remained silent for a while, listening to the hum of the tires on the road and thinking over everything. Sure, these guys sounded like they were in dire need of a couple straight jackets and a padded cell, but my mind kept coming back to what I had *felt*. That strange interaction of energies between me and Duncan. The enormous wolf that had an aura of human power. I mean, yeah, I believe in spirits and what not. But vampires? Werewolves? Demons?

And what of this AEON thing of theirs? A secret government agency for monsters by monsters? Come on! Who would fund something like that?

"Don't vorry," Duncan said, tearing me from my thoughts. "Ve have a secure facility for you to stay in vhile ve vork this case."

"I've been thinking…"

Duncan's violet gaze snapped to Quinn.

"Maybe she can help."

"Vhat?"

"She's psychic. It's possible she has information that we aren't aware of. Even a little detail we might have missed could break the case wide open."

Duncan *humph*ed.

"The cowan constabulary have been known to hire psychic consultants," Quinn said defensively as he steered the car around another corner. "What harm could it do us?"

"Our mission is to protect her, not to use her."

"Hey, if I'm stuck with you 'til Saturday, I may as well work with you. Right?"

"Miss Starr—"

Instant rage erupted though my veins, and I snarled through gritted teeth. "Don't call me that."

Duncan snapped his jaw shut, cleared his throat. "Cybil," he carefully said, "you can't possibly know how dangerous something like this could be."

"Give me a break," I bit back. "What's dangerous is forcing me back to my agi—my grandma. She wouldn't hesitate to beat me to death for running away again. And, no, I'm not exaggerating."

Neither he nor Quinn replied.

In the ensuing silence, I fiddled with the broken strap of my backpack and tried to get my emotions back under my control. It wouldn't do me any good to have a break down now. Especially in front of these strangers. So I breathed in deep and exhaled through my nose, expelling my fear and frustration. It took only a couple of minutes to cleanse myself and relax.

Finally, I looked out the window.

Quinn had driven us to Dark Moon Harbor. Several private speedboats and yachts were floating lazily, tethered to their docks. Only a few spaces were empty, which didn't surprise me considering it was the middle of the workday. Quinn kept driving past them, heading for the farthest dock, where an enormous, white ship had been docked. This ship was even larger than one of those Royal Caribbean cruise ships but smaller than those big, ocean-crossing, freight-shipping ones.

A guard in a green and white uniform stood beside a security kiosk. He waved for Quinn to halt and approached the driver's side once the car had stopped. Quinn rolled down the window, greeted the guard like an old friend. As he did so, I noticed the patch on the guard's shoulder.

Saathoff Academy.

My heart raced with my thoughts. The Saathoff Academy is the most exclusive private school on the east coast. What are we doing here? And where is the school?

The guard waved Quinn through, and the werewolf eased the Bel Air forward. The engine rumbled as he expertly maneuvered the car onto a suspended platform that led somewhere into the depths of the ship.

11 SAATHOFF ACADEMY, DARK MOON PORT, MABON CITY TUESDAY, OCTOBER 21 9:03 AM

Oh! You have *got* to be kidding me! The Saathoff Academy is a freaking cruise ship?!

I kept my attention glued to the windows as Quinn moved the Bel Air through a garage filled with antique and exotic cars. We passed a 1960s Mustang Fastback. One of the new Ferraris. A huge and heavily modified GMC truck. Then my jaw hit the floorboards. Ho. Lee. Crap. They had a Veyron. A Bugatti Veyron!

It sat there in Tiffany Blue and onyx, gleaming like a jewel begging to be touched.

"Oh, good," said Duncan when he finally took notice of where my attention had gone. "They have finished it. Beautiful vork, too."

"As usual," agreed Quinn.

I tore my gaze away from the Veyron. "What are you talking about?"

"Our auto body class did the paint work." With that, Quinn pulled the Bel Air into an empty space beside a school bus and killed the engine.

"What do you mean 'our'?"

"This academy serves as AEON's North American Headquarters," explained Duncan. "Parathropes make up the entire population."

"Everyone here is a monster?"

They both made a noise, and Duncan quickly corrected me. "The term 'monster' vas slapped on us by the cowans during the Dark Ages. Ve use parathrope to describe our kind. It is less insulting."

"Oh," I said. "Sorry."

Duncan flashed a too-white smile. "Come on. Let us get you settled in a room and—" he considered my tattered backpack a moment. "Is that all you have?"

I felt my face grow hot with embarrassment and glanced down at my ugly bag with my meager belongings. "All I had access to."

He pushed the car door open. "Then ve vill get you some things from the school store."

I started to protest, but he and Quinn had already left the car. With a sigh, I grabbed my bag and joined them. I admired the enormous collection of cars as I followed them through the garage. I think they have at least one vehicle of every make, including some old, three-wheeled thing. A pair of Audis had been parked apart from the others and a group of young people stood around them. A tiny woman in a dark green jumpsuit circled one of the cars, pointing out things with a wrench longer than my forearm.

"Professor Tekna Johnson," said Quinn when he caught me watching. "She's our auto body and automotive maintenance teacher."

"Neat," I replied. Then I looked at him. "Are all the classes that relaxed?"

We came to a stop at an elevator door. He hit the button and faced me with a cheeky grin. "If you think that's relaxed, you should meet the yoga club."

"Now there is a laid back group of students for you," agreed Duncan.

The elevator arrived with a polite chime. Duncan led the way into the car, pushed the button for a floor marked D2. He took the lead again once the car stopped. "This is vone of the dormitory decks," he explained as he navigated the halls with practiced ease. We were moving so fast that I couldn't remember which direction we had come from. We came upon a door marked D2-78 and walked right in. "This shall be your room vhile you stay vith us."

"Okay." I followed him inside to take a look. Duncan flicked on the light, and I my jaw dropped in awe.

The room must have measured twenty feet long by fifteen. A door to the immediate left of the entrance led to a bathroom. A closet the size of a small house filled the opposite wall. At the far end of the room, centered beneath a single large window, sat a full bed flanked by nightstands. Between the bathroom and the bed, and against the left wall, stood a long desk straddled by cupboards that ran floor to ceiling. A small flat screen TV sat on a shelf of the cupboard closest to the bed allowing it to be watched from anywhere. A sofa with a matching ottoman had been set in place just opposite the desk. A bookshelf with a small handful of tomes filled the void between the bathroom wall and sofa, and an armchair had been parked in front of it. Everything had been decorated in neutral tones of beige and gray, which matched the rest of the ship.

I set my bag on the bed, took another look around. The room may have been huge compared to my former prison, but it had a kind of hotel-ish feel to it. It wasn't a Motel 6, but it wasn't exactly the Ritz either. I had to remind myself that this was a dorm room on a cruise ship, not a mansion's master bedroom. Plus, I wouldn't be staying here very long anyway.

I felt a pang of disappointment as I thought that, shoved it away. There's no point in getting attached. I have to leave. Before agilisi could find me. Otherwise I might as well just start walking back to Obsidian Grove right now.

"Now, vhat do you say ve get you some clothes and little necessities?"

As much as I wanted to protest, I knew it would be a losing argument. Besides, I needed the stuff. I still felt obligated to say, "I'm not used to charity."

He stopped in the entryway, turned to face me. "Vell, you could vork off the debt, but that vould extend your stay here. Vould you prefer that?"

I shrugged, glanced around the room again. It had almost everything I had ever dreamed about having. And Duncan could easily get me the rest. Heck, he even offered me a job. Staying here would be great. At least until agilisi found me and dragged me back. I don't think I'd survive that encounter. Tears clawed at my eyes at that thought.

"Is it your grandmother?"

I nodded, not trusting my voice just then.

"I promised you that I vould help you disappear. I give you my vord that she vill not find you. Not if she searched all of Mabon City. Not even if she searched the entire vorld."

I swallowed the lump in my throat, looked down at my dusty, old moccasins.

"Come," he gently said. "Let us get you some of life's little necessities. You can decide what you vant to do later."

He led me back to the elevators, pointing out the student lounge and laundry facility along the way. Then he explained that the bulk of the classes took place on the upper decks and ran nearly 24 hours every day. The weird schedule meant that even nocturnal beings, such as himself, didn't have to contend with the sunlight. The cafeteria and the school store were one level below the classroom deck and one above the gym slash fitness center.

By the time we reached the store, I could almost admit that he had convinced me to stay. The lingering doubt came from the terror that agilisi would find me.

"Ah, good. Zero is vorking," he said as we went inside. I hadn't been sure what to expect, but it wasn't a mini mall. It had a section for clothing, another for food and drink, a third for books and collectibles. Shoes. Crystals. Bath and body. You name it, this store probably had it.

I stopped dead in my tracks and gaped at the young Asian lady behind the counter. She looked about sixteen or seventeen, with creamy skin the color of sand. Her black hair had been tied back in dreadlocks that bore beads or blue ribbons. She wore a turquoise tank top and accessories that spoke volumes as to her character. On her hands were black leather gloves with the fingers cut off, and several bracelets dangled off her wrists. A royal blue, Chinese-style dragon scrawled the entire length of her right arm, from wrist to shoulder. It was so detailed I almost believed the creature would come alive.

But it wasn't any of that which grabbed my attention.

Liquids of various types tumbled around her in lazy acrobatics as if she were Saturn and they her rings. They would catch the light and break it into a riot of color. And she had only to twiddle the fingers on her right hand to do it.

"Good morning, Zero."

She looked up from the magazine she had been reading, smiled. "*Zǎoshang hǎo*." Then her sapphire gaze shifted to me. "Good morning."

"I need you to do your thing."

The liquids followed her as she rounded the counter. She waved her hand, and sent them rushing towards the sink beside the coffee station. She pursed her lips as she looked me over.

"Let me guess," she said as she started pulling shirts off the hooks. "Runaway."

I blinked. "How do you know?"

"I've been there. Lived on the streets of Louyang for two years, wound up forced into service by a street gang who discovered my hydrokinesis. Myth—" she paused, looked at me, "she's in charge of AEON's Asian branch—" then she continued pulling clothes off the racks. "stumbled upon me about eighteen months ago. At first, I was returned to my father, here in the States. But he found out about my abilities too, so now I'm here. This place is a life saver, believe you me. Here, give these a try." She handed me a small mountain of clothes, and pointed me towards the fitting rooms. "I'll scrounge up some other stuff for you."

I dutifully made for the short row of tiny rooms, pausing only a moment to look back at her before stepping inside. I broke down in silent tears as I sifted through the shirts and pants and underthings. She had even grabbed a couple pairs of pajamas for me. Everything except one pair of pants fit me like a glove. For the first time in ten years, I had brand new things to call my own. That feeling is indescribable.

And I couldn't stop crying.

It took over two hours to get me sorted with enough supplies to last for a long while and return to my room. I had been glad to finally be alone, and went about unloading everything. I thought about what I might do as I sorted the new clothes and hung them. I could stay here. I wanted to stay here.

Zero had snuck in a couple goodies when neither Duncan nor I had been watching. Snacks. Sodas. Body lotion. And, for some odd reason, bright red hair dye. It had taken me all of two minutes to decide to use the dye, and I scurried into the bathroom. The first thing I did was chop off my hair. I hated it long, but agilisi had never let me cut it any shorter than the middle of my back. I hacked it into a messy pixie cut that exposed my neck. Then I turned the red dye on my bangs. I snacked while it set. The Doritos and Mountain Dew were like ambrosia after going twenty-four hours without food. I showered, dressed in my new pajamas, and fell into bed, thoroughly exhausted.

12 SAATHOFF ACADEMY, DARK MOON PORT, MABON CITY
TUESDAY, OCTOBER 21
11:17 PM

I woke with the sun's setting and the ghost of a familiar nightmare echoing in my mind. Even after all this time, I could still smell the smoke choking the air. Feel the blast that shook the house off its foundation. And that scream. That horrible, gut wrenching scream.

My throat tightened as I battled against the tears. I threw the covers off, my fury at the decade-old memory's resurgence causing them to fly wildly. They landed on the floor in a dishevelled mess. I crossed the room to the sofa. My tattered backpack lay there, the last remnant of my tortured life. I delved into it, removed the notebook that protected my most precious treasure: the photograph of my family.

I stared at the little Polaroid for a while, willing my emotions back into check. I thought I had gotten over this pain. That I had numbed myself to it. Why, then, had I suddenly succumbed to it again? Perhaps it had something to do with what Duncan said earlier; that I'm a demon. That one of my parents was a demon. As I stared down at the happy family, I came to the conclusion that Duncan just made it all up. My parents were—what was the word he used?— cowan. They were normal.

A little voice deep inside told me to stop deluding myself. If my parents really were just vanilla human beings, there's no way I would have the abilities that I did. I mean, they had to come from somewhere. Right?

Right.

A sudden noise at my door made me come crashing back to the present. Curious, I extended my senses in search of the source only to find them blocked at the inside edges of my room. I felt a jab of pain behind my eyes and jerked my senses back with a curse.

The room had been warded.

Wards are a type of security defense system, sans expensive equipment. You would use them to keep energies or beings out of somewhere or, in this case, contained. Some wards are relatively simple to set up; just pour salt across where you don't want the bad stuff to get in. Across a threshold, for example, or in a circle around you. Graveyard dirt and brick dust will also work, but they're harder to come by. So why salt, you ask? Aside from the fact that you can buy it from almost anywhere, salt, in it's natural form, is a rock called halite. Because it's a rock born of the earth, it has the ability to ground out energies.

And that brings me back to wards.

There are other types, of course. Runes and sigils are common and relatively simple to set up. They can even be used as traps. I heard they pack one hell of a punch if you trigger them, too. The ward around my room didn't employ any of the methods I mentioned. This was an energy-based one. They are the most complex to use and sustain. I had absolutely no idea how they worked, let alone how to force my way through it with my senses—or if it were even possible. And that meant I had to physically investigate the strange noise I had heard.

I stood up with a sigh and gently placed my photograph atop the desk. I listened at the door a moment. Voices. I couldn't tell what they were saying or who they belonged to the door muffled them so. I unlocked it, cracked it open. A trio of teenage boys were there, goofing around with a hackysack. That must have been the weird sound I had heard.

I had nearly shut my door when I spotted Zero walking up with two other girls in tow; one a bleach blonde, the other with hair the color of moss. Zero spotted me snooping through the doorway and waved.

“I knew that red would look good on you,” she said with a smirk. “Wasn’t expecting the haircut though. Looks great.”

I managed to force out a thanks, then pulled the door open a little more. “Is there a party going on or something?”

“There’s always a party when I’m around.” She winked. “Actually, we’re heading to Paradox to chill. Wanna come?”

I froze. My mind went completely, horribly blank. No one had ever asked me something like that before. Nor had I ever had the liberty to say yes if I wanted. Do I say yes? Am I supposed to say something else? Do I nod? Shrug? I didn’t know what to do.

“Aw, c’mon!” said a cute, white-haired boy. “The more the merrier.”

“O-okay,” I blurted. “Just give me a couple minutes to throw on some clothes.”

Zero and her group agreed to wait for me. I ducked back into my room, fought the butterflies that had suddenly found a home in my stomach. I quickly donned one of the new outfits Zero helped me piece together; black cargo pants and a red tank top with bedazzled gems along the neckline. Then I stepped into my new sneakers, grabbed a couple bucks from the pocket of my old jeans, and slipped out the door.

We took the elevator to the garage deck and exited over the same suspended platform Quinn had driven up. The guard on duty at the security kiosk reminded us that curfew for diurnal classmen was one o’clock. Zero took the lead from there, guiding everyone through the back alleys and side streets as if she had done it a million times. We were coming up on the building less than thirty minutes later. The moment I laid eyes on it, I came up short. I had to admit, I imagined Paradox to be some sort of night club or restaurant or something. A mom-and-pop comic book and tabletop gaming shop wasn’t anywhere on the list of possibilities.

“I never would have taken you guys for gamers,” I said, bemused.

Most of them laughed.

The white-haired boy spoke up. "Hey, D 'n D is awesome."

The bleach blonde scoffed. "You are such a dork, Necro."

"Whoa, now," he said, feigning offense. "No need for name calling. It's 'geek' not 'dork'."

I couldn't help but grin at him.

Zero fell back to walk with me as I followed the group past the storefront and into the alley. "You haven't been out much, huh?"

I shrugged a shoulder, watched as Necro stopped mid-stride. He spun on his heel like an experienced dancer, rapped his knuckles against a brick on Paradox's side of the alley three times. I heard a soft boom, then the wall began to collapse inward on itself brick by brick. Within moments, a purple door appeared in the wall. It creaked as it swung inward as if of its own accord. Soft rock music surged forth from the darkness beyond.

Necro flashed me a cheesy grin before he vanished over the threshold. The others were right on his heels. I hesitated. I'm not entirely sure why. But I didn't want to look like a coward in front of everyone, so I forced myself onwards. Something strange happened when I crossed the threshold. I'm not sure how to describe it; just that it left me feeling a bit exposed.

I looked around the peculiar, little room I found myself in. To my left, a pair of tinted glass doors that cordoned off a long hallway. To my right, an old time elevator, complete with an operator in a gray suit. Directly across from me a stone staircase that arced downward, presumably to Paradox Proper. A little man with sickly, green skin and greasy, indigo-colored hair stood guard beside it. His beady, black eyes glared as he scowled at me. I tried my best not to stare at him, but his ugliness was remarkably captivating. Long, crooked nose. Warts. Flared ears longer than his face and adorned with multiple gold rings.

Only one word came to mind to accurately describe him: Goblin.

"Evening, Mister Grumbal," Zero said in a way-too-enthusiastic tone. I hadn't even noticed she had appeared behind me.

The goblin grumbled something incoherent.

Zero grabbed onto my shoulders, pushed me forward, towards the stairs. "I know! It *is* lovely weather we're having."

He shot her a dirty look.

It took willpower I didn't know I possessed not to laugh.

"Don't mind him," She murmured in my ear. Then she navigated around to walk beside me as we descended the stairs. Keeping her voice low, she continued. "He just has his panties in a bunch over his wife kicking him out of the kitchen."

A grin tugged at my lips, but it didn't last long. Midway down the stairs, the stone wall fell away revealing Paradox and I couldn't help but stop and stare. A huge cavern stretched a couple hundred feet before me. Thirteen rough stone columns placed at random intervals ran from the floor of the cave to the ceiling. Glowing crystals the size of my head clung to their jagged surfaces and illuminated the space with pleasant tones of color. Thirteen stone tables were scattered between the columns. Running under part of the hallway from upstairs was a bar with thirteen wooden stools. Opposite the bar, where a natural rise in the cave floor formed a stage—and I'm not joking here—six skeletons played soft rock. A fairly good sized crowd of beings—both human and not—had gathered before them to dance.

Zero chuckled, and I tore my gaze from the spectacular cavern to look at her. "Welcome," she said, "to the world of the paranormal."

I continued gawking as I followed her down the arcing staircase. Then she told me to go on ahead to the table Necro had picked out for us; she had just caught sight of a friend. I watched for a moment as she headed off for the bar, which, as it turned out, didn't serve alcohol. It said so on the sign behind the bar tenders. Instead, they served a huge variety of coffee and fruit juice mocktails (I wanted to give the Razzeled Vamp a taste).

I practically followed Zero as she wove through the columns and tables. Eventually, my path forked away from hers, and I joined the group at a table between the kitchen doors and another set of stairs. Before I even sat down, the bleach blonde faced me.

"I have been dying to know," she said, and I got the impression that she was a preppy bitch that I'd normally have nothing to do with. Still, I gave her the courtesy of my attention. "What are you?"

"What am I?" I repeated, bemused. I'd never been asked that before. This new world I had suddenly found myself a part of certainly had its quirks. "Well," I said, sitting. "I'm psychic."

She made a disgusted sound that the moss haired girl echoed. "Another lame psychic."

"And a demon." I don't know why I blurted that, but I instantly had the group's attention.

The blonde looked absolutely horrified, and she stood up so quickly that her chair fell over. She shrieked, "Your kind have no place here!"

I blinked, read the expressions on their faces. Everyone in the group glared at me with such hate that I believed I would spontaneously combust. Everyone, that is, except Necro. The white-haired boy looked at me with sympathy and understanding.

"Get out of here, monster!" the bottle blonde continued to screech. By now, half of the people in the cavern had their attention locked on her.

"Knock it off, Felicity," growled Necro.

"Not until *that,*" she jabbed a finger at me "is gone!"

A little person with an impressive beard and clad in an expensive suit rushed up. "Is there a problem here?"

Felicity kept her finger pointed at me as she shrieked, "That thing is a demon!"

A murmur swept through the cavern like wildfire unchecked, and I suddenly found myself under a lot of furious glares. Even the little man had a reserved look locked on me. I didn't see a point in trying to convince them that I wasn't a threat. They had already made their minds up about me. I'm a demon, which, I guess, means I'm evil by default.

And I had overstayed my welcome.

I slowly stood. A vision of something hitting me in the head flashed in my mind, and I turned in time to catch it. My fingers burned and tingled with the pain, but I didn't let it show. Instead, I set the object—a rock about half the size of my palm—gently on the table. Then I looked at the little man in the suit.

"I apologize for the disturbance," I said, keeping my tone flat despite how hurt and furious I felt. He obviously had no idea how to respond to that, so I merely turned and strode away. I kept my head held high as I made my way through the cavern. I refused to let them see me cry.

I passed Zero and her lanky friend with a tree trunk for an arm, and kept going. Nobody tried to stop me. Nobody uttered a word. But everybody watched me as if I were a mouse among starving hawks. It felt like forever before I reached the curved staircase. My footfalls echoed in the silence as I ascended. At long last, I reached the violet door.

The music started up again as I let myself out.

I stopped well before the mouth of the alley, leaned my battered back against the brick wall. After having spent years burying my emotions, I had gotten pretty good at it. I just settled into the right mindset and took several measured breaths. It took maybe five or six minutes for me to calm down from the hurt and the rage.

"Should have known better, Jinx," I berated myself. "Idiot."

"Jinx, huh?" said a vaguely familiar voice.

I shoved myself away from the wall, glared at the icy-eyed demoness lurking at the opposite end of the alley.

Khione's mulberry lips peeled back in a smirk. "I'll be sure to remember that."

I scoffed, turned my back on her. After a moment, I bade her good night and started to leave.

"It's not safe for you to be alone," she said at my back.

"It never is."

"If I found you this easily, how much longer do you think it will take the others?"

I stopped at the mouth of the alley. "Others?"

Hautiness stained her voice as she said, "I am not the only NEST demon in this realm, little one."

"What are you getting at?"

Her spiked heels clicked against the asphalt as she closed the distance between us. "I am saying, Jinx, that there is a bounty on your head. I'm here to collect."

I whirled around, slapped her hand away.

She glared at me as if I insulted her.

"Why?"

Silence.

I repeated myself, this time more forcefully. "Why is there a bounty on me?"

"Because of what you stole."

The snort escaped me before I could stop it. "And what have I allegedly stolen?"

Doubt flashed in her cat-like eyes. "You do not know?"

I crossed my arms and said nothing. If I were to admit to robbing agilisi's store and stealing her car, I'd only be digging my own grave. It's a little something called entrapment. You don't give a cop—even a demon one—that kind of ammo to use against you. So I snapped at her, "I'm not in the mood for guessing games."

"A mirror."

A mirror? That's right. She said something about that at the train station. Could it have been me she had been sent to collect? She could have taken me by surprise when the lights went out. So why didn't she? "Where did you say this mirror was stolen from?"

Her lips drew into a frown. "The Elysium Royal Vaults. It's the one the Infernas have had in their possession for nigh on a thousand years."

"Facinating," I flatly stated. "I have no idea what you're talking about."

She said nothing, but her scrutinizing glare never faltered.

We simply stared at each other for a handful of seconds before I once again turned my back on her and started away.

"Three days," she muttered at last. "I'll buy you three days to prove your innocence. If you cannot, your head is mine."

I glanced over my shoulder. "What time is it?"

"Seventeen minutes after nine."

I kept walking.

She didn't follow.

As if I didn't have enough problems in my life, now I have to prove that I hadn't stolen some old mirror. Gods! I wish I could be a normal teenager.

13 LOCATION: UNKNOWN
TIME: NONEXISTENT

Darkness.

Sweet, sweet darkness. Ever present yet ever changing. It comforted me as only a loving mother would. And now I knew why. Shadow, they called me. Unholy wretch. Fiend. Demon.

Even the monsters feared me.

And I thought I had escaped all of that.

My eyes fluttered open.

I suddenly found myself standing in a cavernous box of a room. Blue candlelight, borne by candelabras recessed in stone walls, revealed the barrenness of the space. Behind me, a single, narrow hallway cut into the wall. Before me, wide stairs leading down, disappearing into the gloom beyond.

Something compelled me to move forward, and my footfalls echoed off the stone. With each step, the darkness seemed to condense more and more until I was all but cutting my way through it. The stairs quickly leveled out, and I reached forward blindly, counting each step.

One...

Two...

Three...

At seven, I stopped.

In the endless darkness, two eyes like glowing embers appeared. I immediately readied myself against an attack, but the eyes never moved. An eternity passed within a minute, and I forced myself to relax again.

Was that the thing had been getting me into all this trouble?

TROUBLE? came a raspy whisper.

I shrank back. *So it can hear my thoughts. That's kinda creepy.*

The presence laughed, low and dark.

Right, I thought and crossed my arms. *Like I wasn't freaking out already. Let's add a maniacal laugh to the soundtrack.*

The eyes blinked.

I worked up the courage to finally confront the presence instead of simply thinking about it. 'So... uh... How long have you been here?'

ALL YOUR LIFE.

I felt my eyebrow twitch in annoyance. 'If you've been here my whole life, then why am I only now learning of your existence?'

I CANNOT GET OUT.

'Why not?'

YOU HOLD THE KEY.

'How can I have it if I'm just finding out you exist? That doesn't make any sense.'

YOU'VE KNOWN. YOU'VE ALWAYS KNOWN.

I frowned at it. 'Since I'm new to this whole multiple personality thing, perhaps you can explain how you are able to influence my life when you're locked in here.'

The eyes narrowed ever so slightly.

I realized it didn't understand, sighed. 'You get me into fights, and then force feed me superpowers so that I can win. How can you do that if you can't get out?'

EVERY PRISON HAS FLAWS.

'What prison?'

I heard it make a low sound that a human throat couldn't possibly mimic. Then the eyes began to move, drawing closer. There were no footsteps or rustle of clothing as the presence moved, almost as if the creature was nothing more than eyes ever burning in the darkness.

It got within arm's reach of me and finally stopped. Something tapped against an unseen force and violet lightning exploded into existence. It zipped over an invisible surface in a messy grid to reveal a net that spanned from the floor to a ceiling thirty-some feet overhead. It lasted barely an instant before the energy vanished and I was once again plunged into total darkness.

I returned my gaze to the monster's. 'You mean you can feed your power through the gaps in the net?'

The eyes retreated back into the gloom. *ONLY A TRICKLE.*

'Why so litt– Scratch that. Why do you even bother sending me power? Do you have any idea what it's been doing to me?'

I heard the presence exhale. *I GIVE YOU BUT THE TINIEST FRACTION OF MY TRUE POWER TO PROTECT YOU.*

'Protect me?' I scoffed at the idea of this thing pretending to be my guardian angel—or demon, in this case. 'You've done a crummy job in that department.'

It snorted.

'Well, look at what you've done! You got me into so many fights that I've been expe–'

IT WAS IN YOUR BEST INTERESTS.

'Oh really?' I snapped. 'I find that hard to believe.'

The eyes narrowed dangerously. *I DO NOT CARE WHETHER YOU CHOOSE TO BELIEVE MY INTENTIONS WERE TO AID YOU OR HARM YOU, BUT IT WAS NOT I WHO SOUGHT THOSE MEAGER SQUABBLES WITH THOSE PATHETIC HUMANS. AND, SHOULD YOU DESIRE I REMOVE MYSELF COMPLETELY FROM ACTION, YOU MERELY NEED DECREE IT.*

'Then consider this my decree.' I turned my back on the presence, started for the stairs and the way out of here.

VERY WELL. BEFORE I TAKE MY LEAVE, MAY I OFFER THEE SOME ADVICE?

I paused with a sigh, looked sidelong towards those fiery eyes. 'Advise away.'

ASK YOURSELF THIS, KEEPER MINE: WHY WERE YOU *THE ONLY ONE TO SURVIVE?* Then the red eyes were simply gone.

I *humphed*, strode away.

The way up the stairs was harder.

14 SAATHOFF ACADEMY, MABON CITY
WEDNESDAY, OCTOBER 22
3:43 AM

I came back to myself with a shudder, cast a glance around. It took me a minute to recall what had happened earlier. I had left Paradox only to run into Khione, who warned me about the bounty on my head. After that, I had stormed to the ship and sealed myself in my room. My emotions were too out of control for me to do much of anything, so I had slipped into the shower in the hopes that the running water would ground out my excess energy. Some time during that, I must have slipped into a meditative state.

I thought back on that waking dream, frowning. My inner demon's final, cryptic message echoed in my mind. Why *had* I been the only survivor that night ten years ago? I had tried for years after it happened to remember the events that night. I could recall the explosion that woke me, the terrible scream that continued to haunt me. Then, suddenly, I had found myself in the arms of a police woman. What happened between those two events remained a complete mystery. Surely I didn't have that wretched thing to thank for saving me.

I shuddered again, admired the way my skin turned to goosebumps. What an alien sensation! It must be a sign that my inner demon had done as I commanded and stopped force feeding me its power.

So this is what it feels like to be cold. For a brief moment, I wished I hadn't given that command, then I remembered all the trouble the damned thing had gotten me into.

"Good riddance!" I turned the shower off, wrapped a towel around myself. I dressed in the same pajamas as before and wandered my room in search of something to do. Normal people would probably sit down and watch TV or play around on the net. I'm not one of the former and I didn't have a computer to do the latter. So I settled into the arm chair with a sigh. For a long moment, I just sat there and soaked in the silence of the night.

Finally content, I glanced over the bookcase behind me. I didn't recognize any of the titles, but one in particular stood out from the rest. It was bound in plain black leather that had seen many years of use. I grabbed it and started flipping through the pages. I discovered that everything had been written by hand in weird, curvy symbols.

I remembered seeing these once before. A lady had come to agilisi's store with some antiques to unload. A book similar to this had been among the many in a box I got stuck sorting, and I had to flip through it to figure out where to put it on our shelves. I would have suspected some sort of foreign alphabet, but some of the pages had intricate drawings with perfect English beside them. I ended up setting that old book aside and less than an hour later, discovered it gone.

"Maybe it's a code," I muttered to myself as I continued scanning page after page of the strange tome, admiring the intricate details of the drawings and pondering the cryptic writing. Eventually, the look and feel of the pages changed. The paper was of a new, thinner material; something between printer paper and parchment. And the ink and the way the curvy symbols were drawn had subtly changed as well. So too had the formatting.

Now, instead of being textbooky, this section had a more cookbook-ish look to it. Some of the words I presumed to make up the ingredients lists had been crossed out and replaced with English in yet another subtly different penmanship. There were things like Adder's Tongue, Bloodroot, Foxglove, and Hyssop.

None of which sounded like anything that would go into a cake or dinner.

I kept turning. The pages continued to get newer the further into the book I got. With each new generation of paper came an ever-so-slightly difference in penmanship. It became obvious that this journal–for lack of a better word–had been passed down many times through its life, rather like a special heirloom.

"I wonder why somebody would give this away?" I muttered and continued flipping. I had almost reached the end of the book when something gave me pause.

Scrawled across several pages were circles. Intricately decorated circles, sort of like the ones used for transmutation. Some had fancy sigils scribbled in shapes positioned along the edges while others had the astrological signs in a ring around a variety of shapes or intersecting lines. Among the many, only one was a simple, undecorated circle. Scrawled beside it in all capital letters the writer warns:

USES: BIND, IMPRISON, OR SHIELD
- BREAK TO RELEASE
- SILVER BEST
- GEMSTONES EMPOWER

I had no idea what any of that meant, but I found it fascinating. Mostly because whoever wrote it had different handwriting than the person who had penned the rest of the English in this journal. And, judging by the nice handwriting, I felt certain that it belonged to a female. Too bad I had no idea who she was. If I did, I'd ask her what all these symbols mean.

More importantly: why had she left the book here?

I continued leafing through the pages, this time in search of a name or some other way to identify the author. I had nearly reached the end when someone came knocking at my door. Not wanting to deal with more hysterics prompted by my demon side, I ignored it.

"What?" I furiously snapped when another round of knocking broke my sheltering silence.

Though muffled, a familiar voice seeped through from the other side of the door. "It's Quinn. Got a sec?"

I slapped the tome shut, dropped it into the armchair as I made for my door.

"Everything okay?" he asked when I jerked the door open. He hadn't changed from the sweatpants and tee-shirt he wore earlier, but his eyes had gone pale blue. And he held something tucked under his arm.

I shrugged, not really wanting to get drawn into a long and personal discussion. That's the reason my shrinks hated me—I don't talk. So I changed the subject. "Why are your eyes blue?"

"The moon is out," he stated as if it were obvious. Then he gestured to the thing tucked under his arm. "Duncan said your room didn't have it's laptop, so I dug one up for you. Can I come in to set it up or are you busy?"

"I was just reading." I stepped aside so he could enter.

He crossed the threshold asking, "Anything good?"

"Educational."

He made a noise like he approved and knelt beside the desk where he dug around for something. A gray cable suddenly surfaced from the little gap in the desk's surface, and he moved to grab it. He froze, staring in wide-eyed fascination at something on the desktop.

My Polaroid!

I rushed forward to retrieve it, and he looked at me. Recognition dawned in his eyes, and he pointed to the photo. "Your parents?"

I nodded.

"Your parents are Salem Starr and Cassandra Lilley?"

How did he know them? I nodded again, more slowly than before.

He set the laptop down, gaped at the photo again. "You need to come with me."

I blinked.

His moon blue gaze fell on me. "You need to come with me right now."

15 AEON HEADQUARTERS, MABON CITY WEDNESDAY, OCTOBER 22 5:18 AM

I slipped into my old moccasins, ran my fingers through my hair, and followed Quinn out the door. I practically had to run to keep up with him as he rushed to the elevators.

"What's going on?" I breathlessly complained and tried to adjust my foot in its beaded leather slipper.

He impatiently mashed the down button. "You wouldn't believe me if I told you, and Duncan needs to know about this immediately."

The elevator arrived in time with my eyeroll. I followed Quinn inside, watched as he passed a white card over a sensor and jabbed at a button marked O. The car began its descent.

"You knew them," I stated. "Didn't you? You knew my parents?"

He was quiet a moment, then, "Not personally, no."

"Yet you recognized them on sight. You even knew their names."

"You'll see why in a couple of minutes." He finally looked at me. "I promise."

The elevator gave a polite chime and the doors opened. Quinn led the way into a small room with only a single door and a wall composed of a dark mirror. I recognized the one-way window from my stint in police custody after a failed attempt to escape agilisi.

"Agent Fenrir with material witness Cybil Starr," announced Quinn, and he recited a sequence of numbers. I heard a buzz and a soft click before he pulled the door open. Quinn led the way down a long hallway that screamed of hospital. The linoleum floor tiles were cream but a border in dark gray hugged close the pale green walls. We passed a door that looked like it could withstand a nuclear blast and turned right. Five more security doors were set into the left wall while the right one was glass and steel. The latter was an extensive laboratory with a few people still working despite the hour.

Quinn stopped at the last security door and started punching in the code.

At the end of the hall, few paces ahead, I could see a door with a piece of paper taped to it. I read the hand-written, blocky letters aloud."WEIRD?"

"Hm?" Quinn glanced up from the keypad, saw where I was looking. "Oh. Yeah. That's their new office."

"What are they?"

The door clicked open, and Quinn held it slightly ajar. "They're the Astral Plane's version of AEON."

"Oh." I muttered and followed him. A door had been left open at the end of this hallway, spearing light into the otherwise dark area. I could hear voices coming from within; a man and a woman. They were saying something about the jewel theft when Quinn and I reached the doorway.

I paused at the threshold to look around. It reminded me of an ultra-modern lawyer's office, with a seating area formed by leather couches surrounding an oval, glass coffee table. A small conference table sat against the far end of the room, and an abstract watercolor hung centered on the wall behind it. An L-shaped glass and steel desk made up Duncan's workspace. Here and there ferns and shelves of knickknacks were set, giving the room a welcoming, yet professional look.

The blonde driver from yesterday sat on one of the couches. She gave me a passing look and returned her attention to the tablet she had with her. Duncan sat only a few steps away, seated in the chair behind the desk and looking very worried. Someone stood between me and him… Someone I could see straight through.

Though mostly transparent, I could still make out a blonde man with green eyes who could not have been much older than twenty-five. He wore a beat-up Roman legionnaire's leather and iron chain mail armor, greaves, and leather sandals. His arms and legs were muscular, and scars marred the skin in a few places. I had no doubt that he had been in a war or two during his lifetime.

"Hi, Specter," Quinn said as he stepped past me and into the room. "This is Cye. Cye, this is Tiberius Sempronius Atratinus, aka Specter. He's our IS – Information Specialist… And, obviously, a ghost."

"Nice to meet you." I had to admit, talking to someone you can see through is rather awkward. Just imagine talking to dead air (no pun intended).

Duncan's frown grew ever deeper as he eyed Quinn.

"I know. I know," Quinn said, his hands raised defensively in front of him. "But this is important." Then, ignoring Duncan, he turned to the ghost. "Specter, pull up Forlorn's file."

That instantly drew a curious reaction from the three.

"Vhy the sudden interest in him?"

Quinn hooked his thumb back at me, which was, apparently, the only explanation needed.

I watched as Specter brought his hands up before him as if holding a soccer ball. A spark of ghostly blue-green light flickered between his fingertips, then, suddenly, an orb appeared. It was as transparent as Specter and covered in hundreds of symbols I couldn't even begin to recognize. The ghost's fingers flew over the glyphs like mine would a keyboard, each one lighting up for an instant before returning to its normal glow. Then, he turned his attention to the conference table.

The watercolor painting on the wall suddenly went black, and I realized that it wasn't a painting at all, but a television. And within it appeared my father. He had shorter hair when the photo had been taken, but there was no mistaking him.

"Incredible," I heard Duncan whisper. "How did you learn of this?"

"She has a photograph of him taken years after he retired," said Quinn. "And that's not all. In the same photo is Cassandra Lilley."

A riot of exclamations swept the room.

The ghost went back to manipulating his ball, and a photo of my mother appeared on the TV beside the man they call Forlorn. I stared at the familiar yet alien people on the screen. It upset me… no; it royally pissed me off that these people knew my parents better than I did. I'm their daughter. Their flesh and blood. Shouldn't I have known they were part of this AEON Agency? A part of this horrific and terrible paranormal world?

"Finally!" Duncan thumped his desk. "Some answers."

I tore my gaze away from the television to glower at him. I all but snarled, "Maybe for you."

His eyebrows disappeared beneath his bangs.

Quinn looked sidelong at me, his mouth agape and eyes wide.

Out of the corner of my eye, I saw the blonde woman begin to move. A subtle gesture from Duncan made her stop. "Please accept our apologies, Cybil. Ve are just ecstatic to learn that you are the daughter of von of the greatest AEON Agents in history. If you vould like, I can explain everything."

I allowed my glare to lessen.

He took it as the sign that it was, licked his lips. "The man there," and he pointed to the television "is your father, Salem Starr. Correct?"

I nodded.

"That vas just one of the many aliases he's used over the centuries. His true name is Lord Draethius Inferna, and he ruled over the Netherworld Province of Elysium."

Elysium? Isn't that where Khione said the mirror had been stolen?

"Vhen he defected to join the AEON Agency, he took on the codename Forlorn. *He* is your demon parent. And Cassandra Lilley, his wife, your mother, vas von of the most accurate psychics ve have ever had the pleasure of vorking vith."

"Besides being the only psychic Shadow in recorded history," Quinn quickly added, "you are the legitimate Heir of Elysium. The *only* heir."

"And that is vhy these demons have been after you."

I remained silent for a time, letting the information sink in. It just didn't seem real. My mother was a psychic. My father, a demon lord who had defected. Something clicked at that thought. "Is that why my parents were killed? Because my father joined AEON?"

Quinn and Duncan both grimaced.

"It is what we believed," answered Specter. My gaze snapped to the ghost. He had been so quiet that I had forgotten he was in the room. He flashed a wry and understanding smile. "Because Forlorn was the Lord of Elysium, he had rivals. Lots of them. We suspect that when he came to work with us, those rivals saw it as a legitimate reason to have him assassinated, and they sent one of the worst demons possible to pull it off."

My heart skipped a beat. "You know who it was!"

The ghost balked a little before nodding solemnly. "We found that demon's energy at your house the night your parents were murdered. If we had known you existed back then, we would have taken you into our protective custody."

I stepped towards the ghost. "Who was it? I want a name."

"Cybil—"

I cut Duncan off with a glare. "Ten years! Ten years of not knowing who or why. Ten years of living alone and suffering with that wretched woman. I deserve to know. I *need* to know." My focus returned to the ghost.

"Tell me!"

Specter's gaze darted towards Duncan. The vampire hesitated then gave a curt nod. The ghost looked me in the eyes and solemnly said, "His name was Taboo."

16 AEON HEADQUARTERS, MABON CITY WEDNESDAY, OCTOBER 22 6:37 AM

At long last, an answer to a riddle now a decade old.

Taboo.

An assassin sent after my father because somebody had their panties in a bunch. The person responsible for turning my life into a living hell.

Taboo.

A torrent of barely-contained emotions surged through my veins. Hate. Rage. Pain. All kept carefully hidden behind a mask void of emotion. It wouldn't do me or my parents any good getting childishly emotional but this revelation. And I'll be damned if I'm going to break down in front of these weidos.

I cast a glance around the room, noting how everyone had their eyes locked on me. Obviously, they were awaiting my reaction. I didn't know what to say to them. Did I even have to say anything? Then the words of the demon in my dreams came back to me. *Why were you the only survivor?*

And I stunned the room when I calmly asked, "If this Taboo is such a brutal killer, how come I'm still here?"

A handful of seconds ticked by while they recovered from their stupor. Then Duncan cleared his throat. "Vhat can you remember from that night?"

I felt my lips stretch into a frown, and I stared at Duncan for a beat. I hated talking about it. Hated being forced to relive that terror. But if it provided me answers, then… "We had been travelling, so I went to bed early that night. It was dark out when a scream woke me. Then I heard sounds of a struggle. I hid under my bed just as an explosion rocked the house. Everything grew hot and I must have blacked out because the next thing I remember is being in the arms of a cop as she rushed me to an ambulance."

Duncan nodded solemnly. "Morgan," he gestured to the blonde on the couch, and she looked up from her tablet for a moment. "and I must have arrived on scene mere minutes after the ambulance rushed you avay. Vhat ve saw vas a house leveled and burning, so ve vere not expecting any survivors. How you managed it is…" He shook his head, clearly at a loss.

"There is no explanation for it," said Specter. "It should have been impossible for a child of five to survive the onslaught that tore through the house that night. You really don't remember what happened between the explosion and the ambulance?"

I shook my head. I had spent countless nights trying to remember, but never got anywhere. Something must have happened during those missing minutes. Something important. Or gruesome. The latter made more sense. I could have seen or done something so horrible that my memory blocked it out entirely to save me the anguish of reliving it.

I sighed, looked to Duncan. "So Taboo is dead?"

"Since ve have not seen or heard from Taboo since that night, ve suspected that Forlorn, your father, facing his death, put all his energy into von final, desperate attack which took Taboo out of the picture permanently. Up until a few minutes ago, ve thought Forlorn had done that because of his duty to AEON. Now, I believe he sacrificed himself to save you."

I swallowed the lump in my throat, shifted my gaze to my father's face still on the screen. His crimson gaze stared right back, and I could swear he looked sadder than he had a few moments ago.

Maybe I just imagined it.

I tore my gaze away to look at Duncan. "Are you certain?"

"As certain as ve can be," he said after a moment. "As I said, ve haven't seen or heard anything regarding him ever since that night he attacked your family."

His words didn't exactly inspire confidence, and just the thought of this Taboo monster still running around further infuriated me. My voice was like a snake bite as I said, "In other words, there's a slight chance that he might be alive?"

"I highly doubt it," muttered Quinn. He seemed to gulp when I turned my gaze upon him, and he covered the reaction with a quick smile. "Forlorn wasn't known for pulling his punches in a fight. Even against allies, as Sin can testify."

Morgan scoffed, glanced up from her spot on the couch. "I wouldn't trust anything that psychopath says."

Quinn shot her a look before he continued. "See, Forlorn was a member of AEON's Team Alpha. They are some of the most powerful beings on the planet, and many of them are Firsts— the first of their kind; the origins of their parathropic species.

"In terms of power, Forlorn made them look like cowans. So you can probably imagine the fury he unleashed on Taboo when he was desperate to save you." He chuckled lightly. "I bet it was quite the spectacle to see your father kicking Taboo's sorry ass straight back to Hell."

I chewed over his words in the silence that followed. Everything he said made sense, and I wanted to believe him, but something felt off. What if my father's attack hadn't been enough to destroy Taboo? Could that monster be out there right now, sending these demons after me out of revenge? Or, worse, what if someone else is after me to avenge Taboo's death? An unknown person with unknown power and a vendetta sounds like something from a horror flick. But this ain't the movies; this is as real as the ship I'm standing in.

"Fear not, Miss Sta—"

"Don't call me that."

Duncan closed his mouth. Opened it as if to say something, decided against it. He sighed through his nose, tapped his index finger against the top of his desk. After five taps, he said, "Ve vill protect you. So long as you are aboard the ship, no demon vill ever be able to find you."

My eyes narrowed. It wasn't the thought of a demon finding me that had me terrified; it was my grandmother. And I told him that.

Duncan flashed a too-white smile. "That has already been taken care of. Specter, if you would, please."

The ghost fiddled with his weird, glowing ball for a moment, and the photos of my parents vanished. A newspaper article took their place on the screen. My eyes danced over the page, lingering longest on the photograph of a burning wreck somewhere. I read the headline.

Plane Bound for Chicago Crashes, 153 Dead

"Ve added your name to the passenger manifest," explained Duncan, prompting me to glance sidelong at him. "As of 9:48 Tuesday morning, Cybil Golanv Starr is dead."

A wave of unfamiliar emotion washed over me. I was dead. Agilisi would no longer search for me. At long last, I had my freedom. I could live my life the way I wanted. For the first time in a decade, I felt like I could breathe. I wanted to cheer. To dance. Is this what relief feels like?

Then a strange thought hit me.

I could attend my own funeral. I'd probably be the only one to show up, but I could be there. Hopefully, they'll bury me next to my parents… wherever they were. I should find them before I leave Mabon City.

I nearly jumped out of my skull when a trio of precise knocks hammered against the door frame behind me. Morgan's voice grated on my ears like silverware scratching china as she stood and said, "Commander Cartouche."

I cast a glance over my shoulder. A little girl stood at the threshold, her golden eyes scanning the room from beneath bangs of purest white. White silken robes and glimmering silver armor half concealed her unmarred, gingerbread cookie-colored skin. She couldn't have been more than twelve, yet something about her brought tears to my eyes and fear to my heart.

"Ah, Cartouche," Duncan's voice sounded friendly enough to untrained ears, but I could detect a hint of unease concealed beneath his nearly-forgotten accent. "Vhat brings you all the way to the Mortal Realm?"

The little girl moved with liquid gracefulness as she strode into the room. An air of command buzzed around her like it would a five star general, and I got the impression that she was much, much older than she appeared.

"A theft occurred in your jurisdiction early yesterday," she said, her voice quiet and strong at the same time, and held out a folder.

Duncan took it with a frown. "Another one?"

"Why would WEIRD be called in on a theft in this realm?" Specter asked. "You guys gave AEON full jurisdiction over the Mortal Realm nearly thirty years ago."

Cartouche shrugged a shoulder. "Probably because whomever called it in didn't know that AEON deals with demons as well."

"Demons?" Duncan flipped open the file, scanned it. He found something that made him appear as though his heart skipped a beat… if he had a pulse, that is. He looked up from the page. "Are you certain of this address?"

Cartouche jerked her head in a curt nod.

The vampire passed the file to Quinn, whose jaw dropped a moment into reading the report. He looked up at Duncan. "Isn't that Cynthia's estate?"

Specter groaned. "What did Cynthia go and get herself into this time?"

"Thank you, Cartouche," said Duncan, "for bringing this to our attention. Ve vill take it from here."

The little girl turned to leave and locked eyes with me in the process. Though her face never betrayed emotion, I could practically sense her immediate dislike. In a tone as neutral as mauve, she said, "You look familiar. Do you have an elder brother?"

I almost laughed. "Nope."

She 'huh'ed and quit the room without another word.

"Fenrir." Duncan's voice snatched my attention away from the strange girl.

"Yeah?"

"Ve have a rather large caseload to deal vith, so I think it vould be a good idea to escort Mis—" he cleared his throat. "Cybil back to her room. Plus, she has a good deal to think about."

"Oh," said Quinn, setting the file on Duncan's desk. "Yeah." Then he smiled at me. "Come on, kiddo, let's get you back to your dorm room."

I started after Quinn, paused at the threshold. I cast a look back at Duncan, but his attention had shifted to the file. In the silence, I could hear his pen scrawling across paper as he made notes.

"By the way," I said. He glanced at me before continuing his writing. "Khione found me earlier." The scratching ceased. "She gave me three days to find the person responsible for stealing some antique mirror from Elysium or she'll take my head instead."

17 SAATHOFF ACADEMY, DARK MOON PORT, MABON CITY
WEDNESDAY, OCTOBER 22
8:12 AM

Quinn didn't say much during the walk back to the elevator. That didn't bother me. In fact, I wanted the silence. I used it to help sort through the bazillion thoughts that were running rampant in my brain. Naturally, my parents were at the forefront of the raging torrent. How could they not be? I mean, I learned more about them in ten minutes than I ever knew. But if I had an opportunity to talk to them once more, I'd ask one simple question:

Were you ever going to tell me?

I desperately wanted to know if they had had intentions of telling me about their alternate lives. Would they have told me about AEON? About my true heritage? My powers? Anything?

They had left me with nothing. Or, if they had, it had been confiscated by agilisi a long time ago. The only surviving remnant of that happy life lived on in the tiny polaroid that now lay on the desk in my borrowed room.

Of course, that was here on earth or—What do these monst– uh, these beings call it?—the Mortal Realm. I had an entire province waiting for me in the freaking Netherworld. Of all the places in the whole *universe*, I get to inherit a chunk of Hell. And I'd probably never even get to see it. Unless…

I looked up from the sterile flooring to focus on Quinn's back. "Hey, Quinn?"

He glanced over his shoulder.

"Is there a way to get to the Netherworld from here?"

He stopped so suddenly that I almost ran into him. He stood there a moment before slowly turning to face me, a curious look in his moon blue eyes. "There are ways, yes. The question is: Why are you asking?"

I shrugged.

His expression softened. "Thinking about your dad?"

"Yeah," I mumbled.

"Well," he began, stuffing his hands into the pockets of his jeans. "There are legal and illegal ways to get to the Netherworld. The legal way is to use the Gates of the Fallen, which is sort of like the border between Mexico and the US. AEON controls this side of the Gate, and NEST—they're the Netherworld Elite Special Tactics Force—controls the other side. Getting through requires proper documentation or an AEON or NEST badge.

"For the illegal ways..." he made a face. "I'm told there are secret gateways all over the place, but the only AEON who knows where they are is Sin. And I wouldn't get within fifty miles of that guy."

There's that name again. "Who is this Sin character? And why is everyone afraid of him?"

Quinn cleared his throat, reached up with a hand to stroke an invisible beard on his chin. "He's a Nightmare. Literally; that is his rank in the demon guild he trained in. The Tainted Souls." He shuddered. "Just thinking about those monsters gives me the creeps. They're a bunch of... well, I'd say 'guns for hire,' but they don't use guns.

"Nightmares are the guild's highest ranking assassins, and they make NEST look like children. That's why everyone stays away from Sin. Well, that, and the fact that his being forced to work as an AEON has seriously pissed him off. I don't know how The Lady—she's the agency's founder—keeps him under control, but she uses his knowledge of the Netherworld's politics and persons of interest to our advantage.

"Sin has actually saved several thousand lives during his time as an agent," he begrudgingly admitted. "But he's slaughtered countless more, including AEON and WEIRD Agents. And I was unfortunate enough to see him in action. Gave me nightmares for a month afterwards."

I shook my head in disbelief. "How in the world could someone like that become an agent for AEON?"

"To be perfectly honest, Sin is on probation. When it ends in sixty-three years, He'll probably try to kill us out of revenge."

I snorted, crossed my arms over my chest. "You guys put a mass murdering psychopath on *probation*? You don't have a prison to lock him away?"

"Actually," Quinn fretted at his lip, "your dad was the one who made that call."

I blinked.

"Yeah. Forlorn had been sent to kill Sin because of the threat the guy was." He paused for a beat. "Is."

My jaw and arms fell slack.

"And our prisons, while far more advanced than anything the cowans can make, aren't capable of holding someone with Sin's combination of abilities. We lucked out in finding a way to prevent him from escaping to the Netherworld. And," he sighed. "Before you ask, no, I don't know how your dad discovered how to do that. Or why he spared Sin's life."

Well if AEON can recruit a guy like that, then... "Is it possible for me to join?"

Quinn quirked an eyebrow, shifted his weight to one foot. "You mean be an agent?"

I nodded, smiled at a woman in a lab coat who walked passed.

"I don't see why not. The only thing The Lady would have a problem with on your application is your age. Last I heard, the average age for new agents is sixty-eight. You're not even fifteen yet, so you might have a bit of a wait."

Understandable. "How old was my dad when he joined?"

"Er." He shrugged. "I think he was around eight centuries."

I forgot how to breathe for a minute. Eight. *Hundred*? How the—? What? "If he got to be that old, how could he die? He was immortal!"

Quinn scratched a temple with his finger, softly chuckled. "You're confusing immortality with agelessness. Immortality is perpetual deathlessness. Nothing can kill whatever the immortal thing is. Ever. Shoot it. Cut its head off. Light it on fire. Stake it through the heart. It keeps coming back. Right?"

I numbly nodded.

"Well, contrary to what you may have learned in fairy tales and movies, all parathropes can be killed. Take" he swept a hand up and down over his chest indicating himself. "I died at the age of twenty-two, after a wolf attacked me. And that happened back in the winter of 1691."

I. Blinked.

He grinned, and I got a glimpse of his lengthened canines. "Yup; I'm over three centuries old. But, like with vampires and most other were-creatures, I stopped aging when I turned. I haven't changed physically since I woke up in my grave, and, while I can shrug off getting hit by a bus going sixty, something like getting shot in the head would kill me. And it would be especially painful if the bullet contained silver.

"Cowan-born parathropes, such as human psychics and witches, age like their cowans parents. Other species will age extremely slowly once they reach a certain physical peak, retaining their youthfulness so they can fight longer. Pure blooded demon nobles age rapidly at first, then just stop aging completely. Angels and ghosts don't age at all. But every single one of them can be killed in one way or another. In fact, if you do eventually become an agent, you'll learn what to use against each species so that you are able to defend yourself in an emergency."

All those different creatures. All with different weaknesses and strengths and characteristics. It was already a lot to try to wrap my head around, and I got the distinct feeling I had much, much more to learn. I couldn't imagine what the basic training for an AEON Agent entailed.

Then a thought occurred to me. I'm half demon noble and half cowan... "Will I stop aging?"

Quinn pursed his lips as he studied me with those inhuman, moon blue eyes. After a handful of moments, he shrugged. "Honestly, I have no idea. I've never met a half demon like you."

"But you have met other half demons."

He loosed a nervous, little laugh. "Just one. He's nothing like you."

"How old is he?"

"I think he's about my age. Maybe older."

"So I could live to be ninety or nine hundred."

He gave a slight nod.

I sighed, stepped around the werewolf. I could feel his eyes on me as I made my way to the security door. Quinn appeared beside me a moment later, unlocked the door and held it open while I walked through. I found myself in the small room with the huge one-way mirror taking up one wall. The elevator beckoned to me from across the space, and I made my way towards it.

"Anyway," Quinn said from the doorway. "If you're really serious about becoming an agent, I'll let Duncan know. He might be able to pull some strings and get you on the force early."

I hit the button to go up. "Cool."

He softly called my name, and I faced him. He leaned against the door frame, arms crossed across his chest, but not at all displeased. "How did Khione find you?"

I told him about my excursion with Zero's group, leaving out the part where I had been forced to leave because of what I am. He made a face as he listened. I half expected him to go off on an angry rampage or something about my leaving the safety of the ship.

He didn't.

Instead, he muttered, "I wonder how she knew where to look for you." Then he suggested limiting my excursions for a while, or at least going with a bodyguard.

The elevator arrived, and I bade him good night as I stepped onto it. "And good luck on those theft cases."

He flashed a thumbs up as the elevator doors slipped shut.

18 SAATHOFF ACADEMY, DARK MOON PORT, MABON CITY
WEDNESDAY, OCTOBER 22
9:01 AM

The elevator doors opened to reveal a throng of students, each clad in immaculate white and forest green uniforms. It came as a bit of a shock, seeing a bunch of kids up and ready for school at this hour. I gaped at them stupidly for a handful of seconds before realizing the time. As I ambled through them, I found myself wishing that I could join them. How crazy is that? A teenager wanting to go to school. I must be cross wired or something. The kids at Mabon City Campus just wanted to be at home playing video games or at the mall shopping.

I never got to do either of those things.

I never got to be a kid.

I swallowed bitter tears before they could fall, unlocked my dorm room door. Once inside, I flipped on the light and thought of going to bed. I quickly passed that idea up—I had slept all day; there's no way I'd get to sleep any time soon. So I grabbed a bag of Cheetos from the stash Zero had slipped me and flopped down on the couch to eat.

"I really should find the cafeteria."

As I sat there, crunching away and wondering what I could do in the wee hours of the morning, I noticed the laptop Quinn had brought. It sat there, disconnected from whatever that gray cable was and beckoning me to touch it. I briefly wondered if I'd be breaking any rules by using it.

Probably not.

So I moved over to the computer chair and flipped open the lid. I had used a Macbook in school a couple of times and agilisi never bothered with anything made after 1940, so I had very little experience in computers. In fact, I felt like a two-year-old in the International Space Station. It didn't have any branding I could recognize, but it looked like it could withstand a nuclear blast.

I scavenged for the power button, found it among several other buttons. It powered up quickly, and I suddenly found myself looking at a picture of the Saathoff Academy crest and three icons. I hit the one labeled Browser. A page with a bunch of news stories popped up. I munched on a Cheeto while I read through them, froze when I saw a photograph of a sizable, pale blue jewel wreathed in glistening, white diamonds. It lay atop a royal blue fabric behind safety glass. The headline read:

HOPE DIAMOND: STOLEN!

For several seconds, I forgot how to breathe. I just sat there, gawking at the photograph. *That's the jewel Robert Patterson was guarding when the Shadow came!*

I had to read the article a few times before I could make sense of it. Investigators hadn't been able to lift any fingerprints—No surprise there—and had put out an APB on Robert. I scoffed at the latter. They thought he had played a part in the theft since he hasn't been seen since.

"Apparently, they didn't bother checking any morgues."

The female guard on duty that night had survived, but couldn't tell the police anything useful. It struck me as odd that the demon had let her live. Something about that just didn't feel right. Don't get me wrong, I'm glad she's okay. But I would have figured the demon had killed her to keep its existence secret. So why had the guard survived with just a few scratches?

I shook my head in disbelief, backed out to the other major headlines. There were stories about an earthquake, some rapper I didn't care about, and the freak weather. Nothing really stood out to me until I got to the local news.

ROBBERY AT SANTOVA ESTATE

I knew of Missus Santova, mostly because of the library named in her honor. She worked as a paleontologist or something like that, and lived in an area on the east end of town called the Palisades. That's where most of the rich people in town lived.

Yesterday's date glared at me from atop the article.

A frown tugged at my lips. *Why did that seem familiar?*

I chomped on a Cheeto as I read the article. The only thing that had been stolen was some ugly, deformed bone Cynthia had dug up recently. It hadn't been anything particularly special, so she didn't understand the reason for the theft.

Wait a minute! I read her name again. Cynthia Santova. *Didn't Quinn say something about a Cynthia after Cartouche dropped off that theft report? What had she said? A demon had done it?*

That made two thefts within seventy-two hours. Both by demons.

No, wait. Three.

The mirror from Hell had also been stolen by a demon. Three thefts in three days can't be a coincidence.

I spun around in the chair, snatched a notebook and pen from my tattered backpack. I flipped to an empty page and started sketching. It took a bit of concentration for me to remember as much detail about the mirror I had seen in my vision a couple days ago. What I drew turned out to be something hideous and misshapen, covered in spines, with black glass at its heart.

I sat back, staring at it and wondering what that thing had in common with an old bone and the Hope Diamond. And what the heck the number three had to do with anything.

19 SAATHOFF ACADEMY, DARK MOON PORT, MABON CITY
WEDNESDAY, OCTOBER 22
1:13 PM

I have to admit: Google is pretty freaking awesome.

It is absolutely amazing what you can learn just by searching for it. I had spent most of the last couple of hours learning about police procedures and various schools with online classes. But, perhaps, the most important thing I learned was something known as the *Wiccan Rede*. The *Rede* speaks of the Rule of Threes, which states that everything you do comes back on you threefold. So, basically, Karma. Except that it hits you either three times over and over again or three times as hard.

But there is another aspect to the Rule of Threes, and boy is it a doozy.

Apparently, if you say something three times, like, say, a promise, it becomes binding. You are forced to uphold whatever was agreed upon, be it something good or something bad. And if you break that promise, the backlash can be horrifying.

Of course, that report had been written by a tenth grader on something called a blog, so I couldn't be certain if any of it was true. Still, I made a note of it in my notebook, under the drawing of the mirror.

I looked for that ugly thing as well, but found nothing on it. Since it had been locked away in my dad's vault in the Netherworld for who knows how long, that came as no surprise. Who the heck runs around with a demonic mirror anyway? But the lack of any leads proved to be a huge problem. I needed something to give Khione before Friday night, or I might as well just let her cut my head off now.

The alarm clock exploded in sudden noise, scaring me half to death. I rushed over to it and slammed my fist down on the off button. The clock glared a quarter to five in the morning. I had been awake all night, which sort of threw me for a minute. I hadn't felt even a hint of weariness in that time. Now, as dawn approached, a wave of exhaustion rolled over me. I stared at my inviting bed, argued with myself over crawling into it and hibernating. I knew I should, but I needed to talk to Duncan or Quinn or—Gods forbid—Morgan about what I had discovered. They needed to know about the pattern of threes.

So I fought off the exhaustion, grabbed my notebook, and walked out my door.

A couple of students were already roaming the halls. I felt a lot out of place in a tee shirt and jeans while they all wore matching uniforms. It earned me a couple of stares, and I did my best to ignore them. I must have been doing a pretty good job because the next thing I knew something hit me in the back of the head.

I whirled around, instinct automatically driving me into a fighting stance. The kids drew back in fear.

One started screaming at the top of her lungs, "Demon! She's a demon! She'll kill us all!"

I recognized the girl as the bottle blonde who caused the scene at Paradox and forced me to leave. Felicity.

I grit my teeth in both anger and annoyance. My fists clenched even tighter. I wanted to sock her in the jaw, partially out of revenge but also to get her to shut up. But that would have just proven her right about me. I would truly become the monster she believed I was.

So I relaxed my muscles one by one. The tension bled out of me. And with it, my rage. I relaxed, stood to my unimpressive height. I scanned the crowd of students. Most of them looked terrified. Others stood, ready for a fight. Only one looked at me with sympathy and understanding. A tall and skinny boy with a messy mop of shocking white hair and dark eyes.

Necro.

I might have smiled if Felicity hadn't kept screaming.

He shoved his way through the crowd to stand beside me, turned a scowl on Felicity. When that failed, he yelled at her to shut up or he'll give her something to scream about.

She choked on a sob, and finally—thankfully—fell silent.

"It doesn't matter what we are," he said and eyed the crowd. "What matters is what we do with the powers we have."

"Oh, shut up, Necro!"

"Quit preaching, dude!"

"No demon could ever be good!"

I scoffed. "Thanks for trying, Necro."

He smiled over his shoulder. "We evil stereotypes gotta stick together."

Evil? I stretched my senses out to feel him. Or I tried to. Nothing happened. Nothing at all. *What the hell?*

Behind the growing crowd, the elevator doors opened with a chime. "Vhat is going on here?"

I sighed. *Duncan.*

The crowd parted as he strode through it, looking this way and that. I had enough time to note that he had changed his suit to a steely gray number. Then, suddenly, his gaze landed on me. Curiosity flashed in his violet eyes. It took him less than a second to figure out what had everyone's attention.

He tilted his head back and to one side ever so slightly. "Don't you lot have some place to be?"

The crowd quickly began to disperse.

Necro looked at me. "Sorry I wasn't much help."

I waved a hand dismissively. "Don't worry about it. Happens all the time."

"Well, it shouldn't." His brow furrowed. "You're really a demon?"

"Half," I muttered, glancing around the now nearly empty hallway. I

"Cool."

That single word told me a couple of things. One, though he claimed to be an evil stereotype, he wasn't a demon himself. Two, he actually sounded impressed. He really didn't mind my demon side at all. It came as a greater relief than I had realized to find someone who didn't have their head up their butt.

Yet my mind couldn't get over the fact that I couldn't sense him. He had too much color in his flesh to be a vampire, and he obviously wasn't a ghost. So why couldn't I sense his life energy.

"Listen," he said, and I met his gaze. "Don't pay any attention to Felicity and her peanut gallery of friends; they think they're better than everyone just because they're Daughters of Mab."

"Who?"

He laughed. "Exactly." Then he glanced towards Duncan, who gave him a courteous nod. "Well, I'd better skedaddle. Don't want to miss my favorite meal of the day."

"Okay."

"See ya around," he murmured, backing away a few paces. Then he pirouetted and jogged towards the stairs I watched as he bounded up them two at a time like he had done it a million times before.

Suddenly, Duncan and I were alone. And the vampire regarded me in the deafening silence. At long last, he sighed. "Allow me to apologize."

"There's no need."

"I should have told you that some of the population—"

"Are demon-phobic?"

He paused to consider my words. "Vell, that is von vay to put it."

"Whatever." I waved it off. Racism wasn't anything new to me. Still, it did hurt to be screamed at by kids who were supposed to be like me. *Nobody is like me.*

Duncan must have been reading my mind because he said, "I know how alone you must feel, Cybil, being as uniquely gifted as you are."

Gifted? Right.

"Give the kids some time to adjust to your presence. They vill come around."

"Time is one thing I don't have a lot of," I said, and held out my notebook. My drawing glared up from the page. "I need to find this before 9:17 PM on Friday, or I'm dead meat."

He frowned down at the mirror, accepted the notebook from me. I watched as his eyes drifted over the page. "Vhere did you see this?"

"In a vision Monday morning, minutes before Quinn found me on the sidewalk by the train station."

"And you are certain of the design?" His violet gaze met mine.

I shrugged. "It might be a little off, but yeah, it looked like that." I waited while he studied it again, noting how his brow furrowed and a thoughtful frown tugged at his lips. "Do you recognize it?"

"No." He met my gaze again, passed the notebook back. "But perhaps Specter can pull some information on it from our database. Come."

He led the way to the elevators. We rode down in silence, mostly because I wasn't sure how to bring up what I wanted to tell him. I knew the info I had would help him on his theft cases, but I felt like I would be overstepping my bounds by telling him. I may as well tell the Chief of Police how to do his job.

The doors opened to reveal a lobby half the size of the *Titanic*. There were huge portraits in gaudy frames hanging on the walls. A luscious mini garden—complete with a working fountain—sat between the elevators and the wall opposite. I guess it had been intentionally designed and decorated that way so as to impress the parents of potential students.

(Who wouldn't be impressed simply by the fact that the Saathoff Academy was a cruise ship?)

Duncan immediately made for the double doors across from the elevators, and I followed on his heels. We entered an empty waiting room, the only noise coming from a television in the corner that quietly played the morning news. I spotted a door to the right of the receptionist's desk. It bore Duncan's name. He unlocked it with a deft hand, and ushered me through.

This office looked almost identical to the one I had been in last night. It had more personal items, like framed photographs and little nick knacks, and it lacked the conference table area. However, it did have a wall of shelves leadened with leather-bound books behind the desk. I suspect, like the lobby, all of this had been set up for show; dupe the parents in believing the ship isn't hiding a secret government agency.

Duncan rounded the glass and metal desk, picked up the phone. I stood by the door, patiently waiting while he muttered something into the receiver.

"Specter vill be in in a minute," he announced and hung up the phone.

I nodded, moved a little further into the room.

"Vhat else did you vision show you?"

"Some huge, dark room lit by blue flames." I shrugged a shoulder. "It had a bunch of gold and jewels piled all around the space, with the mirror on a pedestal in the middle of all of it."

He hummed in thought. So much so that I almost believed he knew the place I had just described, but he couldn't recall the name.

At least now I had a segue into bringing up what I had discovered. I just hoped he didn't take my helping the investigations as an insult.

"Speaking of jewels," I said and dared a couple steps closer to his desk. "Did you know that the Hope Diamond was stolen?"

He nodded. “It has been in the news. Vhy do you ask?”

I swallowed. “Because the Shadow that killed Robert Patterson was the one who took it.”

The vampire frowned at that.

“Then the mirror got stolen from a vault in the Netherworld the next day. And your friend Cynthia Santova was robbed the day after that. Also by a demon.” I could see the gears turning in his expression. “Doesn’t it strike you as a bit odd that three thefts occurred within three days, and all of them were done by Shadows?”

I watched as haunting realization rolled over Duncan’s face. He sank into his chair as if someone told him he had contracted a terminal disease. I gave him a minute to recover before hitting him with another whammy.

“I believe the three stolen items—the mirror, Cynthia’s bone, and the Diamond—may have something in common. Otherwise, why go through all the trouble?”

Duncan’s gaze focused on me for a moment, then shifted to something behind me. I realized then that the temperature in the room dropped about thirty degrees and the hairs on the back of my neck were standing at attention.

20 SAATHOFF ACADEMY, DARK MOON PORT, MABON CITY
WEDNESDAY, OCTOBER 22
3:05 PM

Instinct screamed at me to fight. To bite and claw my way through whomever or whatever stood behind me. Tear it to shreds and leave it a bleeding, pummeled mess on the floor. I beat down that ridiculous reaction, forced myself to calm. Only then did I look over my shoulder.

The ghost of a Roman Legionnaire a few feet away.

Specter.

I hadn't even sensed his approach. But that didn't make any sense. I have always been able to feel energies. Especially those given off by spirits. Now, all of a sudden, they're sneaking up on me? I don't like it. I don't like it at all.

What the heck is going on? I nodded respectfully to the ghost.

He flashed a grin before his attention turned toward Duncan. "You wanted to see me, sir?"

The vampire's violet gaze lingered on me. I could read the curiosity burning behind the look, and knew he wanted to ask about my reaction. Thankfully, he didn't. But an eternity passed before he looked away. "Cybil had a vision about a mirror she has been accused of stealing. I am hoping you can find it in our database."

"Sure, but I'd need a—"

I held up my drawing. "Picture?"

Specter looked flabbergasted for half a second before lightly chuckling. He brought his hands before him and summoned his weird spectral ball.

"It's probably not an exact match," I said as I watched him manipulate the ghostly sphere over my drawing. I could feel the cold of his presence intensify and recede with every pass he made. "But it is as close as I could remember."

"That shouldn't be a problem." His fingers flew over the strange glyphs on the ball's surface a moment. Then he drew the ball back towards himself. "I doubt there are that many mirrors to search through."

"Can I ask," I nodded towards the sphere. "What is that thing?"

"Oh," he said, his tone amused. "It's my control sphere. See, I can't manipulate things on the mortal plane of existence without expending huge amounts of energy. If I wanted to, say, move a piece of paper across a desktop, it would require the equivalent of what it takes to power a city block for three and a half minutes."

I whistled. All that energy just to move a single piece of paper? If he had done that before, I would have felt it every time the bus to school drew close to the city. It'd be like feeling a black hole with a tiny but intense pinprick of a presence in the midst of it.

It makes sense if you think about it.

Just picture making a sand mound. In order for the mound to exist, sand must be brought in from the surrounding area. When it goes missing to make the mound larger, it leaves a void. And that void doesn't fill back in unless you drag in more sand to fill it, which would leave even less sand surrounding the mound than there had been before. And it would stay that way until the weather or some other event wore the mound back down or destroyed it entirely.

Doing the latter would create an even bigger mess as sand would be strewn everywhere instead of calmly settling back into place over a few days.

"I take it that's something you don't do very often."

"It exhausts me to a point where I can't maintain this form."

I hadn't thought of that before now, but it explains the intense cold around him. Most ghosts you see are just shapeless clouds of energy or little, fluttering orbs. In order for them to take a more humanoid shape, they'd have to draw in the heat energy from the air. The more they want to appear, the more heat they have to draw in.

In other words, thermodynamics.

(I learned about that reading some of the college books people brought in to agilisi's shop.)

Duncan lightly tapped the butt of a pen on his desk top, his subtle way of getting our attention. It worked. "Vhile you are looking into the mirror, check to see if it has any connection to Cynthia's bone and the Hope Diamond."

Specter pursed his lips.

"All *three*," I said, making sure he understood the significance. "Were stolen by Shadows within three consecutive days."

His mouth formed a silent *oh* in realization.

I made a face that hopefully conveyed that I thought the same.

"Good thing you noticed that," he said, his attention returning to his sphere. "Nothing is a coincidence when dealing with threes."

"Then they *must* have something in common," I muttered, more to myself than to either of them. I still received a half shrug from Specter. *But what?*

I looked down at the notebook in my hands. The drawing of the twisted mirror glared up at me from the page, taunting me with its secrets. I studied it closely, looking for any flaw or sign that would give them away. Every line. Every pock mark. Every shadow.

Nothing.

I sighed, frustrated, and relaxed my arms. It didn't help my agitation, and I wound up impatiently tapping the notebook against my hip. It took more effort for me to stop the fidgeting. And even more to let my eyes slip shut. I breathed, calming my mind and body. It took maybe five minutes for me to reach a meditative state. It used to take me an hour or more to achieve this level of serenity, but I had had a lot of practice over the years.

My back twitched.

I shoved that memory away before it could form.

My mind turned to the mirror, and I directed it to the memory of my vision. The thing had been in a round room, sitting atop a pedestal at the very center. Blue firelight flickered off its jet black surface. The unnatural light gave the ebony glass at its heart a wicked glare, and I fought to suppress a shudder. Even like this, I could sense evil in the mirror.

It took a strength I didn't know I possessed to walk up to the thing. When at last I stood over it, I could see my own twisted reflection on the glass. As I did with the drawing, I studied every minute detail. I had no way of knowing what the mirror had been made of, or how long it had sat untouched in this room. Spines jutted out from the glass at mismatched angles, almost like a porcupine protecting itself. The spines were everywhere.

Except at the bottom.

My eyes slammed open. I turned to Duncan. "Do you have a photo of the bone stolen from Cynthia's estate?"

His eyebrow quirked. "Yes."

"Please, can I see it?"

He studied me a moment as if considering whether or not to do it. He made up his mind, swiveled in his chair so that he faced the filing cabinets on his left. From the lowest drawer, he removed an unmarked manila folder. When he turned to face me again, he had two photographs in his hand.

He set them on the desk.

The twisted thing in the photos didn't look like any bone I had ever seen. It looked more like a gnarled twig that had been stained black with age. Its girth appeared to be a little smaller than my wrist, and it twisted over on itself before tapering to a point at one end. The other end bore evidence of something haven been broken off eons ago.

Now the three thefts made sense.

"They're all part of the whole."

"The whole?" I felt a chill as Specter looked over my shoulder. "You mean they fit together?"

I tapped the top photograph of the bone with my finger. "That's the mirror's handle. And I'm betting there's a weird divot somewhere on it where the Hope Diamond belongs."

Duncan licked his lips, pulled the second photo out from behind the one under my finger. I could see the divot clear as day. His violet gaze locked with mine for a beat before he looked away. "Specter—"

"Already piecing them together," reported the ghost. "Then I'll start my search for matches."

"Thank you." Duncan glanced at his watch, came to some sort of decision. He stood, straitened his suit jacket. "Cybil, please come vith me for a few minutes."

I figured he would round his desk and make for the door behind me. Instead, he went to the bookcases behind his desk and pulled out a thick tome. Artificial light spilled out of the book, and he touched it six times. I heard a click, and watched as he replaced the tome. The bookshelf swung open on invisible hinges.

"Okay," I said as I made my way towards the hidden door. "That's cool."

Duncan grinned over his shoulder and let the way over the threshold. The bookshelf door drifted shut behind us of its own accord. The tiny room I found myself in left me feeling claustrophobic. It may as well have been a closet for all the space it had. Red light glared down from pucks in the ceiling, illuminating a reflective warning on the door.

TRESPASSERS WILL BE SUBJECT TO SEARCH AND IMPRISONMENT.

Well, that's just swell.

I watched as Duncan used a number pad by the door handle. A soft click sounded, and he pushed the door open. We stepped through. I instantly recognized the hospital-like hallway and the glass-enclosed laboratory. We were in AEON Headquarters.

"Quinn told me that you expressed and interest in becoming an AEON Agent."

It wasn't a question, but it had the feel of one. So I answered, "Well, I've wanted to be a cop since I was five, if only to bring my parents' killer to justice."

Duncan led me down a hallway. "But?"

"But they fed me some bull about being too emotionally unstable."

He glanced over his shoulder at me.

"I think agil—I mean, my grandma paid them to tell me that."

We came to a stop at a door bearing Duncan's name. He unlocked it, led me inside. The lights flared on automatically to reveal the office Quinn had escorted me to last night.

"Do you believe you could be an investigator?" the vampire asked as he strode around behind me to reach his desk. He grabbed something from atop it, turned to await my answer.

Is this a job interview? "Yes. I believe I could become an even better one once I learn a how to control my psychic abilities a bit more."

He grinned, pointed the contraption in his hand towards the conference area. The watercolor painting went black.

Then it started to ring.

21 SAATHOFF ACADEMY, DARK MOON PORT, MABON CITY
WEDNESDAY, OCTOBER 22
4:17 PM

The blank screen vanished on the third ring, replaced by some very upscale office scene. A woman sat just left of center. She could have been anywhere between twenty and sixty, and had auburn hair that fell around her shoulders in a curling cascade. Her skin looked even more pale than Duncan's, and her eyes were striking, beautiful jade.

The still image sent chills racing down my spine.

I almost screamed when she suddenly blinked.

"My Lady," Duncan said while giving her a slight bow.

"Revenant." Her voice, though soft and polite, had an edge to it. She gave me the impression that she was someone not to be trifled with. Like some elitist mobster unafraid to kill for even the slightest mistake some underling or innocent bystander could make.

"I apologize for the unscheduled call," Duncan went on. "But I thought it important that you meet somevon."

Those piercing green eyes shifted to me.

I swallowed.

"May I present the daughter of Forlorn and Cassandra Lilley."

Her eyebrows vanished beneath her bangs, and she took another long, reevaluating look at me. I had silently counted to six before she finally asked, "Are you certain of this?"

"Absolutely."

"How many years have you, child?"

I licked my lips, nervous. "A-almost fifteen."

"Incredible."

"Ve are still trying to learn how she survived the night Taboo attacked and killed her family," explained Duncan. "But that is not my reason for calling."

Her jade gaze finally, thankfully, shifted away from me. "I gathered as much."

"Actually, since my Second, Fenrir, stumbled upon her earlier this veek, Cybil has been actively playing a role in assisting us on an investigation."

The woman sat back in her chair, steepled her fingers. "Go on."

"I humbly request that you overlook her age, and allow her to officially assist my team as a consultant."

A man's voice came from somewhere off screen. He spoke softly and in a language that might have been Greek, and the woman frowned thoughtfully. Then he said, "You appear to be dead, Miss Starr."

I clenched my fists. I failed to keep the venom out of my voice as I said, "That's not who I am anymore."

The woman quirked an eyebrow.

I think I might have stunned the man as it took a beat or two for him to reply with, "My sincerest apologies."

A second man, this one with a rough and emotionless voice, said something I didn't catch. I saw Duncan grimace out of the corner of my eye, and wondered what about the third speaker caused such a reaction. Or maybe he caught what had been said and didn't like it.

The woman's peachsicle lips pulled into a frown, and her gaze hardened as she focused somewhere off screen. "I am well aware of that, Sin."

So that *was Sin who had just spoken? No wonder Duncan reacted that way.*

The woman's focus remained elsewhere—most likely on Sin—a moment longer. I found myself hoping that the camera would pan towards him so I could get a look at the person who gave monsters nightmares. Of course, the camera didn't obey my wishes, and remained steadily locked on the woman.

The hardness in her gaze ebbed slightly as someone laid a piece of paper in front of her. I watched as her gaze darted over the page for a moment. She pursed her lips in a thoughtful frown, looked off screen again.

The first man uttered something in Greek.

She exhaled through her nose, turned her focus on Duncan. "Very well, Revenant." My heart hammered in my chest when she looked at me. "I hereby deputize you an Agent of the Three Worlds, subject to the duration of your current investigation."

I battled the surge of excitement that erupted through me like fireworks on the Fourth of July. I wanted to jump or squeal or dance, but I held it all in. Except for the smile that made my cheeks hurt. *Don't embarrass yourself. Not in front of the boss.*

Duncan bowed. "Thank you, my Lady."

She held up a hand. "Should any harm befall her in the line of duty, you shall be the soul held responsible. Do I make myself clear?"

"Yes, my Lady."

"Good," she said. "Now, if you'll excuse me, I am in the midst of a meeting with my own team."

"I understand. And thank you."

"Yes," I added and mimicked Duncan's bow. "Thank you very much."

The woman nodded once, and the screen went black.

It took me longer than I'd like to admit to calm myself. When at last my heartbeat slowed to something more normal, I looked at Duncan. "I hope I don't get you in trouble."

He met my gaze with a soft smile. "I am certain that you vill continue to do marvelously."

I couldn't stop grinning during the trek back to Duncan's public office. After ten grueling years of torture and misery, things were finally starting to go my way. I had my freedom and, in a round about way, I had my dream job—even if it was only temporary. I wanted to sing and dance. To shout it from the rooftops.

I'm a cop! I'm a cop!

I just hoped I didn't mess it up.

Duncan deviated from the path we had originally taken. He turned left instead of right at the end of the hall and stepped through a door labeled 'Supplies'. I held the door open with my foot, watched as the vampire went about collecting a few things. He placed them all in a handy, empty printer paper box, which he then handed to me.

"Procedure guidelines and agency information," he said by way of explanation.

I stared blankly at him for a beat, shook the stupor off. "You do realize that I'm only a temporary asset to your team, right?"

He flashed a too-white smile and strode away.

I rolled my eyes at his back and quickly followed him.

We were back in his public office a minute later. Quinn hand Morgan had arrived during our absence, which seemed to surprise Duncan. The vampire looked to Specter for an explanation.

"I know what we're looking for." His voice held a grim note, and he manipulated his control sphere so that it projected an image of the twisted mirror. Only, in this image, all three pieces were one. "It's the Mirror of Souls."

Stunned, Duncan sank into his office chair. "Are you certain of this?"

"There's only one record of it, and you'll never guess who wrote it."

"Sin?"

The ghost nodded wryly.

"At least we'll know it's accurate," muttered Quinn.

"Vhat does the report say?"

"Not much, I'm afraid. We already know the legend of the mirror's ability to steal the souls of its victims. But Sin's report goes on to say that the powers of those souls can then transferred to whomever wields the mirror."

I raised my hand, which earned me a couple of grins. "What does that mean, exactly?"

"Heh. Uh. Let me see. How do I explain it?" The ghost chewed on his lower lip for a moment. "Ah. Let's say that a fire demon wanted to control ice for some reason. All he would need to do is steal the soul of an ice demon using the mirror, which would instantly kill the ice demon. Then he would need to turn the mirror on himself—I'm not sure how, but I'm sure there's some sort of ritual involved—so that he could absorb that soul. Voila. Instant fire-ice demon."

"That would be a bloody nightmare," Quinn grumbled.

Duncan sighed. "And now it is in the hands of a Shadow."

"A Shadow we cannot find," Morgan added, which drew Duncan's and Specter's attention. "As you know, WEIRD is able to track every demon in the realm, but we haven't been able to locate any Shadows in the last week."

I muttered thoughtfully to myself, "But I've seen at least one up close and personal on multiple occasions."

It earned a stern glare from the blonde. "Indeed."

A little louder, I asked, "Is there a way they can conceal themselves from your tracking thingy?"

Her glare on me intensified. "No."

"Huh." I pondered over what that might mean. I had no idea how the angels' tracking system worked, but if it could detect energies, that might explain why it couldn't find any Shadows lurking around. Life energy can be manipulated to a certain extent. A change of emotion could do it. Or, more likely, the Shadows found a way to suppress their energy, making it appear as though they weren't ever here.

I wondered if I could do the same.

"All right," said Duncan. He pointed to Morgan. "I vant you to keep an eye out for any strange pings. If a Shadow really has the mirror, it vill vant to use it." Then he looked at me. "If you get any visions, let us know."

I nodded.

Quinn started to say something, but Duncan cut him off. "The Lady has given us permission to utilize Cybil's abilities for this case."

The werewolf flashed a thumbs up.

Morgan muttered something under her breath.

"All right, AEONs," said Duncan. "Let's get to vork."

22 SAATHOFF ACADEMY, DARK MOON PORT, MABON CITY
THURSDAY, OCTOBER 23
6:43 AM

That phone had started to ring. The special one she kept in the solarium. The one with the Victorian style base and the mouthpiece that reminded her of a shower head. Only two people in the world had the number to that phone, and if either of them were calling, the news had to be dire. She hesitated to answer it. Perhaps the fears that had been plaguing her in recent days would not come to fruition if the call went unanswered.

A foolish thought, but it gave her a moment's hope.

At long last, she picked up the receiver. By some miracle, she managed to hold the phone to her ear despite the trembling of her hands. She tried to sound casual as she spoke into it, but her voice came out small and timid.

The voice on the other end spoke quietly. Calmly.

She lamented, falling into the chair beside the phone. Nothing could be done to save her. Even if she had had the time to counter the magick—if that's what it truly was—she had no guarantee it would work. She could already feel the power beginning to build up around her. It charged the air with a primal energy even as it settled into her bones with a chill.

Static swallowed the voice on the other end of the line. Then the call disconnected completely.

The phone clattered to the floor.

I bolted upright with a wordless cry. Minutes must have ticked by while I sat there, gasping for air and trying to slow my racing heartbeat. Visions rarely left me in such a state of panic like this. The ones that did were often the results of something terribly evil. But this one felt more like a thunderstorm rolling in. A dark, cold super cell.

Could it have been the mirror?

I sighed, rubbed my eyes. "I need to find that stupid thing."

I cast a glance to the clock on my nightstand. Holy crap! I slept way longer than I thought. Oh well. At least I felt a bit better.

My stomach rumbled in disagreement.

I tore myself from my bed, crossed the room to the sofa. The bag of goodies that Zero had snuck me lay on the farthest cushion. But as I began to reach for something, I spotted the clothes I had worn to Paradox last night. No, wait; the night before. All this sleeping weird hours is confusing me. I never did get to spend any of the money I had pocketed. And I longed for something more than just snack foods.

With my mind made up, I quickly washed and dressed. Blue jeans and an anime tee shirt were the flavors of the day as far as style was concerned. I'd probably stick out even if I wore one of those pristine school uniforms to match the other kids. At least this way, I had pockets to stuff my money and room key into.

I heard voices as I made my way to the elevators, silently counted them as each spoke. A quartet. All students. And they were discussing an assignment for some history class.

Aren't they up a bit early?

I drew to a stop just before the hallway spilled out into the lounge area. The elevators were situated directly across from where the students had gathered. I'd have to face being seen if I wanted to get anywhere, but I didn't want to cause another confrontation. The last one had been bad enough.

But my rumbling stomach refused to let me slip back to my room until it had had a real meal.

So I swallowed my anxiety and calmly stepped from the shadows.

The kids didn't so much as look my way.

Relieved, I made for the elevators and pressed the button to summon one. I silently counted as I waited. At twenty-seven, the doors opened with their chime, and I stepped inside. I discovered a directory hanging on the wall to my right. How I had missed that the last few times I rode the lift, I didn't know. But now I could easily make my way to the cafeteria on A Deck.

The car stopped once during its climb, but the trio who had been about to join me decided it'd be better if they took a different elevator. Whatever. At least they hadn't freaked out and started screaming.

How could I have been so stupid?

I punched my reflection in the elevator's door.

Hi. I'm a demon. Won't you be my friend? Idiot!

I punched my reflection again.

And here I thought I had finally found a place where I could actually fit in. Heck, I had everything I have ever wanted right here on this ship. Everything. Except my parents.

The elevator eventually slowed to a stop, chimed with the doors' opening. A group of students stood in waiting. They had been chatting excitedly about something, but went quiet one by one as each of them took notice of me. It quickly turned into the most awkward silence I had ever been in.

The crowd parted like a split log as I stepped forward and off of the elevator. I battled the sudden urge to beat the snot out of the lot of them, kept my emotions hidden behind a blank mask. Maybe if I played it cool, they wouldn't be so nervous around me.

Yeah. Right. And all my wishes will come true.

Well, I guess, in a weird sort of way, two of them already had. I had freed myself of agilisi, which allowed me to become deputized as a cop. So, perhaps, I had a chance to make friends here. Even one or two would be more than I had ever had.

Then I caught a whiff of roasting meats, and my thoughts turned away from my social problems. My mouth watered as I drew closer to the source of the great smells: a trio of gilded double doors.

I stopped at the threshold, awestruck. The dining hall looked like it belonged in some fairy tale palace, not in a cruise ship. It had two levels, with the upper one being supported by wide, gilded columns. Enormous windows ran floor to ceiling, giving a spectacular view of the sunrise-lit harbor as it emptied into the Atlantic. One huge chandelier dangled in a cone of crystals from the center of the ceiling, drawing the eye back down to the several white linen-covered tables.

Students of all ages occupied some of the tables. Some ate. Others were bent over books, studying. A handful were playing a tabletop game, and I recognized Necro among them. I also recognized Zero when I spotted her winding her way though the tables and towards me. I mentally prepared myself for the worst.

She stopped her approach just out of arm's reach. "What's up?"

What's up? That hadn't been on my list of things to expect. I hadn't prepared to answer something like that, so I merely shrugged a shoulder.

Her weight shifted. "I just wanted to ask—"

"Yes, I really am half Shadow demon."

She made a face. "That's cool."

I quirked an eyebrow.

"What? You expecting me to freak out like Felicity and her ilk?"

"Well, yeah." I frowned thoughtfully. "Isn't that how people are supposed to treat a demon?"

"Naw, girl. Half the people on this ship probably have a demon ancestor of some type or another. I know I do. You're just not as diluted as the rest of us."

I felt my lips form an *Oh*, but no sound came out. She really didn't mind my demon heritage? I didn't know what to say to that. All this time, I had felt like an evil leper. Nobody wanted to be around me, and they certainly didn't know how to take me. Then Zero walks up like I'm just a normal girl. Could I be looking at my first friend?

Don't get ahead of yourself.

"Besides," she continued. "That's not what I wanted to ask you."

"Okay." I drew the word out, stressing my uncertainty in the situation. What else would someone who had heard the rumors about me ask me?

"Yeah. I wanted to know if you've enrolled yet."

I didn't know what to say to that.

It must have shown on my face as she replied, "Still not sure, huh?"

I shrugged.

"Family in the area?"

What would make her guess that?

"Yeah, that'd do it," she said. "But you can't let that fear control you or your decisions. You'll spend the rest of your life looking over your shoulder."

I got the impression she spoke from personal experience. "What made you stay?"

She rocked back on her heels, smiled. "Honestly? My brother. He fell in love with the classes the school offered and the way the staff made us feel like we were part of a family. We had never had that before."

Same here.

"But, hey, if this place is too close to your old life for you to feel comfortable, you can always look into one of the other four schools."

I stared at her for a few beats, trying to let that information sink in. "I thought this was the only one."

"Girl," she chuckled. "You've got a lot to learn about this world."

I had been about to agree with her when an Asian boy at the gaming table called out to Zero in a language I didn't know. She shot him an impatient look, replied in the same language. As I studied the boy's features, I couldn't help but notice how much he looked like Zero. In fact, I could only spot two differences: his hair had been buzzed short and the dragon on his arm had been inked in scarlet instead of blue.

They were twins.

If Zero could control water, and her dragon is blue, does red mean he could control fire?

Zero looked back at me with a weird, little smile. "Would you like to join us?"

I blinked. My gaze returned to the table of gamers behind her. Necro spotted me and gave a wave, which I sheepishly returned.

"We're playing Dungeons and Dragons."

"Uh. Thanks, but no." I hooked a thumb towards the buffet line. "I'm just here to grab a bite. I have some work for Duncan that I need to get back to."

"All right." She backed up a couple of steps. "Take a good helping of the cherry coffee cake. It's amazing!"

I grinned.

"Oh! And if you need anything, I'm on D2, room sixty-six."

D2? That's the same deck as me. And room sixty-six put her just a few doors away. I thanked her, watched for a moment as she rushed back to the table. I turned left and made for the buffet line.

23 SAATHOFF ACADEMY, DARK MOON PORT, MABON CITY
THURSDAY, OCTOBER 23
8:13 AM

I returned to my room with a bottle of vanilla latte and plate-load of sausage and a big ole waffle stacked high with all the good stuff. I set the food on the desk before sinking into the chair in front of it. I stuffed a few sausage links in my mouth before I spun the chair in a one-eighty.

The box of info pamphlets Duncan had collected for me sat untouched on the couch. I unloaded the contents one-by-one, stacking them neatly on the desk. There were booklets and info sheets with titles like 'The Accords of the Three Worlds Senate,' 'Navigating the Three Worlds,' and 'AEON: What You Need to Know as an Agent.' I turned to a new page in the notebook I had already used, and got to studying.

By the time I finished the last pamphlet, I had filled the rest of that notebook and started in another. I couldn't help but feel stunned by what I had learned of the parathropic society. I mean, these beings and creatures have existed side-by-side with cowans since before the start of recorded history. And nobody notices them!

Do you realize how insane that is?

There are people and creatures out there right now with powers and abilities I had never even heard of. Not only that, but there are predators that make Shadows and vampires look like helpless, little kittens. And all of them are governed by the Three Worlds Senate and a set of laws known simply as the Accords.

The more I read, the more I kept coming back to the same bewildered thought: How could I not have noticed all of this before?

More importantly, how could I use all this info to help find the Mirror of Souls?

I sat back in my chair with a muttered curse. I completely forgot to tell Duncan about my vision of the woman with the weird phone. I had no doubt that the mirror had been used on her. But when? Why? What did she do to mark herself as the Shadows' target?

Before I could follow that trail of thought, someone knocked on my door. It took my brain a beat or two to register the noise and inquire who knocked.

"It's Morgan."

Oh, great. What does she want? I trekked to the door, cracked it open. The golden-haired woman stood there, arms crossed and impatient. "Yes?"

"Duncan would like your input on something," she said. "He requests your presence."

"Okay. One sec." I ducked back from the door, grabbed my room key from where I had put it on my desk and killed the lights. Morgan had moved a couple of feet during that time, but at least she had waited for me.

We took the elevator to Duncan's public office and passed through the hidden door and into AEON Headquarters. Morgan led the way to an office down the hall from Duncan's. Although similar in decor to the other, this office felt smaller; perhaps due to the addition of several tall filing cabinets along the right wall.

Quinn sat behind the mahogany desk with Duncan peering over his shoulder. They were studying the photographs sprawled over the desktop. The moment Morgan and I entered, the duo looked up.

Quinn stood. "Thanks for coming in," he said. "I hope we didn't interrupt anything."

"Not at all."

Duncan motioned for me to take Quinn's chair. "Ve finally received the crime scene photos from the two thefts that occurred in this realm," he explained as I rounded the desk. It felt awkward to be taking Quinn's seat, and I tried not to let it show as I listened to him. "Ve are hoping to get your take on them."

I glanced over the sprawl as I scooted the chair in. "My take?"

"See if you recognize anything," said Quinn. "Or get a vision off of them."

"Speaking of vision…" I looked up at Duncan. "I had one earlier."

His brow furrowed. "Vhat did you see?"

I told him.

If there had been any color in his face, it would have drained.

"You know the woman in my vision." I stated it as a fact, not a question. Still, he numbly nodded. "Who is she?"

He started to answer, faltered.

"Cynthia Santova," murmured Quinn.

Why had I not realized that sooner? Of course she'd be a victim! Because of her residence in the Palisades, she likely had some high-end security system. Chances were good that she had footage that showed the thief taking the bone fragment. I glanced at the pile of photos before me, instantly zeroing in on the ones taken in the aftermath of the theft.

"Ve need to get over there," Duncan said, finally finding his voice. I felt his gaze on me as he asked, "Do you know ven she…"

I shook my head.

He reached for the phone, stopped himself.

Quinn grabbed Duncan's wrist, pushed it away from the phone. "I'll talk to her."

The vampire nodded, and Quinn quit the room without another word.

I turned my attention to the piles of photos, trying my best not to feel guilty about the doom I had just levied over Duncan's lover.

24 SAATHOFF ACADEMY, DARK MOON PORT, MABON CITY THURSDAY, OCTOBER 23 1:23 PM

A phone call came in to Quinn's office some twenty minutes after he had left. Duncan froze, staring at the phone and unwilling to answer it. I leaned forward and pressed the speaker phone button, asked who's calling.

"It's me," said Quinn.

I noted the tone in his voice and looked to Duncan.

"Lieutenant LeFae is here," Quinn went on. "She says a call came through to her office about ninety minutes ago." He took a breath. "Cynthia is… She's…"

Duncan's gaze suddenly went distant. He didn't blink. Didn't breathe. He just stood there, stunned. Broken. There wasn't anything anyone could do or say that would make any difference. Sympathy. Condolences. It would all fall on deaf ears.

I know. Because that had been me.

I could only watch as the vampire unsteadily made for the door. Morgan tried to go to him, but he waved her off. She nodded, and he quit the room. I drew a deep breath, let it out slow. There was work to do. I didn't have time to get sidetracked on emotions or memories. I'd just have to deal with those later.

So I shoved it all into the deepest, darkest corners of my mind, looked down at the phone. "We know Duncan didn't call her. Who's the other person with the number to that phone?"

"Specter," Quinn and Morgan replied at the same time.

My lips tugged into a frown. That didn't track. "Would he have had any reason to call her?"

Morgan shook her head negative.

"It's extremely difficult for him to make any phone calls."

"That's what I thought." I sat back in the chair with a sigh. "That number isn't listed, so whoever called it had a strong reason to go digging for it. A motive for murder, for example. So let's get the obvious question out of the way. Did Cynthia have enemies?"

"She was a member of our team," replied Quinn. "But she retired nearly thirty years ago."

Thirty years is an awful long time for someone to hold a grudge, but it isn't unheard of.

"Plus," he continued, and I could hear the phone rustling. He must have been pacing as we spoke. "We use codenames and aliases as precautions to prevent this sort of thing."

"Okay," I said, and thought that over. "What were her powers?"

Morgan stepped up to the desk to stand just opposite me. "She was a witch."

According to the pamphlets I read, witches were pretty commonplace, which meant it was highly unlikely that the Shadow had been after her simply to get a power boost. No; This had personal written all over it. And it couldn't be because of Cynthia's ties to AEON.

What if the Shadow had nothing to do with using the mirror on Cynthia? Sure, it stole the pieces and fused them together, but it could have been under orders from someone else. Now that made a little more sense.

Wait a minute!

I sat forward. "Who called the Lieutenant?"

Though he muffled the phone, I could still hear Quinn asking her. "She thought it was one of us."

In other words, Lieutenant LeFae knew of the AEON Agency. She may even be a parathrope herself. Good to know.

"*Did* we call her?"

"No," said Morgan.

"Nope," Quinn confirmed.

I rapped my fingers on the desktop. "Is there any way we can find out who did?"

I jumped a little when Specter suddenly leaned through the wall to my left. He flashed an apologetic smile and said, "I can do a reverse look-up on LeFae's number."

Quinn told him to go ahead and do it and relayed the Lieutenant's phone number. The ghost phased through the wall to join Morgan and me and summoned his control sphere. A burst of static erupted over the speaker phone.

I frowned down at the phone until Specter moved away and the line cleared. *That's right. His energy would make electronics go on the fritz.* Come to think of it, so would a demon's. So it is possible that the Shadow wasn't behind the murder. That narrowed down the suspects a bit, but nowhere near enough.

"Watch," I muttered darkly. "The call probably came from a pay phone or a burner."

"If you're right," Quinn snickered. "I'm going to blame you for jinxing it."

"Blame away," I countered with a smile.

Morgan quirked an eyebrow in silent query.

I waved it off. "I've been a jinx since grade school."

"And—no surprise—the psychic is correct," Specter announced a moment later. "The call came in from a payphone outside Bad Habits."

I knew of Bad Habits only by reputation. The truck stop had become famous for their Nail Biter burger within a month after opening. I also knew that it's location put it within walking distance of the Palisades.

I looked at the ghost, made a gesture towards his sphere. "Are you able to get security footage on that thing?"

He nodded and went to work on that.

"Why?" Morgan queried, crossed her arms.

I pressed the tip of my left index finger on the desktop. "Bad Habits," I said, watching as Morgan's lips pursed in thought. Then I jabbed my right finger at a point an inch and a half away from the first. "The Palisades."

"She's saying the same thing I'm thinking; that they're too close to be a coincidence," said Quinn. "Someone—most likely Cynthia's murderer—could jog between these places within fifteen or twenty minutes."

That drew another heated look from the blonde. She leaned over the phone and spat, "And you presume the caller is the murderer why?"

"Think about it, Paladin," growled Quinn. "If any of Cynthia's employees had found her dead, they would have called from *inside* the mansion. At the very most, they would have gone running to a neighbor. There's no reason for anyone to run across a busy highway to use the payphones unless they weren't supposed to be in the Palisades to begin with."

I nodded. "Exactly. Plus, we don't know if the Mirror of Souls has a limited range or not. For all we know, the murderer could have been within feet of Cynthia or half way across the planet."

"Another point to the jinx."

I grinned down at the phone.

Specter cleared his throat to get our attention. "I've tapped into the security footage. Unfortunately, I can't make much of it; It's too distorted."

Quinn uttered a curse.

I asked to see the footage. The ghost shot a look at Morgan, who begrudgingly gave a nod. So Specter manipulated the sphere until it projected the footage on a blank space in the wall. Everything kept blitzing out as if someone were playing with high-powered magnets near the camera. I could barely make out something vaguely humanoid in shape approaching the trio of payphones outside the truck stop. One frame gave an instant of near-clarity, and I had Specter rewind and freeze it.

"The caller wore high heels," I stated. Actually, they were more like spiked heels. In fact, you could probably stake a vampire with them.

"And that helps us how?" demanded Morgan. "A demon could have easily possessed a passing cowan and used their body to make the call."

I fretted at my lip. She had a point. A possession would also cause a huge flux of energy, which explains why the footage wound up so distorted. But those heels…

"Hey, jinxed one," called Quinn.

I looked down at the phone. "Yeah?"

"I'd like to get you out here to Cynthia's to see if you can get anything. Deaths—especially sudden or violent ones—leave a residual energy. Sometimes even a shade. Maybe your sensitivity to the energy will get us something we missed."

"Is it all right with the cops?"

"They're going to be busy," he answered cryptically.

Go into an active crime scene and use my abilities to help a police investigation? What an opportunity! I've dreamed of doing just that for years. In fact, I would have leaped at the chance to do it.

So why am I hesitating?

Morgan sighed. "*Mater Dei*, just say you'll do it."

"Paladin!" snarled Quinn. "If she doesn't want to do—"

"I do," I blurted. "Really. I'm just…"

"Scared."

I glared at the blonde. "Wouldn't you be if you had a bounty on your head and at least one Shadow on your tail every time you stepped off the ship?"

She snapped her mouth shut, glowered back.

"Cybil," Quinn said, his voice soft and understanding. It drew my attention away from the haughty blonde and back down to the phone. "I give you my word that, should you choose to come to my aid, I will protect you."

I could almost feel his desperation through the phone. He needed my help. AEON needed my help. We had to find that mirror before it could be used again, and I might just have the ability to crack the case wide open. But it would leave me exposed. I'd be vulnerable to the demons hunting me. And I had no way to protect myself.

I took a deep breath. "I'll do it."

"Great!"

"But I'd really like some sort of defense. Just in case."

"Paladin, arm her," commanded Quinn. "And get down here yesterday."

"I will Light Jump us to—"

"She's a demon, Morgan. You can't teleport with her."

The blonde uttered something in another language. "Fine. I'll take a car."

25 SANTOVA ESTATE, THE PALISADES, MABON CITY THURSDAY, OCTOBER 23 2:21 PM

Morgan flew through the streets as if she were driving in an action movie's get-away stunt vehicle. I sat shotgun with a white knuckled grip on the door and a very bizarre gun resting at my feet. The thing looked and felt like something a cop would use. It measured about ten inches and had been made with black carbon fiber. What made it weird was the clear canister of water directly beneath the barrel.

When she had handed it to me, Morgan told me the canister contained holy water. Squeezing the trigger would fire a jet of the water at whatever I aimed at with more force than a pressure washer. She had also warned me against shooting myself with it.

Like, *duh*! Demon. Holy water. Hello?

Whatever. I just hoped her erratic driving didn't pick up a cop. Who knows what they'd think of the gun.

"I can't believe we're stuck driving," muttered Morgan.

I looked up from the tactical water gun to make a retort. It never passed my lips. My attention fell on the jalopy of a station wagon we were passing. Something about it screamed familiar, but I couldn't figure out why. And we had passed it so quickly that I never had a chance to see who was driving that wreck.

"Incoming call from Fenrir," the sedan's automated voice announced in her monotone.

Morgan pressed a button on the steering wheel. "Go ahead, Quinn."

"Where are you? MCPD is just leaving Cynthia's now."

"Two minutes," the blonde replied, checking behind her and moving over to the turn lane. She pulled onto a private road as two police cars left it.

"I'll meet you at the gate."

"I see you."

The call ended as Morgan pulled the sedan to a stop before a towering, iron gate flanked by white stone walls. I grabbed the super soaker as I exited the car. A refreshing whiff of moisture and pine lingered in the air, and I soaked it up. Trees and shrubs surrounded us, their golden sunset leaves casting shadows that danced in the wake of a breeze. I could just barely hear the Cimmeria River softly gurgling somewhere to my left. Songbirds drowned the sound of the busy highway several yards away.

I had never been in the Palisades before, but I found it remarkably peaceful. *No wonder rich people live out here.*

Quinn approached with a petite brunette in tow. My gaze immediately snapped to the badge on her belt.

Morgan confirmed my suspicion simply by muttering, "LeFae."

The Lieutenant curtly nodded. She looked at me, and I could practically feel here assessing me for the police record. Female. About four feet. Black hair with red bangs. Armed, but not necessarily dangerous. "I bought you guys about half an hour. If you're going to do something, you'd better do it quick."

Quinn divested his suit jacket, threw it in the car. He shrugged into the shoulder rig Morgan had brought for him and led us to the iron gate as he slapped a magazine into the handgun. He shoved the gate open as if it were made of chicken wire instead of heavy iron. I followed on his heels as he crossed onto the property.

The lawn had been nicely manicured, and a rainbow of flowering plants edged the white stone driveway. A white marble fountain sat at the arc of the drive, just a short trek away from the mansion's elaborate front entrance. A stone archway kept the patio shaded, and gave ivy something to cling to as it crawled its way up. The doors themselves were a rich brown wood with stained glass windows. The yellow police tape stretched across their frame mashed harshly against their beauty.

"If I remember correctly, Cynthia keeps a safe under the stairs in the parlor," remarked Quinn. He hopped up the few stone steps that led up to the front patio, ripped the police tape from the doors. "The controls for her video surveillance system should be in there."

"Why are we after that?" I asked.

He looked over his shoulder. "To see if anyone was in the house with Cynthia when she was killed. Anyone besides her maid and gardener could be the murderer."

"We should just rip the safe out and get back," grumbled Morgan. "We're too limited on time to go digging."

"Oh, sure. There's no way the cops would notice if we trash a fresh crime scene," I said as I watched Quinn test the doors. They were locked—No surprise. He didn't say a word as he retreated to the stone pillar a few paces to the right of the doors.

Without warning, Morgan rushed the doors, striking them with a kick. The locks screamed as they came undone and the doors exploded inward with a shower of splinters and twisted metal. What remained banged against something inside and started to swing back. Morgan strode forward, shoving the doors aside.

"Dammit, Morgan!" barked Quinn. "I have just about had enough of your crap today. Do something like that again, and I'll have you recalled to the Astral Plane faster than you can say 'smite me'."

The blonde whirled around, livid. Quinn hurled something at her as he crossed the ruined threshold. She didn't bother catching it, so it fell to the floor with a soft clink. It was a key—the spare. Morgan glared at it and me before following in Quinn's furious wake.

I hesitated outside, unsure of whom to be more afraid: Quinn, Morgan, or the Shadow that could be watching me right now. I took one last long look at the peaceful front lawn before I entered the war zone.

The entryway looked exactly like what I expected of a mansion. The ceiling must have been at least twenty feet high, with an enormous, crystal and gold chandelier dangling like an earring from the center. Exactly beneath the fixture stood a circular table adorned with framed photographs and a fern plant. A small pile of letters and a set of keys now sat gathering dust.

Solid, wooden doors with golden filigree led to rooms on either side of the entry. Two more were tucked away in the spaces on the back wall, nearly hidden from my view by small palm trees and padded loungers. A wide staircase stood between the back doors, winding its way up to the second floor. Suits of steel armor stood like silent sentinels on either side of the bottom step.

Quinn and Morgan had split up to search the wall space under the stairs for the safe's hiding spot. The werewolf gave me a passing glance as I approached. His eyes were bright blue, like moonlight. I had seen that effect before.

"You okay, Quinn?"

"Yeah, just…" he sighed. "Just frustrated."

I gestured to his face. "Your eyes are blue."

His fingers paused in their blind search as he looked at me. "It's because the new moon is tomorrow night. My inner wolf wants out to frolic before the moon goes dark and I lose my powers. I'm still in control… for the moment."

"Oh." I had been so worried about finding the mirror that I had completely forgotten about the rapidly approaching new moon.

Quinn went back to his search.

I had never thought to ask him what he went through as a werewolf. I just figured he could change at will instead of relying on moon phases. His transition into a wolf sounded much more unstable, even dangerous. "Do you need anything?"

He flashed a grin, and I could see elongated canines. "I'll be okay. It's not the first time I've gone through the change. Thank you, though."

I leaned against the banister to watch him and nearly fell over when something gave way. I heard a loud click followed by a sliding sound as a piece of the paneling under Quinn's fingers slid aside. I looked at the banister in shock, only to realize that a lever had been cleverly disguised as one of the rungs.

Quinn pointed at it. "Did you know that was there?"

"I'm just surprised as you," I admitted just in time for Morgan to round the stairs and join us. We all looked at the safe to see what we were dealing with. I don't know why, but I had been picturing something like a huge bank vault. This thing could have passed for a microwave. It even had a number pad on its face.

"Alright, we know where it is. Now let's find out how to get it open." Quinn looked at Morgan. "You start looking down here. Cynthia's office is in the northeastern wing." He pointed to one of the doors. "It might be a good place to start looking for the code."

"Right," she muttered and made for the office.

"And do not destroy anything else!"

She paused as if to say something, but thought better of it.

"Where do we start?" I asked as I followed him up the staircase. I missed a step when he said we would start in the solarium where Cynthia's body had been found.

He noticed, paused to turn and look at me. "Are you sure you're okay to do this? I'd understand if—"

"I'm okay," I said to assure him as much as myself. Truthfully, the idea of standing in the same space as a murdered body kind of freaked me out. I knew the energies left behind would be turbulent, just like in that blighted alley. So much so that I should have been feeling them already. It worried me that I didn't even feel the slightest bit of a tickle. "I've done something like this a few times before, just not… intentionally. I can't even guarantee you that I'll get a vision."

His expression softened. "It's not about whether or not you get a vision," he said and put a hand on my shoulder. "It's the fact that you're here to try. I respect that."

The words drew a smile from me. And when he asked me if I was ready, I nodded. We took a left at the top of the stairs, followed the hall to the last door. Sunlight blinded me when Quinn opened the door. I blocked it out with my hand and looked around the space. I my gaze instantly went to the far end of the room, where a pale blue wingback chair sat beside a tiny table bearing the Victorian phone.

Cynthia's remains had been removed, but the phone still lay on the floor where it had fallen.

I licked my lips. My hand slowly dropped to my side as navigated around furniture and fauna, heading for the chair. I should have been able to feel *something* this close to where Cynthia had died. I didn't even get a chill.

Could it be because there is no energy to detect? I stared down at the phone in wonder. I knew the Mirror of Souls absorbed energy from its victims, but there aught to have been something residual. From what I could recall, Miss Santova had lived on this estate for nearly six decades. And she had bought it from the family who built it and lived in it for over a century. If nothing else, there should have been emotional energies ingrained in nearly everything in the house; the floor, the furniture, even the little nick knacks on the shelves.

It's what creates a strong Threshold.

Think of a Threshold as an invisible force field around a home. They are established around every entryway into a home to protect anyone within from negative energies and beings who want to cause harm. They can be gradually built up over time depending on the environment within the home, which is more common. But someone could also magickally establish a Threshold. It's as simple as laying salt in a line across the doorway or window and empowering it with a little bit of life energy.

I expected to feel a little hint of that energy when I picked up the fallen phone. Instead, I felt nothing. Not even a fading memory of power.

What in the world is going on with me? I put it back in its cradle, sat in the chair. I should have been able to sense the energy here. And Specter never should have been able to sneak up behind me. It's as if someone had flicked off the switch to my powers.

I silently mouthed a curse in realization.

I had done it to myself. Or—more accurately—my inner demon had done it to me when I told it to stop force feeding me its power. That wretched thing had tricked me into leaving myself virtually blind! Heck! I could have a Shadow staring at me right now and I wouldn't know it until it jumped out and started doing *La Macarena.*

Well, my demon and I were going to have a talk after I got back to the ship. Right now, I had an important mission that I didn't dare stray from. I simply didn't have the time for an internal argument. So I imagined throwing a steel lockbox with all my problems in it into a black hole. I'd fish it out later, when I actually had a moment or two to myself.

Thanks to the phone dream this morning, I knew my psychic powers weren't affected by my demon's trickery. I let my eyes slip shut as I turned my mind to the task at hand. I've never tried to force a vision before, so I didn't know if this would work.

I think I nodded off there for a second. I wouldn't have realized it if not for Quinn suddenly moving around. Something was different in the way he walked. He had the footfalls of a predator on the hunt; silent and measured. These were nothing like that. In fact, if I didn't know better, I'd say someone in high heels had passed right in front of me.

My eyes snapped open to a changed room. Night had fallen, leaving the room illuminated only by soft solar lights. In front of me stood a woman I had never seen before.

26 SANTOVA ESTATE, THE PALISADES, MABON CITY THURSDAY, OCTOBER 23 3:03 PM

The woman before me must have been in her late seventies or early eighties. When this event occurred, she had been clad in a pale blue sundress and white sandals with a low heel. She had a file open in her arthritis-stricken hands, and she paced as she fretted at the contents within.

Without warning, she slapped the folder shut and started for the door. I followed on her heels. She moved fast for her age, and navigated the mansion with such ease I had trouble keeping up. Only at the stairs did she finally slow down, and she kept a firm grasp on the handrail as she descended. I beat her to the bottom by thirty seconds.

She pressed the hidden lever to reveal the safe concealed within the stairs. I caught a glimpse of the paper in her folder as she glanced warily around. Satisfied she wouldn't be observed, she punched in the access code, which I recited aloud. She stuffed the folder into the safe and resealed it before I could get a glimpse of what lay within.

I watched in amazement as the vision melted like wax figures in a burning house. The sudden daylight blinded me, and I blinked several times until my eyes adjusted. At last, I could see Quinn as he stood before the exposed safe. He pressed the numbers in the order I had recited, and the door clicked open.

That's when the gunshots erupted outside.

Quinn's hand blurred and his gun was suddenly out of the shoulder rig and held at the ready. I felt a little foolish bringing my water gun to bear as I followed him through the busted doors. I struggled to breathe normally as I raised my water gun to mirror him. My hands were shaking and I clutched the gun so tightly that my knuckles had gone white.

"Okay, kiddo, do me a favor." He kept his voice low and steady. One, to soothe me; two, to hopefully go unheard by anything but me. "Take a good, long look at every dark spot out there. If you see anything—no matter how small or trivial it may seem—point it out. Can you do that for me?"

I nodded and fought down the panic that had begun to overwhelm me. I couldn't afford to lose my cool right now. Quinn needed me to focus. He needed my help, and I needed his. But how could I be of any help without my ability to sense life energies?

So I studied every shadow like a criminal investigator studies a piece of thread found at a crime scene.

Something out of the corner of my eye moved, and I locked onto it like a heat-seeking missile. I focused everything I had on the shadow cast by one of the weeping willows that edged the estate. A breeze tickled the limbs to life. The curtain of leaves swayed, and I saw it: blood red eyes gleaming in the darkness.

The Shadow.

"There!"

Quinn fired, but the demon vanished before the round ever got off. My ears were still ringing from the gunshot when a sound like a bomb going off came from inside the house. Quinn whipped around, took off like a bullet. I realized too late that I didn't have a prayer of catching up to him. And just as I reached the threshold, the doors slammed shut in my face. Neither of them budged an inch when I ran straight into them. Shoving as hard as I could and even bashing my shoulder against them did nothing (but it did cause pain to knife through the wounds on my back). Since Morgan had destroyed the locks and much of the surrounding wood when she kicked the doors in, it should have been impossible for them to stay sealed.

"Okay, Cye, just stay calm. Think." I took a few deep breaths, but it did nothing to slow the hammering of my heartbeat. I may not have been able to feel it, but I knew the doors had been magickally sealed. That meant someone—or some*thing*—observed me from close by, and now that I had been cut off from Quinn and Morgan, they were free to corner me and… do whatever they had come to do.

I didn't want to think about the tortures a demon would put on me. Agilisi's beatings probably paled in comparison.

"Just find another way inside," I calmly told myself. There had to be a back door. Heck, I could use a window if I had to. I just knew that I had to get to Quinn or Morgan. My life depended on it.

I gripped the tactical super soaker tightly as I retreated from the entrance. My hands and knees were shaking, so I took it one step at a time. First, I merely had to get to the bottom of the stairs. Simple. From there, I'd turn right. A window would be about thirty feet away. I can walk thirty feet.

I stepped off the patio, feeling pretty good. Three strides into my trek to the right, and the stench of rotten eggs on a hot day came out of nowhere to assault me. I loathed the stink, and what it meant—the Shadow had reappeared. I'm not sure how, but I clutched the super soaker even tighter and hoped against hope that it didn't break. I wanted to bolt for it, but something told me not to. Could it have been fear? Curiosity? Or maybe I had just grown tired of running.

A soft growl came from behind me. I took a deep breath, looked sidelong over my shoulder. Nothing. I turned to completely face the mansion's main entrance. I spotted the Shadow in the shade cast by the column. It just stood there, watching, its unblinking eyes glowing like crimson embers. What was it waiting for?

"What do you want?" I shouted loud enough so that Quinn and Morgan could hear me from inside.

The demon on the patio remained silent and unmoving.

This time I roared all my pent-up fear and fury at it, "Answer me, dammit!"

The Shadow snarled.

"Answer!" I pointed the super soaker at it. "Answer me or I swear I'll shoot you!"

In a voice like gravel, the demon finally spoke. "You are a traitor."

"And just how am I the traitor here?"

"You became one of *them*." It jerked its head towards the mansion. "Now you hunt your own kind."

Something slammed against the doors from inside the mansion. The Shadow didn't even flinch, much less look at the barrier. Could it have something to do with their sealing? Duncan never mentioned Shadows having abilities like that. I doubted he was even aware of it. But if that banging had been a sign of Quinn or Morgan trying to break out, then I would have to keep the Shadow busy for a while. I had to buy them time to find another way.

"My own kind goes around hunting and killing innocent people," I said as I lowered the gun slightly. "People like the woman who lived here."

The Shadow laughed in a way that gave me shivers. "That wretch deserved to die for what she has done."

Another bang shook the door. The demon paid it no mind.

"What the heck did she ever do to you to deserve to have her soul ripped from her body and trapped forever in that mirror you stole?"

"T'was not I who wanted the Huntress destroyed," it rasped.

I narrowed my eyes. If this wretched thing hadn't been the one to kill Cynthia, then who did?

"These… *AEONs*," it laced the word with boiling venom, "make a living out of hunting us. They slaughter us like cattle and claim they are doing good because we don't belong to this world. We are only here to escape, but we are forced to fight for our very existence."

I couldn't believe what I was hearing. Duncan had told me that AEON served as a police force, keeping order among the parathropes in the world. Those that opposed that order were radicals that wanted to kill or enslave humans. But the Shadow before me called it a slaughter, and it had escaped something by coming here.

The doors were struck again and stayed as unmoving as ever.

Truthfully, at the moment, I had grown more concerned about what the demon had said. "What are you trying to escape from?"

It extended a hand, a dark mass with talons like daggers. "Come with me, little one. I will show you."

"How about you start by telling me?"

The Shadow curled its fingers one by one, let its hand fall to its side. "You cannot begin to fathom the horrors we face. Showing you would be the wiser course. Come with me, little one, and I will even teach you how to use your full demon power."

That last part piqued my interest and disgusted me at the same time. This twisted creature really could teach me everything I needed to know about my demon side. But I refused to let that side of me take the reigns and rule over my life. I just wanted to be a normal teenage girl, living in a loving home with everything else other kids had; toys, friends, an allowance, clean clothes. I don't think I could live with myself if I let my demon out, much less follow this twisted, evil thing before me.

I looked at the super soaker in my hand. It felt heavier for some reason, or, perhaps, it was just the weight of my decision settling upon me. I knew what I had to do, and I would have to live with it for the rest of my life—however long that would be. I took a deep breath, exhaled slowly. I took one step towards the Shadow. Then another. It reached out to me again, and I slowly closed the distance between us.

Five feet from the demon, I trained the super soaker on it. Before it could react, I squeezed the trigger. The gun jerked with the release of pressure. A bullet of speeding water slammed against the Shadow. It screeched in pain and fury as steam billowed from the strike. I fired again, this time ready for the kick, and held the trigger down. It couldn't escape the rush of water and flailed around helplessly.

Just as the last of the holy water drained from the reservoir, Quinn suddenly burst through the doors. Three shots erupted from his handgun. The Shadow exploded into black smoke and was gone.

I breathed a sigh of relief.

"Cybil!" Quinn came rushing to me. "Are you alright?"

I punched him in the arm. "What the hell took you so long?"

He rubbed the sore spot, muttering, "Yeah, you're fine."

"Where's Morgan?" I asked, remembering why he had rushed inside to begin with. "Is she okay? What caused that explosion?"

He seemed surprised by my question. "She's fine." He pointed to something behind me. "See for yourself."

I looked over my shoulder in time to see a small sun come rushing towards us. I yelped and ducked behind Quinn.

The werewolf chuckled. "Kill the light, Paladin. The Shadow's gone."

I peeked around Quinn as the light faded away. The woman who approached looked completely different than the Morgan I knew. She had long hair of purest white held out of her golden eyes with a delicate barrette. She wore a silver breastplate etched with scrolling filigree and some sort of white, gossamer fabric that formed a skirt. Royal purple ribbons bearing bizarre symbols hung from the skirt. Silver bracers and heeled greaves completed her armor. And from her back sprouted a pair of pearly, white wings.

I looked up to Quinn for an explanation.

"Don't worry, kiddo," he lightly chuckled. "That is just Morgan's angel form."

"Holy!"

Morgan briefly smirked as she joined us. "What happened?"

"That's what I wanted to know," I admitted and finally dared to come out from behind Quinn. "One second, the Shadow appeared in the yard, the next, we hear an explosion from inside. Are you okay?"

She seemed as surprised by the question as Quinn had been. "I am fine. The Shadow must have Jumped, and tried to take me out since I was alone. But what happened out here?"

"Quinn and I ran to help you, but the doors slammed shut right in front of me. I couldn't get them to open, so I was going to try a back door or the window when the Shadow appeared. I kept it talking to try to buy you guys some time to find a way out."

"She gave it a nice shower, and I was finally able to break through the doors." He glanced down at his gun before holstering it. "I think I hit it a couple times, but there's no way we killed it."

"Then we take the safe and leave," Morgan said as she started for the entryway.

"There's no need to be ripping the house apart any more than it already is."

She paused, cast a look towards Quinn as he stepped past her.

"Cybil already gave me the code to open it."

I took a half step back when her golden gaze settled on me. Without a word, she turned to follow Quinn into the house. I entered a moment after the angel, paused to study the doors and verified my suspicions: they were too far damaged to have been locked shut. Did the Shadow have the ability to magickally seal them?

A venomous curse diverted my attention, and Quinn slammed the safe door shut. “Somebody cleared it out while we were distracted. They even deleted the security footage.”

I felt my lips pull into a frown. *‘T’was not I who wanted the huntress destroyed’* the Shadow had said. I looked down at the twisted metal that had been the doors’ hardware. “It has a partner.”

27 THE PRISON OF THE MIND
TIME: NONEXISTENT

I decided it'd be better for me to ride with Quinn on the way back. So, after telling Lieutenant LeFae about the Shadow attacking, the angel vanished with one of the cars in a spectacular burst of golden light. Afterwards, Quinn explained that Morgan had done something called a Light Jump, which is just a fancy way to say she teleported. He also told me that I should be able to do something like that, only through shadows instead of light.

I didn't have the heart to tell him that I had given up my demon side. But, now that I knew that, I thought it'd be a cool ability. I could teleport anywhere I wanted and never have to worry about having fare or a passport. Paris for lunch? Sure. Dinner in Japan? Why not?

For now, I had to settle with riding shotgun in a BMW sedan.

Thankfully, the drive back to the academy turned out to be much more leisurely than the mad ride out. I spent most of it figuring out how to reload the spent canister on my tactical super soaker, all the while wondering if I had done the right thing in shooting the Shadow. I had just finished swapping it out when Quinn pulled the sedan into a parking spot. The two of us climbed out of the car and made for the elevator.

The doors opened some moments later, and I followed Quinn through the tiny security room. The werewolf muttered something under his breath when we rounded the corner to the hallway of offices. I noted that all the doors were closed and wondered where everyone would be.

Quinn unlocked his office door, told me to wait inside while he rounded up the team. Faced with some unknown amount of time alone, I decided it would be best spent hashing things out with my inner demon. So I sat on the floor with my back against a wall and laid the super soaker beside me. Then I rested my hands in my lap, let my eyes close. I let my breathing slow, and with it, my heartbeat. For an instant, I felt weightless. Then…

Blue candlelight danced over frost-blanketed stone. A familiar gloom stretched on before me, shrouding the presence I knew lurked in the never ending dark. The prison seemed more eerie. More ominous than before. And it was much colder. Enough so that my breath formed clouds of ice crystals every time I exhaled.

Such a drastic change of the place in only a short time. Perhaps this was the way my inner demon threw a hissy fit. All because I told it to take a hike.

'Perfect.'

I advanced cautiously into the murk, the whispers that were my footfalls almost like screams in the silence. The first step down came out of nowhere, and I barely caught myself before I flew down the remaining stairs. I paused a moment to let my heartbeat slow before continuing on.

My progress was slowed by the ever-thickening gloom. It felt like an eternity had slipped by before I stepped off the final stair and onto the landing. Then I took seven steps forward, stopped. There, in the middle of the emptiness, I called for the presence to appear.

It didn't.

'Come on!' I angrily thought. 'I haven't got all night, and I know you're in there. Show yourself!'

Still nothing.

I growled, impatient. 'I command you to show yourself. Now.'

Two fiery eyes suddenly appeared in the gloom. They zeroed in on me in an instant, and narrowed dangerously.

'About time.' I crossed my arms, partially out of annoyance, but mostly because I was freezing. I had never truly been cold before, and this experience with my inner demon was maddening enough without the sudden worry of whether my limbs turning into blocks of ice or not.

You require something, Keeper Mine? I picked right up on the venom to its voice that hadn't been there during our last encounter. It felt a fury similar to my own.

'Uh, yeah! I require that you quit screwing with my senses. I was almost attacked today because you–'

I have done only what you commanded of me.

'No. I told you to stop force feeding me your power and interfering in my life!'

The fire in its eyes flared. *That is what you commanded and what I have done.*

'Oh yeah? Then how did I not sense that demon sneaking up on me and Quinn earlier? I should have picked up on it long before he did.'

It snarled like a rabid animal. *I have kept my word and taken back the power I provided you. Now you are nothing. You are powerless and as feeble as a newborn. You are Cowan.*

'Then restore my senses to what they wer--'

No.

'What?' I hissed through gritted teeth.

I will not.

'Fine then. I command you t--'

I refuse to obey the demands of an ungrateful whelp simply because she suddenly realizes that she is not able to fend for herself now that I am no longer sacrificing myself to come to her aid.

'But if I die because you're too stupid to give me back the ability to sense my enemies approaching, then you will die as well!'

If that must truly be the price for the lesson, then so be it.

I roared with frustration and fury. 'Go to Hell, you miserable piece of sh—"

Telling a demon to go to Hell wouldn't even make a footnote in a newspaper. The eyes vanished. *Be gone!*

I stood there in furious shock for a beat. My hands turned to fists. My jaw clenched. And I unleashed every insult and curse I could think of at the top of my lungs until my throat started to hurt.

Silence hung like a bad smell.

28 SAATHOFF ACADEMY, DARK MOON PORT, MABON CITY
THURSDAY, OCTOBER 23
5:12 PM

"And Cybil even had a standoff with the blasted thing," Quinn finished as he strode into his office. I looked up from the floor to see Duncan and Specter both giving me nods of approval as they filed in. Then Quinn added, "Then she gave it a nice shower, and sent it packing."

"Impressive," said Specter. "I can't believe you stood your ground like that. I ran from the first demon I went up against, and I'm a ghost!"

I couldn't tell if his words were meant to be serious or not. I figured he just wanted to make me feel better.

"Indeed," Morgan stated as she entered. "You handled yourself... better than I expected. Well done."

I couldn't believe it. Morgan, the person who basically stars in the role as my arch nemesis and a constant pain in my you-know-where, hadn't just praised me; she did it with a smile—sort of. I began to wonder if the Shadow had replaced her with a friendlier clone. Whatever! I smiled. At least she's not criticizing me… or trying to kill me. Just bask in it while you can, I told myself.

"Well then…" Duncan dug into the inside pocket of his suit jacket. "I think this deserves something special." He held a box the size of his palm out to me. I looked from the box to his face and back again. Finally, I accepted it.

Quinn flashed me a thumbs up as I removed the lid. Some kind of circular broach lay nestled in white tissue paper. The thing measured about the size of my palm, and had been made of a shimmering, black metal. It had two layers of growing circles and triangles stacked within each other. The bottom portion of the largest circle bore a three-digit number: 333.

I heard Quinn and Specter congratulating me on it, but I could only stare at the thing in bewilderment.

“That,” Duncan chuckled, “is an AEON Agent badge.”

I gawked at him. “Badge?”

He nodded. “Yes. Sin dropped it off at the behest of The Lady. She even gave you an honorary rank to go with that special badge for your helping us vith this case.”

“Oh.” I tried not to sound disappointed by the news that I had missed the chance to meet Sin. “But what's so special about this badge?”

“Aside from the fact that The Lady sent Sin to drop it off, vhich irritated him by the vay, that badge used to belong to your father.”

I looked at the black ornament with new appreciation. My father's badge. It wasn't an illusion or dream. This little thing had been an actual, physical possession of my dad's. It’s the closest I had been to a piece of him in ten years.

Somehow, it seemed heavier than it had a moment ago.

An arm suddenly wrapped around my shoulders. “I'm sorry, Cybil,” Duncan murmured in my ear. “I did not mean for it to make you cry.”

I’m crying? It took a moment to sink in before I noticed my eyes were burning as tears threatened to fall, and my throat had tightened with emotion. I despised crying in front of people. I didn’t want them see me as a weak, little girl.

Well, I’m not a weakling. And I’m not a little girl. Ten years at the mercy of agilisi had beaten that crap out of me.

So I battled down the emotions and choked out, “It's okay.”

“You sure?”

I nodded, hugged my father's badge close. “This is the greatest gift anyone could have ever given me." I looked him in the eyes. "Thank you."

He lightly smiled, backed away a couple of steps. "I had some equipment sent to your room as vell."

"And you can keep the super soaker," added Quinn with a wink. "I'll show you to the armory later on so you can stock up on the water canisters."

"Quinn, vhy don't you help Cybil back to her room so she can check everything out? Maybe get some rest."

The werewolf nodded. "Sure thing, Duncan."

I glanced around the room, taking stock of everything in an attempt to find a reason to stay a little longer. My gaze lingered on a short stack of newspapers atop one of the filing cabinets. Hadn't my demon said something about a newspaper, too? Now that's an odd coincidence.

"I vant you to take a break; relax a little." Duncan put his hand on the middle of my back and steered me towards the door. "You'll burn yourself out vorking so hard."

"No. Wait." I planted my feet to prevent him from moving me any further.

"Vhat are you—?"

I snapped my fingers several times. There had to be a connection between the papers and Cynthia. Perhaps I had seen it during the vision in the mansion. I closed my eyes and summoned up the memory of what I had seen.

It had started in the sunroom. Cynthia had been reading something in a folder while she paced. She had slapped the folder shut, but a piece of the document within poked out. I caught a glimpse of that little corner.

Without warning, I spun on my heel and hurried to Quinn's desk. I snatched a pen from among the many I knew lay strewn across the desktop and scribbled on the back of my hand. I released the memory as I opened my eyes, looked down at my hand. I had no words to describe the weird, scrolling symbol I had scribbled.

Morgan immediately jumped on my case. “Where in the Three Worlds did you learn to write in Hellion?”

“Hello!” I snapped. “I copied it from my vision, you idiot!”

“Enough.” Duncan stepped between us before we could come to blows. He tapped his index finger on my hand.“Vhere exactly did you see this symbol?”

I told him the details of my vision.

He frowned at that, turned to Morgan. “I don’t suppose you know vhat it says?”

She shook her head. “We were taught to recognize it, not to read it.”

“Not again,” muttered Specter, stepping towards me. I watched as he summoned his sphere, passed it over my hand. A split second later, Duncan’s cell phone rang.

He grimaced at the caller ID, set it to speaker phone. “He—”

“Why the hell are you bothering me?”

I suppressed my excitement. It was Sin.

“I do apologize for disturbing you, Sin,” Duncan said through a forced smile. “But ve vere hoping you could help us translate a Hellion sym—”

“Who’s the idiot that drew it?”

I slapped a hand over my mouth before a snide retort could escape.

“They missed half of it.”

Duncan’s phone suddenly chimed.

“It says ‘Tartarus’.”

“Thank—”

The phone beeped disconnected.

Duncan sighed in relief.

Quinn exhaled the breath he had been holding. “Must have caught him on a good day.”

"Yeah," agreed Specter. "He was almost cordial."

I swallowed my laughter, cleared my throat. "So, uh, is this Tartarus a person? Place?"

Morgan gave me a steady glare before stating, "It could refer to either the capitol province of the Netherworld or the capitol city."

I pursed my lips.

"And you saw this…" Duncan turned his phone so that I could see the image Sin had sent back. He had added two lines and a squiggle to it. "On something Cynthia vas carrying?"

"Yeah." I nodded for emphasis. "She put it in the safe under the stairs. I think she may have clipped it from a newspaper or something." I thought about that for a second, added, "Do demons even have newspapers?"

"Yes. Yes, they do." A small smile parted Duncan's lips. "As you vill discover, the Nethervorld is very much like our own realm."

"Hang on a sec." Quinn stepped forward. "Are you thinking that Cynthia might have been featured in a Netherworld newspaper?"

"Only if it had this symbol." I pointed to Duncan's phone.

The werewolf frowned, looked sidelong at Duncan. "That's going to be a huge archive to comb through."

"Better get started."

"Um." I nervously raised my hand, which seemed to greatly amuse the centuries old parathropes around me. Whatever. At least I had their attention. "Just a thought; You could try narrowing it down to when Cynthia found the mirror's handle. If the demons knew what that piece really was, it probably got a lot of exposure in the Netherworld news outlets."

Specter nodded in agreement.

Duncan turned to the ghost. "How long vill it take you to comb through such a list?"

"Dunno," he looked down at the sphere in his hands. "A couple of hours at least."

"Okay." Duncan turned his attention to me. "You might as vell get some rest vhile ve vait for Specter to complete the scan."

I wanted to help with the search, but one glance at Specter told me that he clearly had it under control. Besides, I had more important and personal things to worry about. So I smiled and simply said, "Okay."

"I'll escort you," Quinn said around a yawn and gestured for me to precede him from the room.

I did.

We quickly made our way through the maze that made up the bulk of AEON Headquarters and to the tiny room with the huge one-way mirror. I stepped up to the elevator and summoned the lift. I yawned, suddenly exhausted. And if I'm exhausted, I could just imagine how tired Quinn felt. I glanced over my shoulder at him in time to catch the last second of a huge yawn. He could probably fall asleep standing up. "Duncan should order you to bed, too."

The werewolf smirked. "He usually does."

The elevator doors opened with their annoying and polite ding. This time, Quinn rode up with me. It felt like mere moments before I found myself strolling down the hall to my room.

"Mind if I ask you something?"

I paused, looked at Quinn. He had been so quiet that I almost forgot he had come with me. "Sure."

"The other day, you sensed the Shadow in the alley long before it approached you. Today, you didn't even pick up on the danger until I reacted."A frown pulled at his lips. "I don't know. Maybe I just imagined you had gone blind and deaf or something."

I made a face. While technically correct, I didn't know how to answer him. Could I tell him that my wretched inner demon had messed with my senses to get back at me for telling it to take a hike?

"Maybe it was just your nerves. Anyway, I just wanted to make sure you were alright."

"Yeah, that's probably it," I muttered, unlocked my door. "Nerves."

He studied me for a moment more, clicked his tongue. "Well, I've got a lot of work to do. See you tomorrow, kiddo."

"Good night," I said and stepped into my room.

29 SAATHOFF ACADEMY, DARK MOON PORT, MABON CITY
THURSDAY, OCTOBER 23
8:32 PM

I flipped the lights on, crossed my room to set my father's badge and the tactical super soaker on the desk. A smart phone and tablet were there, plugged in and charging. Both of them were flat gray and black and looked like they could take a hit from an F-22 and come out without a scratch.

"Cool."

A brochure for the Saathoff Academy had been set on the desktop beside them. A sticky note had been stuck to the top page with a note. In metallic blue ink, someone had written:

In case you change your mind.

—D.

I scowled at the booklet for a beat before surrendering to my curiosity. I skipped though the first few pages of welcoming messages and statistics and found the list of classes available. Several of them were either ones I wanted to take or piqued my interest. Then I found the page that listed the other locations of the school. They had one in Africa, South America, even Asia!

I really could escape agilisi if I chose to become a student.

I dropped the booklet on the desktop, flopped down in the computer chair. "Why does this decision have to be so difficult?"

My gaze drifted to my dad's badge. My badge.

I'm a cop.

And even though my inner demon had gimped me, I still had my psychic abilities to rely on. And I had to find that Shadow and it's accomplice before they could hurt anyone else.

I sat forward, woke up the laptop.

I don't know what compelled me to look up Cynthia's archaeological finds, but that's where I started. After scrolling past a few local headlines, I started seeing interviews with her in all sorts of languages. I clicked on a few of them just to look at the photos of all the stuff Cynthia had dug up.

I quickly realized that my idea of an archaeologist being some kind of daredevil explorer delving into tombs to unearth ancient treasures was completely wrong. It's more like the game Minesweeper; a cautious, little peck here or there in the hopes of stumbling upon something of significance. And most of Cynthia's findings were, well, garbage. Busted pots. Some ancient tools. Disfigured statuary. Nothing even remotely close to stumbling upon the next King Tut.

She did have one great find.

In some remote corner of the jungles of India, Cynthia had discovered what I could only describe as a horrifying necropolis. (I've always wanted to use that word.) Photographs from within the underground grave site gave me chills and immediately brought to mind the story I heard of Mount Vesuvius. Like the people of Pompeii, those in the grave had died still carrying on about their lives as if they had no cares in the world.

But, as far as I knew, there weren't any volcanoes in India.

The handle for the Mirror of Souls had come from that site, which explained why the thing had been mistaken for a deformed bone. Now I couldn't help but wonder if the mirror had had something to do with the deaths of those people.

I scrolled through picture after picture in complete awe.

And then I saw it.

It took a handful of seconds for it to register in my brain. I checked the back of my hand. Then the screen again. Back and forth three more times.

I snatched my badge and rushed out the door. I sprinted past students and teachers who yelled for me to slow down, ignored the elevators—they'd take too long—and took the stairs. I flew down twelve stories, finally reaching the deck where I'd find Duncan's office.

"I need to speak to Duncan," I breathlessly told the receptionist, who looked at me like I had rabies. "It's an emergency."

"I'm sorry," she drawled. "But Mister Thatcher isn't avail—"

I slapped my badge on the counter. "He's available."

She stared at the badge for a beat. Then at me. At long last, she reached for the phone, pressed a button. "Sorry to bother you, Mister Thatcher. There's a girl here with an AEON badge who says she needs to speak with you." A pause. "Right." Then she hung up.

The door to Duncan's office jerked open. I thanked the receptionist and rushed to the vampire. "Cybil, you can't just—"

I flashed him the back of my hand as I passed him. "I was right about this symbol."

He sealed the door, faced me with a thoughtful frown. "How so?"

"It's not Hellion; It's from here on earth."

He blinked.

"Okay." I shoved my bangs out of my face. "Cynthia's last discovery was a necropolis in India. It made headlines in a couple of newspapers including one that's written in symbols like this one. I don't know what language it is, but there's a photograph of Cynthia in the necropolis and this thing..." I pointed to mark on the back of my hand. "... appears in the top right corner like a watermark. That's what I saw Cynthia putting in her safe.

"Now, I know I'm overstepping—and I do apologize for that, really, I do—but I believe there's something in that photograph that frightened Cynthia. Maybe it even got her killed. But I don't know how to manipulate an image to bring out the little details so we can see what it is."

"And you are hoping that Specter can."

I dropped my arms to my sides. "Yes."

Duncan stood there a moment or two just thinking before spinning on his heel. I watched as he made for the hidden door behind his desk. I waited until after he had punched in the access code to unlock it before moving to follow him. His long, quick strides meant I had to jog to keep up with him as we moved through the halls. It took less than five minutes for us to reach Quinn's office.

He burst through the door saying, "Morgan vas mistaken."

The three AEONs looked up from their work, and I could see the confusion on their faces. Morgan's gaze fell on me, and her expression quickly turned to fury.

"The symbol Cybil saw vas, in fact, a Mortal Language." Duncan shocked me when he turned the floor over to me.

After a moment or two of panic, I managed to tell them about my online search. I watched Specter out of the corner of my eye while I spoke. The ghost had suddenly started fiddling with his glyphed sphere. By the time I reached the end of my explanation, Specter had already found the photo I had seen of Cynthia and had it projected onto the wall.

"Well," said the ghost. "Cybil is correct. The symbol she drew is Sanskrit, and there's only one newspaper in the Mortal Realm who uses it. Sudharma." He looked at me. "I presume this is the image you want adjusted."

I studied the photograph of a woman in filthy jeans and a khaki vest. Cynthia had been kneeling beside some twisted construct within the cave. Shadows of petrified people and debris closed in all around her, illuminated only by giant flood lights that bathed the grave site in a weird, pale blue light.

"That's the one," I confirmed.

"All right. I'll see what I can do with it."

I watched as colors were enhanced and outlines sharpened. Then Specter began to manipulate the contrast. When the shadows were reduced to little more than gray masses, one remained darker than the rest. It could have been another person, but something about it just seemed off.

I pointed to it. "Specter, can you do anything to clear up that shadow?"

"One sec."

The image shifted, zoomed in on the shadow. It pixelated as Specter adjusted things. Then it cleared.

Quinn growled a vicious curse.

The others echoed his disdain.

I could make out a face, but it didn't look human. The cheeks were too sharp and the ears too long. Its eyes were huge—like a Martian's—and it seemed to have a lightened mark on the forehead.

I looked sidelong at the werewolf. "You know that demon?"

"So do you," he gravely said, looking into my eyes. "You were just too young to remember."

The name immediately jumped to my lips, and I felt my blood boil. "Taboo."

"Taboo is the most elusive demon in history," seethed Morgan, "and Cynthia's in the same room as him? Impossible!"

Specter looked at me. "Where did you say this picture had been taken?"

"Somewhere in the jungles of India. In a cave."

"Oh no," he muttered, glanced at the image again. Then he faced Morgan. "Remember the *Kaanch ka Bageecha* Massacre?"

Her eyes widened in shock.

"Never heard of it," said Quinn.

"You might know it as the Glass Garden Massacre," explained Duncan.

But Quinn just shrugged. "Doesn't ring a bell."

"Vell, it vas von of the more infamous demon attacks on the Mortal Realm during the var."

I frowned at the word war. *What war?*

"The rumor was the Mirror of Souls had been housed there for a time," said Specter. "Along with some other artifacts." He waved a hand dismissively. "Of course, the Netherworld saw it as too good an opportunity to pass up, so they sent a small army to take possession of the mirror. We're talking A Class and S Class—maybe even a few B Class—coming in from all corners of the Mortal Real and Netherworld.

"There were no known survivors, so nobody knows what happened in the ensuing battle, but given this photo…" He glanced at it with a thoughtful frown. "I'd say an earth demon of some sort lead the attack. It's why we see the petrified people so calm and unassuming. I'm betting things are way different further into the cave."

I turned my back on the image. "Given the fact that Cynthia found the handle of the mirror there, I'm willing to bet that it actually was at one point. And something must have happened once the demons got a hold of it, seeing as how it had been in three pieces up until a couple days ago."

"But why would it have been broken up?" asked Quinn. "I mean, the handle and the Hope Diamond both remained in India, but the mirror itself somehow found a way into—and out of—Cybil's family's vault in Elysium."

I looked to Specter. "Could my dad have been at that battle?"

The ghost made a face. "I think it was before his time."

So how did my family get the mirror?

"We also have no clue why a Shadow…" Quinn paused for a beat. "Or anyone, really, would use the mirror on Cynthia."

"It wasn't the Shadow," I stated. "It told me someone else wanted her dead. I'm guessing its accomplice is the one it meant."

Morgan roared, "And you kept that fact to yourself?"

Quinn stepped between us before she could throttle me.

It did nothing to stop me from snarling; "I didn't even remember it until a second ago, and it's not like I was ever asked about it!"

"Ladies, simmer down!" shouted Quinn. Quieter, but just as forceful, he added, "Please."

"Um…" All eyes instantly shifted to Specter, who balked under the collection of glares. "Are you saying that Taboo has the Mirror? 'Cause that would be very bad."

I thought about that for a moment, frowned. "I don't know."

Quinn groaned. "If he does have the Mirror, you can bet we'll never see it again, and that's if he doesn't use it on us first."

30 SAATHOFF ACADEMY, DARK MOON PORT, MABON CITY
THURSDAY, OCTOBER 23
10:11 PM

Talk of impending doom at the hands of Taboo continued for a while until Duncan put a stop to it. The vampire reminded the others—and explained to me—that Taboo preferred to work alone. Not to mention that the Shadow we'd been chasing is a B rank, which falls far, far below Taboo's particular standards.

Finally, I had to ask, "Demons are classified?"

"They are ranked according to their brains and brawn," Quinn explained. He held up his hand and counted off his fingers. "Five classes. D Class we don't really get bothered with because they're basically just brainless drudges, but they are freakishly strong. C Class demons are quite a bit smarter and, thankfully, weaker than D Class. B Class is where we start having problems. They're stronger and faster than your everyday cowan, and they can put up one hell of a fight when they're cornered. A Class makes the B Class look like helpless kittens. And S Class," he grimaced, dropped his hand to his side. "S Class demons are your worst nightmares. As powerful as Taboo is, he's lower on the S Class totem pole than others."

"Thankfully," said Specter, "there are significantly fewer S Class demons than all the other classes. It seems to be limited to the nobles."

"Rumors of a sixth class have begun to float around WEIRD in the last century," Morgan added. "Celestials have taken to calling it Z Class. Supposedly, they make the S Class look harmless, but we have yet to find any evidence to support this."

I gulped. If the Shadow that has been chasing me and giving everyone trouble is only a B, I couldn't imagine what A and S were like in comparison. And a new and more powerful Z Class? Holy crap!

"That's news to me," muttered Quinn. Specter agreed with him.

Morgan shrugged a shoulder as if she didn't care whether anyone knew about the rumors or not.

"What about Khione?" I asked, glanced at the clock on the wall behind Quinn. "What Class is she?"

The AEONs chorused, "S."

Well, isn't that just perfect. I had less than twenty-four hours to prove that I didn't have the Mirror of Souls or an S Class demon would be taking my head to whomever put the bounty on me. How in the world am I going to get past this?

Calm down, Jinx. Think. What do you know?

I looked over my shoulder at the image still projected on the wall. Okay. So Taboo is alive and works alone. Disturbing, yet irrelevant at the moment. But we have a Shadow lurking around town, and now we know it's working with someone. Whoever that someone is had to know not only how to contact a demon but something about Cynthia Santova that justified murdering her. It's even possible that our mystery person knew about the Mirror of Souls. One thing they did know for certain: Cynthia had a security system. Otherwise, why steal into her house and empty the safe and destroy the footage before the AEONs could get it?

So… "Find the accomplice, find the mirror."

"My thoughts exactly," said Quinn.

"Yeah," Morgan drawled. "But we don't know who the accomplice is."

"You guys said Cynthia used to be an AEON, right?"

The four of them nodded.

Then Duncan fell in line with my thinking. "Go through every case the Huntress vorked, starting at the time she retired. If any of the parathropes she arrested knew how to call up a demon, find them and bring them in."

"On it."

Then the vampire looked at me. "Ve need to talk."

I waved my hand in a gesture that said, lead the way. He did. And the two of us strode down the hall and into his private office. I stood just inside the threshold, watched as he retrieved the remote from his desktop.

"Calling that lady again?"

He nodded. "Ve need to report in about Taboo."

"Makes sense."

He pointed the remote at the watercolor painting. As before, it went black and started to ring. The woman appeared on screen.. Her auburn hair had been released from it's bun to curl around her shoulders. She looked more relaxed that way.

"Revenant." Her voice held a note of impatience. "This is becoming a bit of a habit for you."

Duncan didn't reply, but the way he clenched his jaw spoke volumes in the silence.

"Very well," she continued. "What is so important that you hastened to call upon me?"

"Ve have evidence that Taboo is alive."

Her lips parted in a small but silent gasp. Then the fire in her jade eyes blazed and her brow furrowed. "Do not jest of such things, Rev—"

"I'm not." He folded his arms. "Actually, it vas Cybil here," he nodded to me "who made the discovery."

Her jadefire gaze settled upon me.

"It's true," I said and took a couple steps closer to the screen. "He appears in a photo taken in a necropolis in India dated a little over two weeks ago."

She fell silent.

"Ve are certain it is him. The pale starburst on his forehead is visible in the photo."

"Impressive," she said at last. Though her tone hadn't changed, I could tell that that little revelation had actually awed her. "You were only made an acting agent hours ago, and in that time you managed to find the most elusive demon in history."

I shrugged. "Happy accidents."

"Even so," she said. "You have proven to be quite the asset to Team Beta. Have you considered staying on and eventually becoming a full agent?"

"Eh." I shrugged again. "I've been arguing with myself over that this entire week. It mostly boils down to whether or not I want to remain so close to agili—er. I mean, my grandma."

Her lips pulled into an understanding, little smile. "AEON has ways to conceal you in plain sight so that your grandmother will never see you even if she's standing right in front of you."

My heartbeat quickened. Such a device would open up all sorts of opportunities for me, and I wouldn't ever need to fear being found by agilisi again. I could hang out with friends. Graduate from high school. Have a home with everything I've dreamed of since I turned five.

I'd finally be safe.

"If you were to receive one of our concealers, would you feel more comfortable remaining in the area so as to continue working with Revenant and his team?"

This time, it took me all of two seconds to decide. "Absolutely."

"Very well. I will have one delivered to you on the marrow."

Somehow, I managed to choke out a thank you.

It took Duncan over just under hour to register me for nocturnal classes at the school after the call had ended. He helped me choose the electives that would serve me best in my budding career as an AEON Enforcement Agent.

Then, with a pair of new uniforms and a schedule for my classes, I headed upstairs to my room.

My home.

31 SAATHOFF ACADEMY, DARK MOON PORT, MABON CITY FRIDAY, OCTOBER 24 12:01 AM

By the time I had reached my room and hung my new uniforms in the closet, I felt much better about myself than I had in a long time. In fact, I felt as if the weight of the last ten years had been taken off my shoulders. I knew eventually the nightmares would cease. The scars would fade. And at long last, I would be a normal teenager.

Well, as normal as a half-demon girl living in a private school for monsters could be.

Unfortunately, I still had to find the mirror. And I had just twenty-one hours left to pull it off. Otherwise I might as well kiss this sparkling new dream-come-true life goodbye. Everything hinged on the Shadow's accomplice. I just have to figure out who that is.

I fell into the computer chair with a sigh.

"Okay." I steepled my fingers, closed my eyes. "What are the facts of this latest fluster cluck?"

With the hardware as messed up as Morgan had made it when she kicked the doors in, and the Shadow focused on me, someone else had to be there. And not just to keep the doors shut despite an angry werewolf slamming into them. He or she had also cleaned out the safe and erased the security footage. All in the time it took for me and Quinn to catch a glimpse of the Shadow outside.

But how were the doors held shut?

I felt my lips pull into a frown. Were wizards and witches considered parathropes? Do they even exist?

I snorted. "Stupid question."

A sudden scratching at my door roused me into action. I snatched the super soaker from atop my desk, rushed to the door. I unlocked it and jerked it open in one swift move. Gun held at the ready, I stepped into the hallway. Darkness lay beyond the quaint pool of light that spilled out from my door. A chilling panic settled over me.

Shouldn't there be lights? Where are the lights?

The door slipped shut, and the darkness deepened. My heart raced. A second passed like an eternity.

My eyes finally adjusted to the gloom, and at last I could see the faint yellow-pink glow from the security lights that ran along the floor.

"Strange." I glanced up and down the length of the hall. I didn't hear the sound again. Nor did I catch any signs of movement. But I didn't dare move to investigate. I was already pushing my luck being out in the hall after curfew.

I silently slipped back into my room, locked the door. A handful of moments ticked by while I stood there, listening. Wondering what could have caused that scratching noise. The mystery would likely plague me until I discovered the answer.

I thought about my badge, wondered if I could use it as an after-curfew hall pass. I really didn't want to abuse my privilege as an honorary AEON Agent—provided I even had privileges. But if I could take a quick look around, maybe it would put my mind at ease. Then it occurred to me, I'm technically a nocturnal student. My curfew wouldn't roll around for several more hours. So I slipped out the door before I could talk myself out of it.

I navigated by using the glow of the security lights. The ship's forward elevators were only about a hundred feet from my door, and no one occupied the little lounge area opposite them. For a moment, I thought I heard receding footsteps on the stairs, but the sound quickly faded. A guard, maybe?

I kept going.

The student lounge proved to be empty. As did the laundry room and bathrooms.

I exhaled in frustration as much as relief, started back the way I had come.

I had barely managed a few steps when a soft voice shattered the silence. It sounded like it had come from the elevators.

Water gun at the ready, I started towards the elevators again. I kept to the shadows as much as possible as I approached. Two people stood in waiting at the elevators. One had long, dark hair styled in dreadlocks. She shifted her weight, and I caught a glimpse of a dark mark running the length of her arm.

Zero.

The girl with her had dressed in jeans and a hoodie, with one arm bunched at the elbow. A cast covered the rest of her arm and, like her clothes, appeared to be stained with dark splotches. Only when she turned her head to scowl at the elevator did I recognize her.

Anjie Cross' little sister.

What on earth is she *doing here?* I closed my eyes to listen.

Here's something you probably didn't know about yourself: When you lose one of your senses, say, sight, for example, your other senses grow more acute as a result. Having been agilisi's prisoner for ten years, I taught myself how to eavesdrop on her so I could be wary of her presence at all times. All I needed to do to improve my hearing was close my eyes and put very little effort into concentrating. Though they were whispering, I heard them loud and clear.

"—real reason you have come here tonight?" Zero asked.

Little sister remained quiet for a moment before stating, "I came to you because I need your help."

"I can see that. You look like you got hit by a bus. What happened?"

"Remember those stupid jocks that got the weird girl at my school expelled?"

"They did this to you?"

Little sister nodded. "That's why I came to you. I need your help getting back at them."

"Heh. Say what?"

She made a disgusted noise. "I want you to help me beat them up."

"What? Now?" Zero paused long enough for her to nod. "Are you out of your mind, Aiden? It's after midnight. I'm not sneaking out to break into people's houses just to beat up some stupid bullies."

Little sister's voice turned to venom. "I thought you were my friend, Rhea."

"Oh, don't even start that shit," seethed Zero, and she jabbed the elevator button. "I am your friend, Aiden, whether you choose to believe it right now or not. But what you are proposing to do is not only illegal, it's freaking stupid. If you want to go breaking into people's houses in the middle of the night to beat up kids, then that's on you. Don't come crying to me if you end up in jail."

"Fine!" Little sister spun on her heel and rushed to the stairs. Zero and I both listened as her footsteps faded into the silence. Then, with a sigh and a muttered curse, Zero turned to go back to her room.

32 SAATHOFF ACADEMY, DARK MOON PORT, MABON CITY
FRIDAY, OCTOBER 24
6:38 AM

'Monster Mash' woke me.

Something buzzed a beat that didn't match the song, and the ruckus quickly got on my nerves. Then it went blissfully quiet. I had just about dozed off when the routine started up again. This time, I popped my head up from my pillow to find the source of the noise with a promise to graveyard smash it when I did. The disturbance came from my desk.

The cell phone!

I threw off the covers and sprang out of bed, missing the call by only a second. Before I could return the call, I heard a pounding on my door.

"Cybil? It's Quinn."

"One sec!" I said as I rushed to unlock the door. I opened it with, "What's up? Were you just calling?"

"No; Duncan was." His tone sounded as serious as I had ever heard him, and he appeared to have just gotten out of bed himself. His hair looked messier than usual, and the buttons on his shirt didn't line up, never mind the fact that it didn't match his smiley face pajama pants. "He wants us in the office ASAP."

"Something wrong?"

He shrugged. "Duncan didn't say anything except to hurry down."

"Okay. Just let me grab my key." Now I couldn't help but feel worried. Duncan had woken Quinn, tried me, and probably Morgan too. But why? Did it have something to do with last night's unexpected visitor?

I snatched my key, threw on my trusty pair of moccasins and rushed out the door. Quinn was just hanging up a call when I joined him. Together, we rushed down the hall.

"Told Duncan he can stop calling you. He still didn't say what in the Three Worlds was so important though."

I hit the down button for the elevator. The doors opened within moments to reveal Morgan inside. With a pristine, white smock and heather gray pants, she had put together far better than me and Quinn. But she also looked like she had been asleep just minutes ago.

"You, too, huh?" she muttered as Quinn and I got on.

"Don't suppose Duncan told you the reason for this crack of dawn wake-up call?" Quinn hit the button to close the doors.

Morgan shook her head negative as she stifled a yawn. She pointed to Quinn's shirt. "Missed one."

He looked down, rolled his eyes. "I was in a hurry."

"We both were," I said as I ran my fingers through my hair in an attempt to fix my bed head. I might as well have been stapling Jell-O to a tree for all the good it did.

The elevator finally stopped, and the doors opened with their friendly, little ding. The three of us rushed through the little security room and down the halls. Light surrounded his door like a halo until Morgan jerked it open.

Specter and Duncan were by the desk opposite the door, standing in wait. Duncan surprised me with how dressed down he was. His black hair fell like a curtain past his shoulders. A matching set of navy blue pajamas, wrinkled from his sleep, and bare feet made up his attire.

His usually violet eyes were yellow as he glanced at me. "You sleep like the dead."

"So I've been told," I shrugged sheepishly. "Why did you set Monster Mash as your ringtone?"

Specter failed to hide the amused snort, and Duncan shot him a look that said, 'really?'

Ah ha! So the ghost is the culprit! "And why are your eyes suddenly yellow?"

Duncan returned his gaze to me. "I'm hungry."

A hungry vampire? That's not good. I really hoped that he didn't see me as a snack.

"Care to explain the reason for the six AM wake-up?" Morgan asked rather crossly. The question effectively sobered Specter right up.

"We have a huge problem." He hit a few glyphs, and the monitor on the wall to my left began to play the morning news.

All eyes were glued to the screen. The Asian reporter from Channel 31 was on the scene, at a house surrounded by police and rescue vehicles. In the corner of the feed were a couple of pictures. I knew both of the boys; the pimple-faced football captain at Mabon City Campus and one of his lackeys.

The reporter went on, "For those of you just joining us this morning, we are coming to you live from the scene of a tragic double murder. Jonathan Davis, the quarterback of the Mabon City Campus football team, and Louis Nettles, a forward on the school's basketball team, were found dead in the Davis' house earlier this morning.

"Officials have stated that the cause of the boys' deaths is still under investigation, but could be related to the mysterious murder of Cynthia Santova earlier this week. Police are asking for an—"

The monitor clicked off.

My mind reeled from the shock.

Two of the boys who had gotten me expelled from school had been murdered on the same morning the youngest Cross girl sneaks on board? What in the world did she do? No. It had to be a coincidence. It just had to be! Sure, she had been furious enough to spit nails… But to murder someone – two someones? There was no way!

"Cybil."

I numbly moved to look at Quinn. His moon blue eyes were studying me closely like he suspected I had something to do with the killing of those boys.

His voice was stern as he spoke. "You knew those boys. You were fighting them when we first met."

Tears were burning my eyes, threatening to fall. He's accusing me!

"She had nothing to do with it!" exclaimed Specter.

Quinn looked sidelong. "I'm not saying she did." He sighed, shifted his gaze back to me. "The girl you were with that day—Would she have any reason to go after those boys if she had the power to do so?"

Reason? He meant motive. Of course she had the motive. Heck, I had a motive. I wanted to kick those brats so hard they'd hit the moon. They had harassed both me and her—the new girls—numerous times. I had the power to seek my own revenge against them, but she didn't look like much of a fighter. That must why she had snuck on board to see Zero.

"Cybil, answer," Duncan commanded.

I licked my lips and hoped I wouldn't get myself or Zero into trouble for what I was about to say. "The youngest Cross girl came here a few hours ago." I held up my hand to stop any questions or comments they were about to fire at me. "She snuck in at about midnight to see Zero. I witnessed the two of them whispering by the forward elevators. While they talked, I heard her say that those boys had beat her up earlier, and she asked Zero to sneak out to go beat them up for her.

"Trust me, that girl is *not* a fighter. Not like me and Zero. She doesn't have the will or the strength to take on a ballerina, let alone two jocks from school. Anyway, Zero told her no, and she stormed off ."

Quinn's gaze finally softened up a bit, and he looked to Duncan. "How in the Three Worlds did a human girl manage to sneak on board this ship in the middle of the night?"

"I'm checking the security feeds now," Specter answered.

"I know how," declared Morgan, effectively earning everyone's attention. "She's no human girl," the angel glared at me. "She Jumped aboard. Your little friend is the Shadow."

I wanted to sock Morgan in the jaw and chew her out for even suggesting that that girl is the Shadow we've been chasing all week. Unfortunately, it made sense. Young Cross had been visiting agilisi's shop when the Shadow appeared in the alley. And I had seen the Cross' station wagon heading towards the Palisades before the Shadow appeared at Cynthia's estate. And Whatever-Her-Name-Is had been badly wounded when she snuck on board, but could holy water have caused the injuries I saw?

It all fit. As much as I didn't want to believe it, that little girl really could be the Shadow.

"What is your friend's full name?" Duncan asked as he crossed the room to his desk.

"I have no idea. Something Cross. It starts with an A. Why?"

He typed something in his computer, glanced at me. "I'm going to see if we have any record of her. Specter, you do the same in the cowan databases."

"Sure thing."

"What will you do to her if she does turn out to be a demon?"

"She's killed innocent people, Cybil," Specter said, his voice grim. "Her sentence would be death."

My heart skipped a beat. "But that's only after you've proven she's really the Shadow, right?" I looked at Quinn and Duncan. "I mean, it could just be a huge, royally screwed up coincidence. She could be innocent."

"I knew it!" spat Morgan. She was suddenly looming before me, her eyes blazing with golden power. She had moved so fast that it hadn't even registered in my brain. There still wasn't time for it to sink in before she slammed me into the wall six feet behind where I had been standing. "This little wretch is playing us for fools! She's in league with the Shadow!"

Duncan and Quinn immediately began playing hostage negotiator, desperately trying to get her to release me. My head started throbbing so loudly I couldn't hear them. The angel wanted to kill me. Me. A half-Shadow who hadn't done anything wrong except try to protect herself.

My intentions were always misunderstood.

And that seriously pissed me off.

Anger overpowered my terror in a tidal wave of rage.

Blinding.

Seething.

Rage.

I loosed a wordless roar. My first punch wasn't as hard as I wanted it to be, but it had been enough to shock Morgan into releasing me. The second one connected with her jaw and sent her spiraling to the ground. Quinn caught my arm and pulled me back before I strike the angel a third time. I screamed my fury at her in Tsalagi as she rose to her feet.

"That's enough!" roared Duncan. I clamped my mouth shut but continued to glare daggers at Morgan. "Morgan, once this case is closed, you are to report to your superiors in the Astral Plane for disciplinary drills."

Her jaw dropped.

"Pull another stunt like you just did and I will personally see to it that you remain there. Are we clear?"

Her shoulders sagged, and she looked away. "Yes, sir."

"Cybil," the vampire turned to me, scowling.

"*Uyo ayelodi*," I muttered, letting my fury evaporate. A little louder, I repeated it. "I'm sorry."

Duncan sighed, nodded. Quinn released my arm, and I let it fall to my side.

"I vill overlook this assault on an AEON Agent as self-defense," stated the vampire. "But please understand that if your friend is proven to be the Shadow behind the murders, her punishment vould be death. Demons like that are too much of a risk to the Mortal Realm to let them live."

I swallowed tears of frustration, sat myself down in one of the chairs at the conference table.

"However, since she is not in our system—at least not as Aiden Marie Cross—ve vill have to figure out how to prove or disprove her innocence in the matter."

"She may not be in the AEON system, but she has been in headlines in the cowan news," replied Specter. Without being told, the ghost restored the feed from his sphere to the monitor on the wall. He had pulled up several articles from newspapers all over the county. Every one of them said the same thing. "Lisa Janelle Cross, mother of Anjelah and Aiden Cross was killed in this head-on crash, dated just last weekend. Aiden survived with a broken arm and some minor injuries. "

"Holy crap!" I cried in sudden realization. "That's what they were talking about!"

Quinn gestured for me to explain.

"Okay." I shoved my bangs out of my face. "So Aiden and Anjie came into the MCC theater for homeroom Monday morning and sat near me. I heard them whispering about something, and, when I listened in, I felt some intense negative energy."

The werewolf scratched his chin. "What were they talking about?"

"One of them said something about punishing someone. A woman." I sagged with a groan. "Cynthia. They wanted to punish Cynthia."

"Vhat?"

I looked into Duncan's inhuman eyes. "I found it while searching online. A couple of news stories mentioned Cynthia being in a car crash. It's gotta be the reason why they went after her. How they found out about the mirror or called up a demon, I don't know. But there's our motive."

Quinn quietly agreed with me. "Wasn't one of them sitting with you when those boys started the fight?"

I nodded.

"If you didn't know her, why was she sitting with you?"

"I don't know," I said with a shrug. "She wanted to talk to me about something, but never got the chance. It must have been really important because she also showed up at agilisi's store."

"I take it she vas the girl vith the cast on her arm?"

Quinn and I chorused a yes.

"Odd," murmured the vampire. "I didn't sense anything from her."

"Let me try talking to her." I half-expected Morgan to say more crap about that, but she chose to remain silent.

I was grateful when Specter chimed in with, "Well, it could work. I mean,it might get this Aiden to drop her guard and confide in Cybil."

Duncan fell silent as he considering things.

"If we are to set a trap," said Quinn. "We'll need a day to prepare. Catching Shadows isn't like catching butterflies."

"Tomorrow may be too late," replied Duncan, sighing. "It vill have to be today."

I got the impression that Quinn wanted to argue further, but chose to drop it.

"Do you have a plan?" asked Specter.

"Ve vill have to get Aiden out in public," Duncan replied thoughtfully. "Hopefully, vith cowans around, she vill be less inclined to transform. It should also be an area vhere there's very little darkness she can utilize as escape routes."

I smiled, looked up at Duncan. “I know just the place.”

33 MABON CITY CAMPUS, MABON CITY FRIDAY, OCTOBER 24 10:02 AM

Ten o'clock had rolled around when Quinn pulled the car to a stop in Mabon City Campus' parking garage. I climbed out of the sedan's back seat, made a final adjustment to the concealed holster at my ankle. Duncan had been adamant about me going in armed. 'Just in case,' he had said. But the super soaker I had wouldn't fit in my bag. So, I had been given a little rig only slightly bigger than the size of my hand instead. And the flare leg of my jeans hid it perfectly.

Quinn was also packing. Since he had chosen to wear cargo shorts and a tee shirt, I couldn't figure out where, but I knew his gun had real bullets and not holy water. Morgan didn't need a mortal weapon. She could simply summon one from the light if she needed.

Cheater.

Specter had joined us for this outing. He had been given the important job of being my bodyguard. More importantly, he was going to help me interrogate Aiden. All while invisible. That should be interesting.

Once the car had been locked up, I took the lead. Quinn and Morgan were right behind me, but I couldn't see Specter anywhere. We exited the parking garage, headed for the football field on the south side of the school. The festival was just kicking off, and air was a sweet and delicious mix of candies and roasting meats.

Immediately to the left as we approached, a group of people were playing a game in the mowed grass. Quinn paused to watch as one of the players tossed what looked like a baseball onto the field. Scattered applause from a few onlookers followed.

"It's called digadayosdi. Marbles," I said without being asked. "It's sort of like golf meets shuffleboard. Players throw the balls to try to get them into the holes while trying to keep their opponent from doing the same."

"When I played marbles," he looked at me over the rim of his sunglasses, "the balls weren't the size of your hand."

I flashed him a cheeky grin. "When you played marbles, dinosaurs still roamed the earth."

He tilted his head back and laughed. Even Morgan cracked a smile.

I led the way around the Marbles field, towards the small stage and dancing area. A familiar voice suddenly shouting my name made me freeze. I looked in the direction of the school's outdoor food court. Mister Roan marched a weaving pattern through the tables, making his way towards me on a mission—most likely one to kick me off school property again. The little man's hands were fists and his mouth bore a scowl so deep it practically cut his face in half.

I braced myself for the worst.

To my great surprise, Morgan cut him off before he could get within ten feet of me.

He stabbed the air with his finger, pointing at meas if I were an ugly piece of furniture. "Get that murderous witch off school property!"

I didn't know whether to be shocked or furious or embarrassed. Not only did he believe that I had murdered someone—most likely those two boys from the school's sports teams—he shouted it so loudly that almost the entire gathering of people stopped to gawk. I grit my teeth so hard it felt like my jaw would break just to keep from saying anything back.

A terrifying thought passed like a ghost through my mind. Could that horrible man be the Shadow we've been after all week? I firmly told myself no. Roan couldn't be the demon. Sure, the guy had issues with me, but he cares too much for the school's athletes to kill them or stand by and let someone else do it.

“Principal Roan,” said Quinn, facing the man. “That was completely out of line.”

“She,” Roan snarled, “isn't allowed here anymore.”

“Oh?” Quinn crossed his arms, cocked his head to one side. “Why? Because of that bogus expulsion you slapped on her?” He paused long enough to flash his badge to the approaching school security guards. They promptly stopped in their tracks. “Oh, wait. I forgot. That expulsion was illegal, and—if memory serves me right—you haven't even submitted the required paperwork to the school board to actually begin the process. One could almost say you're desperate to get hit with discrimination and harassment charges.”

Roan's eyes flew wide.

“Now, I suggest you apologize to Miss Starr before you embarrass yourself further.” The werewolf just coldly stared at him, smiling as if he was the principal's old friend.

Mister Roan's scowl grew even deeper, and he turned his heated glare on me. “Not one toe out of line, young lady!” He wagged his finger at me. “I mean it!”

I kept my mouth clamped shut to prevent a snide remark from slipping past my lips, but I managed a curt nod. He eyed me suspiciously a moment more, then turned and rushed away muttering something. The gathered spectators began to thin.

“Thanks for that,” I said to Quinn.

He frowned at the principal's retreating back. “What a jerk.”

I agreed with him. Then I pointed out the patio tables and asked, “Do you think our little friend could fit through those?”

“It would be a tight squeeze,” said Morgan, “but a cornered demon will try to escape via any route it can.”

Quinn was quiet a moment, his brow creased in pensive concentration. Then, "Specter."

For barely a moment, the scent of rain overpowered the smells of candies and roasting meats. Then an echoing whisper said, "Deployed."

I watched as Morgan took her phone from her pocket, tapped an app. The screen changed, dividing into quadrants that reminded me of four-player mode in one of my PlayStation games. A live video feed of the food court appeared in one of the squares.

Morgan muttered a confirmation.

I led everyone on a short tour through the festival in search of more shadows deep enough to serve as doorways. We passed the food pavilion (and my mouth watered in anticipation of the roasted meats), glanced over the little kids' gaming area, and ventured through the double row of vendors. Each time Quinn or I pointed out a particularly large pool of shade, Morgan and Specter repeated the procedure they had with the outdoor food court. Morgan's phone continued to fill with video feeds.

At long last, it was on to Mabon City Campus' prized football field.

It was all sunshine and freshly-mowed grass until the end zones, where the field goal posts formed long and thin shadows that could make for quick doorways. We als worried about the bleachers, whose shadows were so vast Quinn worried about the Shadow summoning in an army for backup.

Specter deployed even more of… er, whatever those invisible things were, and Morgan's screen filled with twelve additional feeds.

"I think that's it for out here," I said with a shrug.

Quinn did a slow three-sixty, nodded. "This is a lot more ground to cover than I had been expecting."

Morgan looked up from her phone. "What about inside?"

I frowned at that thought. If Quinn believed the outdoor setting to be more ground than expected, adding the interior of the school was only going to complicate things even more. I took a minute to recall the layout of the school's interior before finally breaking the news.

“Well, there are two sets of bathrooms inside—one on either end of the cafeteria, through there,” I pointed at the double doored entrance that served as a gateway between the food court and interior of the school, “that visitors are allowed to use. They can also go to the library, which is where the students have set up art and science displays. The seven designated women for the festival are allowed in the kitchen as they are responsible for most of the food. Then there's the students who can come and go on their off hours or lunch breaks and when school lets out.”

Quinn exhaled his dismay in a gust of breath. “Specter?”

“Already on it.”

Morgan muttered something about needing a larger screen, asked for the car keys.

After she left, Quinn looked to me. “When's your friend's lunch hour?”

“She’s not my friend.” I glanced at his watch, told him that if Aiden had come today after being out so late last night, her lunch would begin in about forty minutes. He nodded, and we settled in to wait.

34 SAATHOFF ACADEMY, DARK MOON PORT, MABON CITY FRIDAY, OCTOBER 24 11:18 AM

I sighed and released the string of my bow. My arrow sprinted a hundred yards down range and sank into the foam target three inches above the bullseye with a *thwump.* I made a frustrated noise, nocked another arrow.

Another sprint down range.

Thwump.

Another miss.

My aim was usually much better than this. I wanted to blame it on the lousy design of the bow, but deep down I knew it wasn't the one at fault.

Aim.

Thwump.

Miss.

A bad feeling had been plaguing me for the past hour. It started when Aiden didn't show up for lunch. Quinn had even gone inside to search the cafeteria for her. When he returned without Aiden, he had had Morgan dig up the Crosses' phone number. I had left a message on their answering machine.

Thwump.

I tried to ease my worries by telling myself Aiden could have stayed home from school and is now comfortably asleep in her bed.

Thwump.

Anything to keep me from imagining the Mirror of Souls being turned upon her. I may not know the girl, but no one deserves that fate.

My last arrow sailed right past the target and headed for the backstop. It sank into the foam and carpet with a barely audible *pfft.* I shouldered my borrowed bow with a frown, stared at the stray arrow.

It took a minute or so for the other archers to empty their quivers, and for the range officer to call the all clear. I followed them downrange to pull my arrows from the foam target. I was nearly to the backstop to retrieve my last arrow when my phone suddenly rang. I quickly pulled it out of my back pocket, checked the caller ID.

Blocked.

The hairs on the back of my neck started to rise.

I took a deep breath, put on my resting witch face. On the third ring, I pressed the answer button. "*Osiyo?*"

Static pulsed over the connection. Then a distorted voice cut through the noise. "Good afternoon, Jinx."

I frowned. Whoever was on the line couldn't have been a Shadow. The last time I bumped into one, its voice was like gravel and it kept referring to me as 'Young One.' No, this was a human. A human who knew me by my nickname. And they seemed to be using a device of some kind to disguise their voice, which meant that the odds were good that I knew them as well. That list of people was pretty short, and none of them struck me as someone willing to kill for something.

But with the static on the line, I was willing to bet that a Shadow lurked near enough to cause the disturbance. Perhaps Morgan and Duncan were right and the demon had possessed someone. Even that didn't explain why the caller used my nickname.

"Who are you and how did you get this number?" I demanded, pulling the arrow free of its cushy prison.

"Before —u say something you might regret, *bzzt* –ould consider the fate of your AEON frie– *kshh* –vr there by the tent..."

My blood ran ice cold. I rushed to the exit of the archery range, peered over the kids' gaming arena. Quinn stood at the far side of the food pavilion from me, watching the area around the dance floor and food court.

"... an— vendors."

I spotted Morgan's golden hair in the midst of the little market row. There were too many people around her for me to know if someone had gotten to her. I got the impression that, had she been confronted, she would have made a scene that astronauts on the International Space Station could see.

I may not have been able to pinpoint the threat against their lives, but I knew it couldn't be anything but real. And my teammates were too far away for me to warn them without alerting whomever I had on the phone. I truly hoped Specter had been hiding near me when the call came in. He would be able to warn Quinn and Morgan of the threat without drawing attention to himself. Maybe he could even trace the call.

But I doubted he needed to.

Almost nobody had the number to my phone. The only one way our enemies could have known how to get a hold of me and where to find me. They had listened to my message on the Crosses' answering machine. That simple fact brought to light a whole new and terrible circumstance. If Aiden wasn't the Shadow in disguise, she was a hostage. Her whole family could be hostages. And there was no way in hell I was going to let that slide.

I tried to keep my voice steady and calm. "What do you want?"

"Meet me."

I licked my lips. "Where?"

"*bzzt*— theater. Come alone or the AEONs will die."

The phone disconnected.

I looked at the school's southern entrance, already knowing that Quinn wouldn't miss seeing me if I went that way. I couldn't afford to have him follow me. Good thing I knew the east wing had a door that led to a hallway that was a straight shot to the theater. I made for that door at a dead run, paused long enough to check that I wasn't followed. Then I pulled the door open and slipped inside.

The lights were out and I fumbled in the dark, sunblind, but I had navigated this route too many times to not know where to go. Fifty steps ahead. Turn left. The theater doors would be right there. I couldn’t see anything lurking in the simulated night, but I could feel it. A sinister presence had settled over the area like a dense fog. It crept into the back of my mind to fill me with overwhelming terror and doubt.

I don't have the luxury of being afraid now, I firmly told myself as I nocked an arrow on my borrowed bow. With a deep, calming breath, I strode forward, shoulders squared and chin held high.

35 SAATHOFF ACADEMY, DARK MOON PORT, MABON CITY
FRIDAY, OCTOBER 24
11:58 AM

The doors swung shut with a barely audible click, cutting off the easiest escape route. My sight was rendered useless in the asphyxiating gloom. Everywhere I looked, an unnatural darkness loomed before me. I had been in here five days a week for the last two and a half months. I knew the theater's emergency overhead lights and little, golden step lights needed to be lit at all times. Yet none of them were on. Either someone knew where to find the fuse box to turn all the lights off manually, or the Shadow had blown them out simply by appearing here.

Ten bucks says it's that wretched Shadow.

I got my bearings, continued forward with measured steps. The deeper I plunged, the more my eyes grew accustomed to the dark. I began to make out the shapes of chairs, the positions of guard rails, and I felt a little more confident than before.

The flight of stairs eventually came to an end. I paused at the front row of seats, adjusted my grasp on my bow. I cast my gaze about the room, even way up into the rafters. The theater was empty. And cold—not physical cold, but something terribly nefarious.

Had I missed something?

I brought my bow up and dared to tiptoe closer to the stage.

Movement out of the corner of my eye made me freeze. An utter darkness yawned where there hadn't been one a moment ago, and the stench of rotting eggs assaulted my senses. I threw myself into a forward dive, rolled up to my knees, and loosed the arrow.

The Shadow let out a hissing snarl, yanked the arrow from the spot between its glowing ruby eyes. I had no time to admire the luckiness of the shot. It hurled the projectile at me and I lunged sideways to avoid it. By the time I recovered, the demon had vanished. Unfortunately, the stench of its presence didn't.

I scanned the shadows and readied another arrow. "So, was this your plan?" I called to dark. "Draw me to a secluded area for a duel? A little payback for that shower I gave you."

Ear-grating laughter erupted all around me.

I took that as a no.

Something slammed into the small of my back with the speed and strength of a bullet train. The impact knocked the wind out of me and snapped my head back sharply. I crashed to the ground and lay there in agony as stars whirled before my eyes. Through the confusion, I realized the Shadow now stood over me. I felt it grab me by the back of the neck and then the world turned glacial cold.

I suddenly found myself floating in emptiness. There was no sound. No light. No smell. Just total, icy nothingness, as if all my senses had been turned off. I felt waves of panic and despair crash over me. There was just no other explanation.

I was dead.

36 SOMEWHERE IN MABON CITY TIME UNKNOWN

All my senses came screaming back to me in a disorienting flood of color and noise. I felt dizzy and nauseous, and I was grateful to be laying on the ground. My skin crawled as if it was experiencing the feel of air for the very first time. There was a strange pressure on the back of my neck, and I realized the Shadow still had me in its grasp. I belatedly realized that we were no longer in the theater. Hard, cold concrete had replaced the warm carpeting, and the artificial dark now bore the red-orange glow of flickering firelight. The smell of blown-out matches and fresh paint hung in the air.

The Shadow and I had somehow been transported to a dungeon. Or a basement.

"Ah. Good," said a muffled female voice. With my head still spinning from the ride through nothingness, I couldn't discern her identity. But I had the distinct and dreadful feeling there was something familiar about the tone. "The guest of honor has finally arrived. Thank you, Bal'zaroth, for Jumping her here."

At least now I knew how I got here from the theater. The demon—I guess Bal'zaroth was its name—had a teleportation ability like Morgan's Light Jump. Now I just had to figure out where the heck 'here' was so I could leave.

The Shadow snarled something vicious that might have been its language and released its hold on me. I slowly pushed myself to my knees, glanced at my surroundings. The demon had brought me to a concrete box of a room. Metal shelves stacked to capacity with Roughneck tubs and Tupperware containers had been haphazardly shoved against the walls leaving an irregular walkway down the middle of the room. Barely noticeable behind the shelves was a trio of windows that had been smothered by what I guessed to be paint. An oval table, veiled in ebony cloth, filled the space at the opposite end of the room from me. A halo of black candles rested upon its surface, casting a dancing orange glow over the hooded shape who stood before it.

The shape appeared to be humanoid. Concealed as she was, I could only make out a head and shoulders and legs... Legs that ended in vaguely familiar high heels. My eyes ached when I tried to see her face; There was just too much light behind her.

And yet, I felt a familiarity to her presence.

"Guest of honor?" I asked as I rose to my feet. That was when I noticed the nearly perfect ring of metal laid into the floor, and I was standing in the middle of it. To make matters worse, my bow and quiver were gone; probably left behind in the theater when the Shadow Jumped me. The light pressure around my ankle told me I still had the water gun, but that proved to be only a small relief.

"Pardon the metaphor," said the unknown woman. I recognized it immediately and now knew why those heels were so familiar. I think I even knew where this dungeon-wanna-be of a basement—or sub-basement as the case may be—was buried.

"I love what you've done to the place, Anjie," I said, pretended like I didn't hear the sharp intake of breath she took. "Tell me, did you black out the windows at your house too? Or do you just confine your Shadow friend down here?" I looked at the demon glowering at me from less than five feet away. "If I were you, I'd demand better room service."

It snorted, unamused.

"Such impudence," uttered a coarse whisper.

Crap.

The depth of the darkness in the space to my immediate left intensified, and a second Shadow demon stalked into the fetid dimness. This one looked slightly larger than the other, and it had a length of heavy, black chain in its grasp. The other end had been shackled around a young girl's neck.

Double crap.

The Shadow yanked the chain forward, and Aiden crashed to her knees with a cry of terror and pain. Watching the girl be subjected to such treatment immediately had me seeing red. I rushed forward, ready to pound the demon with my bare hands, only to find the air as solid as steel. I pushed against the invisible wall, again and again, to make sure I wasn't imagining it.

"You're not going anywhere, whelp," said Bal'zaroth, the smaller Shadow. "That circle is your prison."

I frowned down at the metallic ring in the floor.

Triple crap.

Wait a minute! That weird book I found had mentioned something about circles. This must be what it was talking about. All I had to do was remember what the heck it said. I closed my eyes and tried to picture the page with the plain circle drawn on it. Scrawled beside that circle had been a short list—the very list I needed to remember right now. I focused my mind's eye on it, and I could almost hear the tip of the pen scratching against the paper.

Used to contain…

… Something about silver…

… Empowered by gemstones…

My eyes flew open.

Break to release!

That's it! I had to somehow break the circle to get out. I knew I had no way to smash up a metallic ring sunk into the concrete. And I had serious doubts that these Shadows were stupid enough to fall for a trick and rush into the circle with me. Anjie sure as hell wouldn't. Aiden might have done it if she wasn't so terrified.

That left me with a single option: I'd have to Jump out.

The demon that dragged me here had done it, so I know it can be done. However, it was going to be particularly difficult since I had never actually done it before. It also meant I'd have to surrender myself to the demonic side, and the very thought of that terrified me. I mean, who willingly lets a demon take complete control over their body? And, as if all of that wasn't bad enough, I'd first have to figure out how convince my inner demon to give me its powers.

I was so involved with my problem that I hadn't been paying attention to what was going on. Aiden had completely ignored the chains that kept her bound and went straight up to Anjie to chew her out.

"Don't you see?" Anjie snapped, shoving her little sister away. "It had to be done!"

Aiden leveled a glare at Anjie. "If you think killing in mama's name is going to make her happy, you're an even bigger dumbass than your ugly pets!"

In that instant, realization came out of nowhere to oh so nicely kick my head in. At long last, the puzzle made sense.

My little 'ah ha!' moment was interrupted by Anjie's exploding rage. Suddenly, the air around her seemed to shimmer like waves of heat from an open oven. With just a simple flick of a finger and a word, Aiden was thrown sideways as if she had been hit by a bus. She slammed into one of the shelving units. It wobbled, tipped, then finally crashed into the one behind it. A cacophony of noise erupted as the storage bins and their contents rained down.

Aiden melted down onto the floor with a groan.

Anjelah hissed at her to shut-up.

"Anjie," I said, my voice dripping scorn as I glared at her. She returned the look with an acrimonious scowl. "When I get out of here—and make no mistake, I will get out of here—I am going to kick. Your. Ass."

Anjie gave me a haughty, little smirk. "Oh, please," she scoffed, half-turning to grab something from the table. "Bal'zaroth already told me that you were stupid enough to stop using your demon powers."

I refused to let myself show any reaction to her words. There are things you just don't let an enemy see. Fear, for instance. Fear works like an aphrodisiac to predators—for that's what Anjelah and the Shadows were: predators. They zero in on your terror and wait, drawing out the tension until you make a fatal mistake. Until you run.

So I couldn't afford to let them know how my courage unraveled like a cheap sweater at her words. Still, I pondered over them. Unless other demons can sense that sort of thing, the Shadows couldn't have known that I had told my inner demon to get lost.

Alright, I thought, crossing my arms. Time to get some answers. "Color me curious, but how did you get stuck working with monsters?"

Anjie took the bait with a cocky little smile, and launched into some monologue I didn't give a crap about. With her occupied, I was free to once again dive into the prison of my inner demon.

37 PRISON OF THE MIND
TIME: NONEXISTENT

I was met with frigid, asphyxiating dark no light could pierce. Icy barbs, hurled by hurricane wind, thrashed at me like ten thousand tiny needles. I threw my arms up to protect my face, and the barbs chewed through them as if they were tissue paper. With furtive steps, I trudged blindly through snow that clung to my hips, ever wary of the stairs I knew lay ahead.

My limbs grew heavier the further into the blackness I pushed. Numb from the cold, and shivering uncontrollably, I didn't feel the floor suddenly give way. Somehow, I managed to catch myself before I went head-first down the stairs. I sacrificed a few precious moments more to descend the stairs carefully. Once I reached the landing, I counted each step forward for a third (and hopefully final) time.

It took a few tries to get my mouth working properly, and I called out to the presence. Or, at least, that's what I tried to do. The cold choked my throat, and wind stole my hoarse whispers away again and again. I turned my back to the onslaught, blew into my hands in the vain attempt to warm them and my voice box. Then I shouted for my inner demon.

Once.

Twice.

Thrice.

At long last, those eyes like smoldering embers appeared.

AH, SO, MINE KEEPER DARES YET ANOTHER RETURN, it said, its raspy whisper laced with annoyance. The eyes disappeared into the dark once more. *HOW BRAVE.*

'Cut the crap!' There wasn't any time to put up with this stupid thing's personal issues with me. 'Turn this damn storm off and give me back my powers. Now.'

NO.

I ignored its response, stamped my feet in the vain attempt to restore some feeling to them. As I did, I filled the demon in on the situation. 'Anjie and a pair of Shadows have us trapped in a circle. The only way we can get out of it to save ourselves and put a stop to their plan is to Jump out. I can't do it alone, so I am asking you to return the powers you gave me.'

THERE IS NO US.

'Listen to me, dammit!' I lurched forward a pace in my rage. As if sensing my anger, the wind picked up and the temperature plummeted to an all new low. There was no point in worrying about the weather if I couldn't get this stupid creature to help me. 'They are going to kill me. And you. Then they're going to kill an innocent girl. I can't let that happen. You need to help me stop it!'

The eyes slammed open with an enraged snarl. *YOU IGNORANT CHILD!*

The fiery glow of the demon's eyes streaked towards me. I fell back, some instinct driving me to a defensive posture in case the demon didn't stop. But it did. Just out of arm's reach.

DO YOU SERIOUSLY BELIEVE THAT EVERYTHING YOU SEE AND FEEL HERE IS REAL? WE ARE INSIDE YOUR HEAD, YOU MORON.

'Of course we are, you stupid thing!'

Its irritated growl reminded me of rumbling thunder. *I MEAN, THIS IS NOT AN ICE STORM. YOU ARE NOT IN A DARK PRISON. I AM NOT REAL. YOU MADE ALL OF THIS UP BECAUSE YOU WERE TOO AFRAID OF THE TRUTH TO FACE IT.*

'I wasn't af—'

YOUR OVER-CONFIDENT ATTITUDE AND TOUGH GIRL MASK MIGHT FOOL

OTHER PEOPLE, BUT YOU CAN'T LIE TO ME. I KNOW YOU INSIDE AND OUT BETTER THAN YOU DO. I KNOW FOR A FACT THAT THE MINUTE YOU LEARNED YOU WEREN'T ENTIRELY HUMAN, YOUR RATIONAL MIND SHORT-CIRCUITED, AND YOU CREATED THIS ELABORATE MIRAGE TO AVOID DEALING WITH IT. THIS PRISON, the eyes swept the darkness, *THE WIND, THE COLD, THE BARRENNESS; ALL OF THAT IS THE LIE.*

YET, HERE WE STAND NOW, AT EACH OTHER'S THROATS, BECAUSE YOU REFUSED TO USE THE POWERS YOU WERE BORN WITH. AND IT'S ALL DO TO THE FACT THAT YOU WERE AFRAID YOU WERE GOING TO LOSE YOURSELF TO THE DARKNESS. WELL, KID, I'VE GOT NEWS FOR YOU: WE HAVE BEEN IN THAT DARKNESS FOR FIFTEEN YEARS, AND WE ARE STILL THE SAME PERSON. WE WOULD WILLING SACRIFICE OURSELVES FOR OUR FRIENDS IF IT MEANT SAVING THEM. IF YOU DON'T BELIEVE THAT, OPEN YOUR EYES AND TAKE A LOOK AT THE SITUATION WE'RE IN.

NOW, SUDDENLY, YOU WANT YOUR POWERS BACK. THE DEMON SIGHED. I HATE TO BREAK IT TO YOU, KID, BUT I CAN'T RESTORE THEM. IT'S IMPOSSIBLE. DO YOU WANT TO KNOW WHY?

Stiffly, and a little uncertain, I nodded.

The demon leaned in closer. I felt hands take me gently by the shoulders. *BECAUSE THEY WERE NEVER REALLY GONE TO BEGIN WITH.*

Never. Gone?

I felt the wind shift into a wild spiral around me. My hair battered my face, and I shoved it aside with a huff.

'My powers were with me this whole time?' I stared into those crimson eyes, desperately searching for any sign of deception. It was a wasted effort. Everything my demon said was true. But it didn't make any sense.

I SAID YOU REPRESSED YOUR POWER. The weight of my demon's hands on my shoulders disappeared. *YOU MAY BE ABLE TO LOCK IT UP IN A DEEP,*

DARK HOLE SOMEWHERE FOR A FEW DAYS, BUT YOU COULD NEVER COMPLETELY DIVEST YOURSELF OF IT.

'How do you know about all of this?'

Its scarlet gaze quickly surveyed the space around us. *IT WOULD BE EASIER TO EXPLAIN IF YOU'D JUST TURN THE LIGHTS ON.*

A frown tugged at the corners of my lips. 'How the hell am I supposed to do that in this win—' I froze.

A playful mischief flashed in those eyes as the demon's focus once again settled on me.

I just stood there like an idiot for a handful of precious seconds, disbelieving what had happened without my notice. The dark prison had gone as silent as a graveyard at midnight, and I no longer felt the biting chill of windblown shards of ice.

I all but cheered, 'There is no wind!'

THERE IS NO SPOON.

I think I'm finally beginning to understand. From the moment I set foot in here, I had been fully aware that this prison was within my mind. What I had failed to realize is that the entire thing was nothing more than an elaborate dream construct. Like with lucid dreaming, I had complete control over every single detail. Including—and I looked into those crimson eyes—my subconscious.

Torches flared to life all around the prison, washing the two of us in warm light. At long last, I saw it. No. Not 'it.' *Her*. From her hairstyle and color to her clothes and posture, my inner demon was a perfect reflection of me in every way, save one: her ruby red eyes.

She flashed a smile. *NOW YOU SEE.*

'Yes,' I said. 'The reason you have all the answers is because you, as my subconscious, remember everything I've ever heard or seen or felt. My entire life's story wrapped up in one neat, little package.'

PRECISELY, she said with a nod. *NOW, THERE'S BUT ONE QUESTION LEFT UNANSWERED.*

'Oh?'

She raised her arm as if she wanted to arm wrestle and held it between us. *ARE YOU FINALLY READY TO KICK SOME ASS?*

I felt a jolt of cold energy pass through me as I gripped her hand.'Absolutely!'

38 SUBBASEMENT,MABON CITY CAMPUS, MABON CITY
TIME UNKNOWN

For the briefest of moments, all my senses were assaulted with a riot of impressions. Then everything was simply right. My vision was sharp and clear enough, even in the dark, to count the stray hairs that peeked out from under Anjie's cowl. I could hear the subtle differences between her footfalls as she approached, babbling on about revenge. The combined stenches of the Shadows and fresh paint was, much to my displeasure, overpowering and unavoidable. I even felt the thrumming and invisible tension of the circle I was trapped in. Despite all of that, all I could think was: Damn! It's good to be back!

Now all I had to do was get out of this circle by pulling off a trick I'd never done before, beat the snot out of a conceited, little witch, take her two minions out of the picture for good, bust up the Mirror of Souls—wherever they were hiding it—and rescue Aiden.

Sounds simple enough. My biggest problem would be figuring out that whole Jump thing with nothing to guide me. Well, that, and finding the Mirror. I just had to trick them into showing me where they put it.

Anjie was still droning on about her plan when I finally tuned back in. Her two Shadow friends merely observed, though, to me, they seemed to be growing increasingly impatient.

"That's the problem with villains these days," I muttered to the smaller demon, earning a quick look. "Get 'em talking about their plans and they'll never shut up."

It snorted; maybe even in amusement.

"What the hell does your plan have to do with me?" I demanded, effectively cutting off Anjelah's annoying yammering. Woo boy! Did she look like she could spit nails.

“Didn't your mother ever teach you not to interrupt people when they're talking?”

“As a matter of fact,” I crossed my arms defiantly “she didn't.”

“Enough!” The larger Shadow roared. Anjelah bowed out of his way, giving me a quick look at her altar. It was just a bunch of candles and an iron pot sitting atop a black tablecloth. There was enough room within the semi-circle of candles for the Mirror to rest, but it wasn't there.

Where else could it be?

“You have but one option to get out of here alive, Half Breed.” The larger Shadow jerked the chain, forcing Aiden to lop sideways with a pained yelp. “I suggest you take it.”

I rolled my eyes, already aware of the demons' sales pitch. I had more important things to worry about than some too-good-to-be-true offer from the Netherworld’s lackeys. The worst part about it was that they’d keep coming, again and again, making the same offer over and over. I should give them a signed note.

Wait! Maybe I didn’t need a note; I just needed the Law of Threes. And I hoped it would work in this situation.

The Shadow continued trying to talk my ear off. “… you could command armies, conquer kingdoms.” Its grin stretched in a perfect mimic of the Cheshire cat’s. “Slay Taboo.”

I looked it dead in its ruby eyes. “Anyone ever tell you that you sound like an infomercial?”

Its grin melted.

“Since you Shadows seem to have a void where your brains should be,” their growls rumbled like a raging storm, “let me be perfectly clear. I. Will. Never. Join. The Netherworld. Twice more I’ll say it, and be done.” I felt the same weird, little pop of energy that happened last time. The demons went insane with rage. Whatever that Law of Threes thing was, it really seemed to pack a wallop among parathropes.

"Then you leave us no other choice!" bellowed the larger of the two. "Kill the wretch!"

"A moment please, my lord," Anjelah said, her voice thick with hollow flattery. That revealed something I hadn't thought of before now. All this time, I thought she had been in charge of this whole train wreck, but it would seem she was merely the Shadows' peon.

"Speak."

"Allow me to feed her soul to the Mirror."

It took the Shadows maybe half a second to approve the idea. I watched in a mix of awe and dread as the smaller Shadow reached into the dark, melding perfectly into the shadows for a moment. Then, slowly, it began to pull back. With its fist came a twisted and pitted sculpture with black glass at its heart. The temperature of the room took a sudden dive, and I shivered in realization.

The Mirror of Souls.

Anjie muttered something, and my arms suddenly had minds of their own. They rose as if I was trying to reach the ceiling, and stayed there. I tried bringing them down, but it felt like I had a Bowflex machine on the highest resistance setting.

"You should feel honored, Jinx," said Anjelah. I felt a shimmering ripple of energy rush away when she reached over the border of the circle, breaking it. She pulled a dainty knife from the sheathe clipped to her belt. With a satisfied grin, she jabbed the blade into the middle my forearm and dragged it down, carving out a path about three inches long. The edges of the wound sizzled like bacon on a hot stove.

Okay.

Ow.

She held the knife there until my blood coated the blade in crimson, and backed away. "Your soul will make the Mirror more powerful than it has been in centuries."

"Why am I not excited?"

Angie backed away, muttered another word. My skin started to crawl as every hair on my body stood on end. The air around me felt like a lightning bolt was about to strike. There was a sudden change in pressure, and my arms were freed from whatever force had held them. I held my hand over the wound to ebb the flow of blood and watched as Anjie accepted the Mirror from the Shadow.

"You never answered my question," I said. She paused to glare at me. "What did I do to wind up on your shit list?"

"Who says you're on my list?" She shot a glance at the larger of the two Shadows.

I pointed at it. "Oh. It's *your* list. Were you the one I shot full of holy water?"

It snarled something I could only guess was an insult.

"That reminds me." My attention returned to Anjelah, and I tried to ignore the sick feeling that settled in the pit of my stomach as she let my blood drip into the cauldron. Disgusting! "What were you doing at Cynthia's mansion? You already had the wonder twins here," I gestured between the two Shadows, "steal the Mirror, and I know you had no interest in the junk in the safe. So, why were you there?"

She was silent a moment, working on her spell, then she glanced at me over her shoulder. "Funny. I thought a psychic would have known that."

I frowned.

"Think, Cybil." Anjie set the tiny knife on the altar. "What one thing did the alley, the mansion, and the festival all have in common?"

Son of a monkey!

How did I not realize it sooner? Of course, I was their target! Both Duncan and Quinn had warned me that Netherworld agents would be coming after me, and that those agents would do everything and anything in their power to try to recruit me. And I just handed myself over to them all willy-nilly. How freaking stupid could I be?

"Figured it out, have you?" Anjelah murmured, regarding me with a serpentine smile plastered on her face.

In a low, ice cold tone, I told her, "I'm going to make you eat that smile."

She scoffed. "I'd like to see you try." With that, she turned her back to me to begin whatever twisted ritual the Mirror required.

It was the moment I had been waiting for.

Anjelah's voice cut through. "*Maledicti invoc—*"

I heard her, but I was too focused on my task to care.

There was a sudden flash of darkness. The feeling of weightlessness. For a moment, I felt like I was adrift in a dream. I thought I saw doorways. Countless doorways. All lining a long hallway that stretched on for eternity in either direction.

Then it was gone.

"*—abo.*" Anjie uttered the last syllable of the word she had been on. However long I had spent floating in the nothingness had been less than an instant here. In that split second, I had crossed twenty feet and now found myself directly behind Anjelah.

A giddy wave of exhaustion shuddered through me. I shoved it aside. Before Anjie could take a breath, I punched her square in the middle of her back. She crashed into the table with a yelp of pain and surprise. The candles toppled, spilling wax and flame onto the tablecloth. I grabbed the back of her head and slammed it against the table top as hard as I could.

She screamed.

The Shadows—probably just now realizing I was no longer caged—bellowed ear-splitting shrieks.

I snatched the Mirror with one hand, freed my water gun from its holster with the other. At least, that's what I tried to do. My hands were shaking so bad from the adrenaline rush that I just ended up yanking the whole thing off my ankle. It didn't matter; one shot from the gun would send the holster flying.

Anjelah was trying to get up. I kicked the back of her knee and heard a satisfying crack. She crumbled to the floor, striking her chin on the table's edge as she went.

I whirled around to face the Shadows.

In the handful of seconds I spent dealing with Anjie, the demons had almost closed in on me. I pointed the gun at the closest and fired. The holster passed harmlessly through the Shadow's head. The water bullet that followed right behind it didn't. The demon's head snapped back at the force of the blast, and the monster burst into a cloud of mucus-like goo. The fluid splashed to the floor with a violent hiss.

The remaining Shadow froze in its tracks, gaped at me.

I stared, mystified, at the rapidly evaporating puddle.

Anjie screeched a word. The water gun flew out of my hands and clattered to the floor several feet between me and a cowering Aiden. I reeled around to strike Anjelah down, but she was already shouting another word. My arms suddenly felt heavy, as if they had been weighed down with anchor chains. The Shadow glommed onto me from behind and wrenched the Mirror from my grasp. I struggled to pull its arm away from my throat before I was choked out.

"I'll kill you!" Anjie snarled. I caught a glimpse of her face before she hammered punches into my ribs. The right side had been caught in the spilled candles, and the flames and molten wax had taken their toll. Where her skin hadn't been blackened by the burns, enormous blisters and strips of dead flesh remained. She would never heal from the trauma. I probably should have felt guilty, knowing I had been the one to cause it, but right now, I didn't give a flying rat's naked, purple butt.

The Shadow may have had a good hold on me, but it was powerless to stop me from completely fighting back. I slammed my foot into Anjie's already injured knee, and it caved with a crunch. She screamed in agony and fell sideways, but I was quick to follow up with a kick to her face. I felt her nose burst before she was thrown backward, missing the blazing table by a hair, and landing in a heap on the floor. The ethereal weight on my arms abruptly vanished.

"We tried to make your death quick," the Shadow grumbled in my ear. "Now you will suffer."

Its hold around my neck tightened, and I suddenly felt myself being lifted off my feet. I thrashed uselessly against the hold. When that failed, I reached up to rake the demon's eyes. The Shadow only squeezed tighter. My heartbeat hammered wildly in my head. For a moment, I thought I heard voices. I would have screamed for help if I could.

I fought to keep my senses, but the darkness was closing in.

And the world went black.

39 SUBBASEMENT, MABON CITY CAMPUS, MABON CITY
TIME UNKNOWN

I came back to myself. I felt cold. Dark. Sweet, sweet dark.

My lungs burned. My head ached. My throat hurt.

I choked down a gulp of air.

Air.

It was heavenly, even infected with mildew and smoke.

I devoured it.

Something was hissing by my ear. My gaze sluggishly rolled to the source.

A puddle of gelatinous goo had splattered on the floor. It was quickly dissolving into nothing, just like the demon I had shot earlier. But the inhuman shriek piercing my eardrums told me the remaining Shadow was still alive. And it was wounded. Grievously.

I was too tired to move, but I knew I had to. At the very least, I had to get Aiden out of here. My arms and legs felt like lead, yet I managed to somehow push myself to my knees. My right hand found its way to one of the shelving units, and I used it to leverage myself to my feet.

The room swayed.

I felt like I was going to be sick. I let my eyes drift shut, breathed in deep and exhaled slow. It felt like it took forever, but my stomach and my nerves eventually relaxed.

My eyes slammed open at the demon's enraged shriek. I found Aiden a couple feet from where she had been thrown into the shelves. She had my gun in her hands, and she blasted the Shadow with shot after shot, tearing it apart piece by piece. The parts immediately turned to mucus that splashed against the floor, the walls, and the shelves, where they quickly hissed into nothingness.

What the heck kind of holy water is in that gun?

A water bullet ripped through the Shadow's sole remaining arm, severing it and sending Mirror of Souls crashing to the floor. Unfortunately, the Mirror didn't break, and the demon's final act was to kick it away in a desperate attempt to keep it out of my hands. Then Aiden put a round into its head, and what remained of the Shadow burst into mucus and splashed across the floor like spilled milk.

Aiden spat on the goo as it sizzled and melted into oblivion. Then she aimed the gun at me. I blinked with surprise.

"Are you with them?"

I scoffed, choked out, "Are you out of your mind?"

She lowered the gun.

I pointed past her, to where the Mirror had been kicked. She followed my gesture. "Smash it, Aiden," I said, my voice barely above a hoarse whisper. Talking made my throat burn worse than every cold and flu I've ever had, and still I urged her to do it. "Just destroy it."

Without warning, she rocketed across the room by an unseen force. She flew over the circle and crashed into the stone wall head first within the blink of an eye. I turned to face Anjelah as her little sister lurched sideways, leaving a crimson trail along the wall while she melted down onto the floor.

Adrenaline and rage exploded into my system, and time slowed to a crawl.

Anjie had managed to get herself sort of upright despite the mess I had made of her face and leg. Most of her weight was on her hip, and her right arm kept her from falling over as she struggled to drag herself across the floor. She muttered something and moved her raised left hand in a come-hither wave. A quick glance back confirmed my suspicions; the Mirror was now speeding towards Anjie's outstretched hand.

I shoved myself away from the shelf, moving faster and smoother than I thought possible. It wasn't fast enough to get between the Mirror and Anjelah as I had planned, and the cursed artifact soared past me. I spun on my heel. My hand rushed out before me, snapping around the twisted bone handle a heartbeat before it flew out of reach.

I skidded across the smooth concrete, bumped lightly into the shelves along the opposite wall from where I started.

Time returned to its normal pace.

Anjie gaped in silent confusion.

I looked from her to the Mirror. An intense hatred towards the thing went through me. I hated it for the souls it took; the lives it destroyed. I was going to make sure this thing paid for every single one of them.

I felt a strange pressure begin to build up around the Mirror. It was Anjelah, trying to rip it from my grasp. For a moment, I was surprised that she wasn't trying to take control of me again. Then I saw how exhausted she looked, and sneered.

She didn't have the power.

I took a step towards her, ready to hit her over the head with the Mirror if I had to. Aiden came screaming out of nowhere to kick her sister in the ribs. Anjie shrieked in pain, and the power around the Mirror vanished. Aiden kicked her again and again, screaming wordlessly.

I blinked. I had never seen such a quiet girl like Aiden so angry. But I set my awe, my pain, my exhaustion aside. I had something far more important to deal with.

I glowered down at the Mirror, snarled, "You deserve to be destroyed for all the death and pain you've caused."

The evil thing pulsed with power, protesting. That's when I learned the Mirror had developed a soul of its own. It knew I was about to destroy it; to end its life like it had so many others. And it begged. It pleaded, desperate for its survival.

When it realized begging had failed, it turned to seduction. I suddenly felt like a child about to enter Santa's workshop and walk away with the toy of my dreams. I was giddy with excitement and high on the rush.

At last, I understood what drew people to seek this twisted treasure out.

For a moment, I was compelled not to fulfill my threat; to hug the mirror close to me and vanish to my own little corner to use its power for myself. It would be the perfect way to retaliate against Taboo. I'd give him a little payback for all he's done to me. Then I caught a glimpse of myself in the flawless, obsidian glass. A stark white sneer beneath glowing, scarlet eyes glared back at me in the dark. The level of anger and malice in that monster's expression left me stunned.

Never. I would never allow myself to change into that.

I turned the black glass away from me. Gripping the twisting, bone handle tight, I raised the mirror as high over my head as I could.

For barely a moment, Anjie's screams to stop gave me pause.

"I fulfill my promise now!" I slammed the cursed thing on the floor as hard as I could. The ancient mirror exploded in a shower of glass and bone. A blinding, green light erupted from its shattered remains. I heard a whoosh as a wave of heat tore through the room. Suddenly, the space filled with countless screaming faces trapped within swirling, green flames.

They were the souls, I realized. Men. Women. Children. Human, and not. I caught a glimpse of Cynthia's face in the frenzy and felt a sense of relief. Unspeakable numbers, harvested over the mirror's centuries of use, all spiraled upwards from the Mirror's corpse.

At last, they were free.

And they were furious.

Several of them homed in on Anjelah, their latest tormentor. They passed through her, ripping a white light from her with a horrid scream. A moment later, she slumped to the floor, staring ahead with glazed eyes. I didn't want to stick around to see what else they would do.

In the madness, I somehow managed to find Aiden. She had been thrown aside—by her sister or by the souls, I didn't know—and stood, leaning against a shelving unit in awe of the green vortex. I ran to her as fast as I could and snatched her arm. The only exit, a simple, wooden door that led into the laundry room, was at the opposite end of the room, through the swelling tornado of souls. It might as well have been a mile away for all the good it did us. I cursed my luck and hoped that I had enough oomph to do that Jump thing one more time.

The air quickly grew hotter. The souls crammed against the ceiling and the walls and started to spread out. They pressed against each other, desperate to escape the cramped basement. I could feel the pressure building and knew I had just seconds to get away. I closed my eyes and concentrated hard on Jumping myself and Aiden out of there. The noise and the heat made it difficult to focus, but one by one, I shut my senses off. I somehow managed to block it all out.

With the little strength I had remaining, I knew I had to pick a landing spot nearby or we'd never make it. I knew there was a spot on the front lawn, where a trio of trees created a haven of darkness. I picked it as my target and hoped it would be far enough from the blast. I visualized it in my head and wished myself there. When nothing happened, I closed my eyes tighter and kept wishing. I put every ounce of my remaining life-force into the Jump. The sudden and icy cold of the void swallowed me. I couldn't say how long I was in that black space, but it felt like days.

Solid ground was suddenly beneath me once again. My knees immediately gave out and I collapsed onto the dew-spotted grass. Aiden slumped beside me. I only had a moment to check on her and catch my breath before a fiery, green explosion rocked the entire area. Too spent to move any more, I just lay there and let the blast wave rush over me. I could only hope that the countless number of souls that I had freed from captivity within the Mirror would see fit to spare the two of us.

My vision blurred and started to fade out. The last thing I could remember thinking was what a crazy week it had been. Then total, peaceful darkness overcame me, and I knew no more.

40 SAATHOFF ACADEMY, DARK MOON PORT, MABON CITY
SATURDAY, OCTOBER 25
8:08 AM

I became dimly aware of whispers close-by. Male voices. Both speaking in low, clear mumbles. I caught ghosts of a British accent in one of the tones. That had to be Quinn. Which means the other was most likely Duncan. Curiosity got the best of me, and I tuned in to their quiet conversation.

"… was stupid, but the caller didn't leave any room for negotiations," said Quinn. He sounded frustrated. "They had us dead in their sights, and we never even knew it. If Specter hadn't told us what had gone down, I doubt we'd have shown up before emergency services. They could have taken her and her friend in, slapped them with some bogus charge of terrorism or something, and we'd be playing hell to get them back."

"I am avare of that," Duncan replied in a patient voice. "And I am not accusing you or Morgan of dereliction of duty. Cybil only saw von vay out of the situation, and I thank vhatever higher power may be out there that she had been smart enough to keep her phone on so ve could track it." He sighed. "But even Morgan had to admit that the fact that she vent up against a Shadow alone, and managed not only to survive, but also to save her friend, is incredible."

Quinn hummed in agreement.

"Two," I muttered, blinking my eyes open. I sat up with a groan and a couple popping joints. My gaze traveled around the room. I had been brought to my quarters and tucked into bed. The lights were off, and the blinds had been drawn, but an uncomfortable amount of daylight still seeped through. I stared longest at my desk, where my phone had been placed and was grateful that someone had retrieved it.

I found Quinn standing at the foot of my bed; Duncan by my couch, where the sunlight couldn't strike him. Both were dressed similarly, in tee shirts and jeans. And both looked relieved to see me awake.

Relieved.

And a little confused.

"There were two Shadows," I clarified before they could ask. Their eyebrows practically disappeared into their hairlines. "And I think they were working for Anjelah but..." I shrugged, winced a little at the tightness in my neck and shoulders. "It might have been the other way around."

They traded a look.

"What?"

"Summoning demons is—at least according to Bones—relatively simple, but requires a talent for black magic." Duncan's voice adopted a pensive tone, as if he was trying to make sense of the details. His hand reached up to absently stroke an imaginary beard. "The Crosses veren't in the AEON database, vhich means one of two things. A, they kept their talents very vell hidden, changing names and associations frequently, vhich is highly unlikely; or B, the talent developed vithin the last generation or two, and they did not know to be registered."

"Interesting," I muttered. Honestly, I was more curious to know, "Who's Bones?"

Even behind his hand, I could tell the corners of Duncan's mouth twitched upwards. "She's a vitch who vorks on Team Alpha."

This Team Alpha intrigued me more and more every time I heard about it. First, it was Lady Saathoff herself, who I knew little about. Then it was Sin, the mysterious and powerful being who terrified everybody. Now, it's this Bones character, who wasn't just a witch; she was the witch. The first one in history—her position among the Alphas told me that much about her at least.

"Well, Aiden is definitely not a witch." I firmly stated. "Or black mage, or sorcerer, or whatever else they might be called. She had had plenty of opportunity to use magick on her sister, but never did."

Duncan's brow furrowed, and his hand fell back to his side. "So it vas the sister?"

I nodded. "Anjie was waving her hands around and muttering words in some language I didn't recognize, and every time she did that, something would go flying. Oh! And she kept me prisoner in a summoning circle."

The vampire blinked, shook his head as if he had just been slapped. "How did you get out?"

I told them about my Jump.

They gaped at me for a long, silent while. Then Duncan had me backtrack all the way to the beginning and fill them in on what went down. I told them about the creepy phone call. The threat against Quinn's and Morgan's lives. The duel in the theater. Everything that went down in the school's sub-basement. Up until the big, green explosion that I narrowly escaped. They listened quietly through the whole tale before they started asking me questions.

"Before I answer all those, I have a couple questions for you."

They each waved a hand, welcoming me to ask away.

"Could you tell me what the heck was in that mini super soaker you lent me?"

Quinn chuckled, adjusted his weight on the bed. "Remember when you shot the Shadow on Cynthia's front porch?"

I said that I did.

"The plain ol' holy water didn't do much except give it what we would call a nasty sunburn. The demon could have healed that with just a quick Shadow Jump to… wherever it was hiding out. The water didn't have the stopping power we needed to go up against a demon of that caliber. So, I beefed up the mixture I put in your concealed carry with a little silver nitrate."

I didn't know exactly what that mixture was, but my attention hung on the word silver. "I thought werewolves were allergic to silver."

Duncan concealed a smile.

"Oh, if only it were a simple thing like an allergy." Quinn made a face, absently rubbed a spot on his right forearm. "The mixture we use actually comes in a soluble capsule that any parathrope can touch; even werewolves and demons. Just so long as you don't accidentally break the capsule."

"I see," I muttered.

"I thought you vould have anxiously inquired about your friend," admitted Duncan.

I grinned at him. "If you had bad news about Aiden, you would have told me already."

He nodded.

"I take it she's here?"

Another nod. "She woke up about an hour ago. She's refusing to talk to anyone except you, so I had a professor escort her to the cafeteria for something to eat."

"She's not a parathrope. Neither is her dad..." I swallowed hard, shook my head. "She can't stay here, can she?"

"Unfortunately, no. The school is a sanctuary for parathropes. And, while she may have been exposed to our world, her cowan status won't count for anything among our population. However, we will be keeping a watchful eye on her in the years to come to make sure nothing goes after her."

Well, at least she'll have some protection.

"Vhy don't you go up to the cafeteria and talk to her?" prompted

Duncan. "I'm sure she is still there."

Quinn agreed, got to his feet. "Yeah, we can finish this Q and A session after things have settled a bit more."

That sounded like a great idea to me.

I threw aside the covers, draped my feet over the side of my bed. As I did, I caught a glimpse of my family Polaroid and was reminded of something. I called Duncan's name before he stepped out of the room.

He looked sidelong at me.

"Any word from Khione?"

His expression turned stone cold.

I took it as a 'no.'

41 SAATHOFF ACADEMY, DARK MOON PORT, MABON CITY
SATURDAY, OCTOBER 25
9:16 AM

I didn't want to go traipsing through the ship with my wild bedhead and yesterday's dirt still clinging to my skin (It's bad for the rep). So I got cleaned up first and climbed into some fresh clothing. Then I took the stairs up to the cafeteria deck.

Okay, I admit; I was putting off talking to Aiden because I was dreading it. Everything that happened to her these past few days was my fault. The jocks beating her up. The Shadow shackling her. Worst of all, I had killed her sister.

Because of me.

No apology in the world could make up for that.

"I might as well try fixing a broken dam with a band-aid," I grimly muttered, pausing before the threshold to the cafeteria.

The place was practically empty save a dozen or so students who had shoved some of the tables together near the middle of the room. Globules of water danced around them in acrobatic feats as they talked over a tabletop game and snacks. I spotted Zero among them, lazily waving her hand while chatting with the girl seated beside her.

Aiden.

She was munching on Doritos and Mountain Dew, completely at ease despite Zero's obvious use of hydrokinesis. Her wounds didn't look as bad as I had been expecting, though the skin around her nose and eyes were dark purple. She sported a Saathoff Academy tee shirt and sweats, and the cast on her arm had been replaced with a clean splint.

She must have felt my stare for she looked right at me. When we locked eyes, I felt like a gunfighter in the Old West, staring down the sheriff until the clock tower struck noon. I half expected a tumbleweed to bounce its way across our path. She broke eye contact first, muttered something to Zero. The water's tumbling gymnastics paused long enough for Aiden to bow out gracefully, and she started for me.

I worked up the courage to cross the threshold. Every step after that felt like my shoes had been turned to lead. I didn't want to face Aiden, but I couldn't run away from her either.

We met beside a table.

I braced myself.

"Hey, Cybil," she said softly, clasping her hands behind her back and digging the toe of her shoe into the floor.

"Hey."

"I'm glad to see you're okay."

That… Wasn't what I had been expecting. Where's the screaming? The hitting? The crying? That's what I deserved; Not a 'glad to see you'.

She pulled out a chair and slumped onto it with a sigh. "I'm sorry you got dragged into our family squabble."

Wait. What?

She wiped at her eyes. "I knew Anjie wanted revenge against Missus Santova for the accident. For our mother. I tried to stop her. Just like I tried to stop her from killing those boys. It was her fault. She abandoned me at the mall and those boys found me."

Holy crap! I knew Anjie was a witch— in every sense of the word— but abandoning her little sister at the mall was a despicable move. At least it explained why Aiden snuck aboard the ship in the middle of the night. She knew Zero and had sought her help.

Aiden choked on a sob. "I'm so sorry. It wasn't fair to you."

I melted down onto the chair beside her. For several long moments, all

I could do was stare at her in awe. Here she was, apologizing to me when I was the one who should be sorry.

I hung my head, swallowed the lump in my throat. "Aiden, you don't owe me anything. Not after what I did."

"Are you kidding me? You saved my life."

"At the cost of your sister's."

Aiden sighed. "I know I should be sad, but I'm not. I know it makes me sound like a bad person, but I…" She looked me in the eye and continued in a harder tone. "I just don't care. She abused me all my life, and she tried to kill you, me, and my daddy, so, I guess, she got what she deserved." Her expression softened. "And it's not like you knew those things were gonna go after her when you broke that weird mirror. I can't blame you for that."

I hadn't realized I was crying until Aiden wrapped me in a tight hug. It wasn't an obnoxious, loud bawl—I've never cried like that—just a quiet release. After all the stress of the last week, it felt good to take a load off. It only took me a minute or two to calm down.

I broke the hug. "Anjie really left you at the mall?"

Aiden wiped away a stray tear with the back of her hand, nodded. "She was supposed to bring me home when she got off work at eight-thirty. I waited until the mall closed, but she never showed. I couldn't get daddy on the phone 'cause he was at work, and I didn't have enough money for bus or cab fare, so I ended up walking. I talked to her boss, and he said Anjie didn't come in after school like she was scheduled."

After school? That was around the time I had seen the Crosses' station wagon on the way to the Palisades. The Shadow attacked us there shortly after. It would have taken Anjelah at least that long to drive from the school to Cynthia's mansion. And I could swear that Anjie was the same height and build as the mystery lady caught on the phone at the truck stop the night before that.

"Anyway." She waved her hand. "I'm sure you've figured out by now that Anjie was a black witch."

I didn't expect Aiden to be so forthcoming about it, but… "Is that what you wanted to tell me the other day? Before those jocks showed up?"

"Sorta," she said. "I saw you Grounding in homeroom, and figured we had something in common. Very interesting technique, by the way."

I quirked an eyebrow at her.

She grinned. "Mama was a green witch. I eavesdropped while she taught Anjie about her abilities. Too bad Anjie chose to dip into black magick."

"So you know all about parathropes and cowans?" A rhetorical question seeing as how Aiden was friends with Zero and knew about Paradox's underground nightclub.

"Yeah. And I also know you're an AEON Enforcement Agent."

It may not have been entirely true, but I didn't correct her. I'm not sure why. Perhaps it had something to do with my pride. Or, perhaps, it was because it gave me an excuse to not blame myself for what happened to Anjelah.

I just hoped that the guilt I felt would eventually wash away.

Before I could tell Aiden that, Zero came running up. "Come on!" she called, grabbing our hands. "We're fixing to start a new campaign, and you guys need to be there to help us beat the dragons."

I laughed and sat down to make some friends.

42

OUTSIDE PARADOX, MABON CITY
FRIDAY, OCTOBER 24
9:17 PM

Paradox was packed tonight, both within the shop and the cavern beneath it. Zero, Necro, Aiden, and a handful of others had already gone inside, but I had something to do first. So I took up a sentinel's post across from the secret door in the alley, waiting. Watching.

She would come.

I knew it.

I had something she wanted.

The heartbeat of the city thrummed on. People moved through the city's streets, blissfully oblivious to the encroaching dark and the creatures lurking within it. Creatures like me and my new friends.

I felt the marrow-freezing energy long before the icy demoness appeared at the mouth of the alley. Khione's snow-blue skin glinted in the light that filtered through the shop windows as she moved. Her outfit tonight mimicked the first one I had seen her in. Silk shirt. Leather pants. High heels. All in varying shades of shimmering blues and purples.

"Right on time," I said and held out the item I had for her.

Her catlike eyes narrowed slightly as she studied the plastic Dollar Store bag. She warily accepted it, looked within. Her grape-colored lips fell open in awe. "What did you do to it?"

"Made sure nobody would ever use it again."

Her eyes met mine.

"Hey, the way I see it, the mirror was mine, anyways. After all, it was stolen from my family's vault."

"And the diamond?"

I scoffed. “Anonymously returned to the Smithsonian.”

“Good.” She tied the bag closed. “I shall see to it that the bounty on you is rescinded immediately.”

“Then our business is concluded,” I said and started for the hidden door that would take me to Paradox’s underground nightclub.

“Thanks for the help, Cybil.”

“Cybil Starr is dead.” I looked back at her. “Just call me Jinx.”

JINX AND THE GANG WILL RETURN IN

THE LYCAN Pharaoh

1 SAATHOFF ACADEMY, DARK MOON PORT, MABON CITY TUESDAY, MAY 6 11:43 PM

I know history as long as it isn't dated. Oh, I can prattle on and on about many things that occurred since the invention of cave paintings; I just couldn't tell you the *when* behind them. It's particularly annoying during school finals, which were rapidly approaching.

The Saathoff Academy was moored in its usual spot at Dock 66 of the Dark Moon Port. It was surprisingly quiet tonight, despite the heavy Saturday night traffic. It would not be quiet for long; I could feel a storm building several miles outside of the harbor. It would still be a few hours before it broke upon Mabon City, but it was already sending dark waves to lap lazily at the ship's hull. To some of the inhabitants within the enormous ocean cruise liner, the gentle sound was a lullaby. But for those like me, the night was too young for sleep. And I found myself on the outdoor recreation deck, studying for a final.

By studying I really mean that I was trying to kick some serious butt.

I dipped under the open palm strike and swept my right leg in a rapid arc. My counter attack did not land; Quinn was much faster than that. He had leaped back a few feet and probably thought he was out of my range. Actually he was right where I wanted him, and as I twisted in a full circle, I called upon an itsy bit of my true power. In a wink, the deck of the ship vanished into total, icy darkness. A quick count of three and I was meandering within the Rift.

It is a funny place, the Rift. It is best described as the space between the Mortal Realm and the Veil, which is sort of like the Great Wall of China that prevents most of the beings in the Spirit Realm from crossing over. Think of the Rift as an extremely large shopping mall—far bigger than any mall in the world. And instead of shops or outlets, the Rift is full of nothing but doorways; lots and lots and lots of doorways. It had taken me quite a while, but I finally learned how to control my Shadow Jumps. Instead of just flashing through to some random location, I slowed down so I could actually see the Rift, and pick out the perfect door to land in strategic positions.

How do I know which door is which? Good question, especially when you consider that each doorway changes as the shadows change and they are never in any particular order. If I know where I want to go, I can usually just feel the right doorway. Not knowing where I am going makes Shadow Jumping rather tricky. I could potentially Jump out of any shadow in the universe (I told ya the Rift was huge). Sometimes I am able to just look at the doorway for a minute, and in the swirling blackness, see where it would lead. Like this one to my left; it won't return me to the Mortal Realm, but send me someplace deep within the Rift's other side. Yeah, a scant few of these doorways actually allow passage through the Veil. The doors on that side of the Rift lead to various places within the Spirit Realm.

The Spirit Realm really freaks me out. It looks almost identical to the Mortal Realm except everything has this sort of blue-gray coloring to it. Even the grass over there is blue. And then there are the creatures who call such a place home. Most of them are ghosts, who want nothing to do with you and tend not to notice your presence unless you are the one who killed them. There are also all kinds of creepy crawlies lurking there; beings of pure energy that can only be seen by someone with True Sight. And then there are the Fae. Fairies are probably the first thing you think of when someone mentions the Fae, but these wee ones are nothing like your tinkers and tooth collectors of the Astral Realm. No, these ones would eat your face off faster than you can say "There's no place like home." You definitely do not want to go wandering into one of their gatherings… which was exactly what I did. Thankfully Morgan came to my rescue. She is an Angel and a bit annoying, but that might just be the Shadow Demon in me talking.

Yep, I am a demon. My name used to be Cybil Ulasigvi Starr. These days, I am known only as Jinx, Daughter of Forlorn. I have chocolate eyes, mostly black hair—I dyed parts of it and this month's flavor is purple—and at just four-foot ten, I am freakishly short. Really, though, I am actually only half Shadow Demon. I get that and my Cherokee heritage from my dad. My temper and stubbornness I proudly get from my mom. At least that is what my agilisi used to say. Both of my parents were murdered when I was five years old. Another demon that goes by the name Taboo killed them, and it has become my goal to track him down and make him pay. That is why I joined the AEON Agency.

AEON is a top secret organization tasked with protecting the Mortal Realm from attacks. What sort of attacks, you wonder? It actually varies. Sometimes the attacks come from a ghost of person who died too suddenly or with a lot of hate. That is where you get your poltergeists and vengeful spirits from. Very rarely does a bored Fae pass through the Veil and start mixing up trouble as entertainment. Possession is one of their favorite things to do, despite the fact that it breaks one of the Laws—One cannot take away someone's free will. Most of the attacks, however, are caused by the creatures of the Netherworld. These guys make the Fae look like jokes. I should know, since I am technically one of them, and I have sort of become my team's go-to person for all things demon.

When the demons of the Netherworld come out to play, that is when

AEON really goes to work. There are AEON teams all over the world. Most of them are small, two- maybe three-person units. They take care of the little stuff. Then you have the heavy hitters; teams that are actually given ranks depending on their success and strength. I work with Team Beta, which is led by a vampire named Duncan, aka Revenant. We have a ghost that we call Specter because his real name, Tiberius, is apparently too hard to say (I just think of Captain Kirk). He died alongside Spartacus, and has remained in the Mortal Realm since, so he is a plethora of information—all the volumes of Encyclopedia Britannica have nothing compared to him. Morgan, or Paladin, is our Angel, who keeps us up to date on the happenings of the Astral Realm. There's me. And, of course, Quinn. He is a werewolf codenamed Fenrir, and he is our team's second in command. He is also my combat instructor at the Saathoff Academy. And I just found the doorway that would let me pop out right behind him and kick his butt.

Whoever said homework couldn't be fun?

As I had planned, I popped out of the shadows right behind Quinn, ready with a roundhouse kick. He managed to spin around and block it just in the nick of time. He immediately countered with a right hook that left my shoulder tingling. I smiled in spite of myself, and reset my fighting stance. He wiped his shaggy, brown hair out of his green eyes, smirked and sank into his own stance.

Our martial dance continued.

The helicopter was almost upon the ship before Quinn and I took note of it. He called a halt to the training session, and we stood together to watch the chopper make its descent. Air buffeted us in choppy waves that left me fighting for my next breath. It seemed like forever before the chopper touched down on the helipad. The engine was cut. The rotors slowly drifted to silence. The door slid open, and Quinn gasped at the man who stepped out.

I had never seen him before. He was tall—much taller than me, but shorter than Quinn's lanky six foot, two—with black hair held in a loose braid that fell all the way down to his hip. The man was dressed in simple, yet matching, black clothes: shirt, slacks and shoes — probably socks and underwear, too. He would fit in very well at a funeral, I mused. He spotted us watching, jerked his head in a stiff nod. Even at this distance, I could see that his eyes were bright blue, very similar to Quinn's when the full moon draws near. But the moon would not be full for a while yet.

"Is he a werewolf?"

Quinn licked his lips, swallowed nervously. "Lycaon isn't just another werewolf; he is *the* werewolf."

My jaw fell slack in surprise. It was especially rare to have a visit from one of the Firsts.

How do I explain the Firsts? Let me see… I guess you could say that the Firsts are the original bad boys and girls of various paranormal species. Just like Dracula is widely believed to be the first vampire in history, Lycaon is the very first werewolf. That is why his kind are often referred to as lycanthropes or lycans. I could not believe my luck that I was actually getting to see such a renowned figure in the flesh.

Lycaon stepped aside as someone else started climbing out of the chopper. A moment later, a woman stood at his side. She was clad in a burgundy dress that hugged her curves and reached down to her ankles. A black bodice with a frill similar to one an evil sorceress would wear covered her shoulders and waist. A ribbon choker with a pendant was against her throat, and a black veil shrouded her face. Her auburn hair was curled and half-tucked under a small hat. She also held a fancy cane with gloved hands. I had recognized her the very instant she had stepped out of the chopper. She was The Lady. The founder of the AEON Agency and a living legend among the schools that bore her name: Lady Zabrina Saathoff.

Something big must have gone down if The Lady and one of the Firsts have come here, I thought as I watched the pair draw closer. The Lady moved like a queen; back straight, shoulders squared, cane aloft in one hand. And her footsteps fell silently despite the high heeled boots she wore. Lycaon walked like a shadow a pace behind her. His manner sent out a clear message: Mess with The Lady and I will rip you to shreds. Moon-blue eyes sought hidden threats in the shadows, but there were none. He seemed to relax slightly.

"Lady Schroeder, Lycaon," Quinn said a bit breathlessly once the duo were a few feet away. "What an unexpected surprise. To what do we owe the honor?"

"I must speak with Revenant at once." The Lady spoke in a soft voice, thick with an accent that immediately made me think of Dracula. He is real, by the way; Dracula. Yup, the ol' boy is still alive and kicking. I know this because Duncan—the man whom The Lady calls Revenant—had to go to a meeting with the Vampire Clans a couple months back. I so badly wanted to go, but he told me I would only be seen as lunch if I stepped foot in Drakul's halls. And when a vampire tells you that you look like lunch, trust me, that is when you back up few paces and start looking for a quick exit.

"Absolutely," said Quinn. "Please follow us. We'll take you straight to his office."

SELENA INALI RAYNELIF DRAKE is an American author best known for her paranormal mystery series titled *The AEON Files*.

Drake is a martial arts enthusiast, a Wiccan with Cherokee roots, and an award-winning artist. Her love for writing started when she was eight, and she has won a number of Editor's Choice awards and a Shakespeare Trophy of Excellence for poetry. Her works have been published in *Thrice Fiction Magazine*, *Emerging Poets 2018* (Midwest Region), and *Emerging Writers 2018* (Horror Edition).

She currently resides in Minot, ND with her dog Pipsqueak, where she continues to work on more books.

VISIT SELENA ONLINE AT

SIRDWRITES.COM

ALSO BY SELENA IR DRAKE

THE AEON FILES

The Archfiend Artifact

The Lycan Pharaoh

The Lullaby Shriek

The Bone Prophet

WEIRD CHRONICLES

Episode One

DRAGON DIARIES

Ascension

Culmination

Made in the USA
Monee, IL
19 March 2020

23089518R00152